# BELLS OF SAINT MICHAELS

*A Christmas Story*

## BRYAN MOONEY

*Also by Bryan Mooney*

*Summer of '68*
*A Christmas Flower*
*Been in Love Before*
*Christmas in Vermont*
*Once We Were Friends*
*Love Letters*
*A Second Chance*
*A Box of Chocolates*
*Indie*
*The Potus Papers*
*Eye of the Tiger*

*Should you enjoy this story or any of my other works, please feel free to leave a review on your favorite reading site. Thank you.*
*—BDM*

*Dedicated to My Loving Wife,*
*Bonnie*

# Chapter One

The old, unlit freighter, the *Holy Cross*, was flying the Maltese flag as it slowly lumbered into the darkened harbor of Saint Michaels, Maryland. It was well after midnight that night in the heart of winter. Though the crossing was in rough seas and dangerous waters, the ship had crossed the Atlantic in record time and managed to escape the ravages of the Nazi submarine wolf packs. But others in their ragtag convoy were not so lucky and sank beneath the frigid black waters off the coast.

The journey had been a long one for the rusty old ship, but now her voyage was complete. With military precision, the boat docked at the deserted harbor at the end of Willow Street, not far from the sleepy downtown of the backwater eastern shore town. The tired group of rugged sailors huddled in a circle rubbing their hands together, trying to keep warm in the frigid winter air. Those waiting ashore secured the mooring lines as the captain walked down the gangway to greet them.

"*Buona sera,*" the captain said quietly as he shook each of their hands in turn.

"English," insisted the woman dressed in black, the apparent leader of the group.

"Yes, of course. I bring you greetings from Saint Paul's."

"Greetings. No U-boats, I see."

"We were the lucky ones. However, you never see them until it's too late."

"Glad you made it." She was quiet for a moment. "We don't have a lot of time, and we have a lot of work to do." The wind blew stronger, gusting through her hair, as she lifted her eyes toward the brooding sky. "Let's hurry."

"Yes." The captain raised his hand to signal the men aboard to begin unloading the cargo.

The lightning in the moonless sky was the only light that guided them that night. Over the next four hours, the crew, and their helpers—all sworn to secrecy—labored under the heavy loads, trudging up the narrow cobblestone alleyways before turning onto Willow Street. The crew finished their backbreaking assignment just as dawn began a new day in the sleepy town of Saint Michaels.

"We must go," said the captain, wanting to leave the same way he had arrived: unobserved.

"Godspeed," said the woman in black.

The ship departed as quietly as it had arrived, heading back home across the ocean, just as a fierce offshore storm began to batter the old transport.

Weeks later, remnants of an unidentified ship washed ashore on the outer islands that dot the Maryland coastline. That was the only telltale sign of the visit by the *Holy Cross* to Saint Michaels harbor that cold winter night.

The ship's visit then faded into history.

# Chapter Two

## *Many years later*

The small hamlet of Saint Michaels was waking. The morning fog lifted slowly off the harbor waters as fishing boats chugged out of the port. The watermen began their long day at sea, just as their fathers and grandfathers and great-grandfathers before them had, fishing the rich waters off the Atlantic seaboard. Marauding seagulls followed them in hopes of securing a stray piece of chum. Fishermen tossed fragments of bait high above them, laughing as the seagulls performed their aerial acrobatics to try to reach their meal before one of their fellow kings of the air beat them to it.

Just before noon, in old Saint Michaels church—the town's namesake—choral director Grace Albright listened from the front pew with an attentive ear to her young Christmas choir group. She preferred to conduct her Christmas music classes in the church, hoping it would inspire her young charges. Over the years, Grace's blindness had made her hearing even more acute, and in turn, she detected a young voice not in sync with the rest of the group.

The aromatic smell of fresh Christmas trees filled the air inside the two-hundred-year-old church, and she breathed deeply. She loved Christmastime: the music, the shopping, the cookie and pie-baking, the cheerful demeanor of everyone she met and the pleasant scent of pine trees. While everyone else seemed to dislike the nonstop Christmas music on the radio, she loved it and always sang along. But none of that distracted her keen ears from the task at hand.

Finally, she stood and clapped her hands three times to stop their singing; she knew who the culprit was. "Billy Collins?" she said, reaching for her walking cane.

"Yes, Miss Albright?" said the shy boy in the rear row, slinking backward.

"I know you're new here, but I need you to harmonize, to blend in with the rest of us." She softened her tone and said, "Join the group, enjoy your singing. You have a wonderful voice; don't be afraid to use it, okay?"

"Yes, Miss Albright. Sure."

"And Alison, I need you to stay in key with the rest of the group."

"Yes, ma'am," said Alison Parker, "it's just that—"

"I know, Ali," she said, unfolding her cane; she walked from the wooden pew toward the front of the altar, stopping halfway. "You have an angelic voice, but I need you to join in with the group. Let's sing 'Silent Night.'" She heard mumbling in the background and clapped her hands.

"Okay, okay. Let's try this again. Listen to my pitch and follow my lead. But first, stand tall, head high. Breathe deep and don't slur your words. Most importantly, caress the words. Love the words you sing. Now, listen to my voice."

Low and strong she sang, then she breathed again. It was her favorite Christmas hymn. She sang loud and clear, inspired, lost in the glories of the song, and motioning with her hands for her class to join her. She began to sing, but her voice was the only one she heard as it echoed in the church. When they didn't join her, she stopped singing. "Class? Class? Hello?" She laughed. "I know you're there; I can hear your breathing. Hello? Class?"

Alison spoke up. "I'm sorry, Ms. Albright, but your singing was so awesome…well, we were afraid to join in and spoil it."

Grace smiled, embarrassed. "Thank you for the compliment, Ali, but my singing—while not beautiful, as you call it—is disciplined. Much the same way yours will be after you practice. And practice and more practice. Now, once again, from the top. 'Silent Night.'" As she motioned for them to start singing, a voice spoke out: Joanna Sayles.

"Excuse me, Miss Albright, but I have a question."

"Yes? What is it, Joanna?" *We'll never finish our practice at this rate.*

"Why are we concentrating so much on this one song?"

"Well, because it's the perfect song for us to sing without an organ accompaniment at Christmastime," said Grace—as a former history teacher, she jumped at the chance to explain why. "You see, two hundred years ago during a blizzard in a small Austrian mountain village, a church discovered two days before Christmas that their organ was broken. So they worked day and night to write a song to express their holiday joy. The result of their efforts was the beautiful hymn 'Silent Night.' So let's begin—"

"But Miss Albright, we have an organ. And church bells too. Why can't we use them? I'm sure they must sound wonderful."

"Many years ago, our church bells were said to be the most melodic on Maryland's Eastern Shore, and people filled our church to listen to them. But during the war, it was decreed by the bishops that all churches stop ringing their bells out of respect for our fighting men overseas. When the war ended, our church tried to ring them again on V.J. Day. Unfortunately, the bells had gone sour from lack of use, or maybe from the salty rains of the many hurricanes we had over that period. They haven't been rung since, nor do we have the funds to replace them."

"But what about the organ? It's so beautiful, but we never use it."

"It's old and very delicate. And, like most church organs, it needs to be tuned every six months to maintain a perfect pitch. Ours hasn't been tuned in a very long time."

"But I'm sure it would sound so wonderful if—"

"Yes, you're right," interrupted a deep voice from the darkness behind her. "It would sound wonderful, but the church has decided to spend its meager financial resources on ministering to our flock." She heard the footsteps coming up from behind her, she stopped, listened- a man's broad step- ah familiar footsteps. The man behind her leaned in close and whispered, "Good morning, Gracie. I missed you at breakfast."

"Morning, Dad," she replied with a smile. "I came here to practice. I love it here early in the morning." Then, turning to her choir, she clapped her hands. "We are done with our lesson for today. It's time to return you to Mr. Howard for your computer class."

She heard the students' groans. "So come on now, be off with you or you'll be late." Computer science was one of the few subjects that Grace did not teach at the school.

Her father touched her elbow. "Grace, sit, please." Sitting next to her, he said, "You seem so worried. You must have faith and courage to do some things and perseverance to do others. You're working very hard. Perhaps too hard. I think perhaps…"

"But Christmas is not far off, and the bishop and the school and—"

"What will be, will be, Grace," he said. "We can do little to change things. Just continue to pray."

She touched his arm, shaking her head. "Dad, I have a confession to make. I couldn't help but overhear the conversation you had with the bishop last week on your speakerphone. If we can't increase attendance soon, the bishop will announce the closing of both the school and the church when he comes here on Christmas Eve. Isn't that what I heard? Right?" Her hands began to shake.

"Have patience," said her father. "I've been the pastor for thirty years. We've lived here our entire lives. We have been very fortunate, and I sincerely doubt that they are going to move us."

"Well, I don't want that to happen any more than you do," said Grace, "so I'm doing everything in my power that I can to prevent it."

"You're doing a fine job working with your choral class. They sound better every day." He paused. "And you sounded like an angel today. Better than I've ever heard you sing before. It sounded so natural."

"It's in my genes, I guess," she said. "If I can only get some additional people into the group, then maybe more families will come to hear us sing on Christmas Eve when the bishop is here. You know, I was thinking, we could invite all the people from the new housing development down at Saint Michaels Landing, and the families that moved into the new homes at Saint Michaels on the Miles River. Most of them probably don't even know we're here. And in town, we can—" She rambled on when excited.

"Perhaps."

"But, Dad, if we could get—"

He relented, as usual—he knew how stubborn she could be when she had her mind made up. "What would you like me to do, Grace?"

"Make up some flyers for me. Ones that read like this." She reached into her sweater pocket and handed him a note written in her unmistakable scribble.

As he unfolded the paper, he read:

*Come join us!*
*We are actively seeking singers interested in joining our Christmas*
*Choir and Holiday Caroling Group.*
*Anyone interested, should call Saint Michaels school and ask for*
*Grace Albright.*
*Merry Christmas!*

The picturesque seaside town with just a thousand inhabitants on the remote Eastern Shore of Maryland was far from the hustle and bustle of Baltimore and the politics of the nation's capital. The distance to the eastern shore was measured not in the two-hour drive but in taking a step back in time, back to a simpler era.

People recently had begun to discover the small seaside town as a good place to live and raise a family. But Grace knew they did not have the luxury of time. She and her father could only pray that more of Saint Michaels' residents would show up for church services and school. But they were running out of time. Christmas was not far off. She would do anything.

"Okay. I'll have this flyer made up for you. Then what?"

"Well," she said, her hands nervously twisting her handkerchief around her fingers, "I'll tack them to our bulletin board out in front of the church and ask the shops on Talbot Street to do the same. If you could mention it during Sunday services, that would be helpful."

"Okay, okay. I can do that. What else?"

"I have loads of ideas, but this will do for now. Oh, by the way, I did want to mention to you that when I stopped by the church this morning, I heard noises. Like I wasn't alone. I think someone was here with me, watching me. It felt weird and gave me chills." It was true, earlier that day, a slow unknown shuffling sound had made Grace think someone was there with her.

"Well, Grace, we don't lock the doors to our church."

"But it was early and—"

"Everyone is welcome here, Grace. You know that. Anything else?"

She faced him the same way she had before she had lost her sight. "Dad."

Now he knew it was serious when she addressed him in that tone. "Yes, Grace? What's on your mind?"

She bit her bottom lip and brushed her hair away from her face. "As much as I hate to admit it, Joanna Sayles does have a point. Why can't we try to use the church bells again? I hear from the old-timers in town that people came from miles around to hear them ring, especially this time of year. It might help our recruiting efforts for new parishioners if we can get them working again. What do you think?"

"I suppose we can give it a try. Let me start up the equipment and see what happens. I'm willing to try anything at this point to fill these pews. Give me a day or so to look through the manual. It's been a long time since the bells have been used." He looked at her and coughed. "What else?"

"The kids also asked about the organ. From what I remember, it sounded so majestic. Heavenly, even."

"Grace, it costs a lot of money to have the organ tuned, especially since it hasn't been tuned in years. I'm sorry, dear, maybe next year."

"But Dad... there might not be a 'next year.' We need to have it tuned now before the bishop comes. Let people hear the organ, and then I'm sure they'll feel more like singing and maybe they'll..."

"I know, Grace, but I've already told you—"

She interrupted him. "I can ask Sam Carpenter the next time he's in town to come by and take a look."

"No, Grace. I've asked you not to mention his name in my presence."

"Dad! This has to stop. He's my best friend. We grew up together, and I heard somebody in town say he may be coming back home soon for a visit. I just thought—"

"He's not welcome here."

Her back stiffened. "He's not wanted in church? A minute ago, you told me everyone was welcome here." Grace's voice rose. "Just not an old friend of mine."

"That's not what I meant, and you know it. Sam Carpenter is not welcome in our home. It's because of him that—"

"Father, my going blind wasn't Sam's fault. The doctors told us they don't know what caused my blindness and—"

"I don't want to talk about it."

"Dad, it's been three years since the accident, and I think it's time for you to—"

"No. Can we just leave it at that, please?"

"No, we can't," she said, standing while reaching for her cane. She paused for a moment, deciding whether to continue. "Karen, my old roommate, stopped by yesterday and asked if I wanted to move back in with her, and I think it's a good idea. I told her I would think about it. I have to learn to stand on my own two feet again and do things on my own."

BELLS OF SAINT MICHAELS

Her father looked at her, standing there, before him. He looked at her and said, "You remind me so much of your mother," he sighed. "But every time Sam Carpenter's name comes up, we fight. We don't want to, but we always do. Grace, this has to stop. I must go now, sweetheart. I have calls to make." He kissed her forehead. "See you at dinner. And if you're lucky, I'll let you beat me in chess tonight."

Her fury spent, Grace could not stay mad at him for long. "Ha, that'll be the day."

"Don't be long, sweetheart."

Grace heard his footsteps retreat down the aisle. And then she listened to the door leading to the school close behind him. She was alone in the church and sat back, perfectly still. The church was empty. Finally, she stood and shouted, "Is there anyone here? Anyone at all?"

Her voice echoed off the walls. But no response. "Hello?" she said again.

She took her cane, unfolded it, and tapping on the floor back and forth in front of her she walked to her favorite location towards the front of the church. Many months before, she had located the musical vortex of the building, the heart of this beautiful old church. Laying her walking cane in a nearby pew, she stood tall, back straight, with her head held high and began to sing.

"Hallelujah, hallelujah." Then she sang it higher, "Hallelujah, hallelujah!"

She loved to sing, just for the pure joy of singing—something she could never tell her father. He would never understand. Her spirits rose high. She smiled as she sang to the heavens, and she sang as if no one was watching.

But she still felt someone was watching, sitting somewhere in the church. Watching, listening...waiting.

# Chapter Three

Sam Carpenter listened intently, as he finished tuning the last of the organ pipes at Saint Marks Church in downtown Baltimore. He closed his eyes, remembering what his father had always told him: "Sam, you need to listen with your heart." Unfortunately, his boss Oliver Matz had always insisted on using the latest gadgets to test the sound instead, like a sound meter.

As a tuner, he knew that each pipe, regardless of its size or composition, had to sound good alone, with the help of the sound meter. "It will never fail you," Ollie would say. "Besides, it's faster." But what his boss never understood was that though they had to sound good separately, more importantly, they all had to be harmonious together, and no sound meter could ever measure that. The sound of each had to blend with all the others, not compete or overwhelm, and that was always the challenge faced by an expert organ tuner. And Sam Carpenter was one of the best.

Sam loved his job. Often, he would just close his eyes and listen to the beautiful sounds that he loved: a perfectly tuned church organ. Like the voice of an angel. Some pipes sounded like trumpets, while others like trombones or harps, and many times when they were tuned to perfection, he could hear them, like voices, voices in a choir. So wonderful.

It was then Sam stopped and remembered her angelic voice, her smile, her laugh. Grace. He thought of her often, more and more every day, especially around Christmastime, their favorite time of the year. It had been three years since he had seen her last, and he missed her. More than he realized. *Focus, Sam. Focus.* He crawled from the innards of the organ chamber, brushing the gathered dust and grime from his pants.

"All done?" asked the pastor, a youngish man in his early to mid-thirties, with a young congregation. He was about the same age as Sam.

"Yes sir, Reverend," said Sam as he removed his white cotton gloves. "Would you like to try it?" he asked the pastor, who was hovering over the keyboard like an expectant father.

He beamed. "May I?"

"But of course," said the expert tuner, stepping away from the keyboard. It was a dual MKII keyboard which controlled over four hundred pipes.

The young reverend was a longtime customer, a friend. He made himself comfortable on the old leather bench and turned on the machine. Sam could hear the air rushing through the lines and filling the bellows with a long whooshing noise until it subsided, signaling that the organ was ready. The reverend opened three stops and began to play. The deep baritone sound of the organ responded enthusiastically, as it roared its approval, performing loud and deep. The pastor moved to test the sweeter sound of the shorter, smaller pipes, numbers 43, 399, and 156, and smiled. Perfect.

Nodding his approval, Sam knew his tuning work was done.

To both men, it sounded superb, but Sam glanced at his sound meter per Ollie's mandate. *Hmm, long pipe number 12—may be off by one decibel. Minor tweak. Almost perfect.* He closed his eyes and listened. *Yes, number 12.*

The young pastor played with a smile spreading across his face. "I don't know how you do it. It's wonderful! In all my years, I have never heard a sweeter sound. You're a maestro, Sam Carpenter."

"Thank you, Reverend." Sam smiled. "But if I can suggest, let me make just one minor tweak to number 12 and then…"

The minister held up his hand to stop him. "Listen to it yourself, Sam, listen with your ears. Don't mess with perfection, my friend. And don't ever believe those electronic machines." He kept playing, then said, "However, if you could persuade your boss to lower your company's fee, life would indeed be perfect."

The company he worked for, Carpenter & Matz Tuning Company, was the oldest and largest organ pipe tuning service in a five-state region and the most expensive. Sam's father had started the firm, with the home office formerly in Saint Michaels, Maryland, and expanded to offices in Baltimore before merging with his business partner there. Oliver Matz now ran the company after Jack Carpenter passed away the year before.

It was rumored that Sam was in line to be the next Vice President of Operations for the company. Sam wasn't sure about the job. If he took the job, he would be desk bound and knew he would miss the field work, working with churches he had serviced with his dad over the years. He recalled working in the field with his dad during summer vacation when he was younger. But, he rationalized to himself, it's the cost of career progress.

"Can't help you there, Reverend. I just do the tuning work." As he began to pack up his tools, he said, "With the growing size and makeup of your congregation, Reverend, you may want to consider investing in a new trio multi-keyboard organ. I've heard that attendance grows substantially at other churches that have done it. You would also love the sound. Just something to consider. Or let our shop rebuild this one for you next summer."

"You say that every year, my friend, just like your father," he chuckled. "But you're right; it's something to consider." He smiled, sporting a huge grin. "Merry Christmas, Sam."

"Merry Christmas, Reverend."

The small church, decorated in its holiday finest, was preparing for the upcoming Christmas holidays. The altar was filled with red poinsettias, flanked by twenty large live Christmas trees. Pine wrap and wreaths were attached to the end of the pews. The church had that fresh pine Christmas smell to it.

Sam closed his old brown leather satchel, the one his father had used for years, and walked towards the door. It contained all the instruments of his trade, most accumulated over the years by his dad.

"Is all your Christmas shopping done?" the young reverend asked him as they walked.

"Yes sir," he lied—sort of. He did not have a lot of people in Baltimore to buy presents for, other than the secret Santa pool in the office. "All done. See you at Easter, Reverend."

"Tell me again, why must I tune the organ twice a year?" he asked, with a puzzled look on his face.

"Because pipe organs are made from many different materials, including specialty woods, and metals that are very sensitive to heat and cold. It does not take much to take them out of harmony. So when you turn on the heat or the air conditioning for the change of seasons, they must be retuned and rebalanced. If you want them to sound good, that is."

"I see," said the young pastor.

Sam laughed. "If you want to extend the time between tunings, all you need to do is close your doors and keep the temperature exactly at 72 degrees every day and the humidity at 50 percent."

"That's a tall order for a church, close your doors," he said with a chuckle.

They reached the front door, and the young tuner shook his hand. The minister said, "I miss your father's visits every year. He was one of the few people who would argue politics or religion with me. I'll say some prayers for him at Sunday services. And he played a great game of chess. Do you play?"

"Yes sir, just not as good as my father." Sam recalled the countless hours that he and his father had spent in the cabin, in front of the fireplace, playing chess and talking. His father may not have been well educated but was well versed and well read. He knew a lot. Sam loved those talks…he missed those days.

"Practice, my boy, practice." He paused. "Your father was a good man. I miss having him around."

"Thank you, Reverend. I miss him too."

"So long, Sam. See you at Easter. God bless."

"Merry Christmas, Reverend." Outside, the grey sky threatened snow, but it was a rare year when they had a white Christmas in Maryland. It seemed to him they had more snow when he was growing up on the Eastern Shore. Christmas in Saint Michaels, a white Christmas—heavenly, if only…

His phone beeped, and he read a text message. From the office: *All appointments canceled–return to office–employee meeting with Oliver.*

*Just what I need today*, he thought to himself, *a staff meeting with Ollie. The third meeting this week. I'll never get my work done if this keeps up.*

Sam drove the twenty minutes back to the shop and parked his old red Jeep at the rear of the building. It was a century-old former foundry his dad had stumbled across one day, after getting lost in downtown Baltimore.

The building was the former home of The Baltimore Steel Company. They made steel rails for the railroads that proliferated on the east coast around the turn of the century. The company had prospered at a time when the port of Baltimore was a busy seaport transporting raw materials, agricultural products, and finished goods west to West Virginia, north to Pittsburgh, and south to Roanoke. Baltimore Steel was driven out of business by the Pennsylvania Steel Company, and the only remembrance of its history was the faded, weathered name painted on the side of the old building.

By the time his father stumbled across the building, it had been abandoned for over twenty years, last being used as a leather tannery, then as a warehouse. But his father had loved the building, and always told him that if he closed his eyes he could still smell the molten steel, the carbon, and tungsten in the air, that it was a perfect place for an organ tuner's workshop.

Sam made his way through the organ refurbishing and repair area. The smell of welding, braised leather, metal pipes, aged and fresh cut oak, poplar, and walnut woods filled the air. Vast hides of custom leather hung from the high ceilings. He loved the smell of the shop—it was familiar and comfortable.

Growing up, Sam had worked at the company during his summer vacations as an apprentice with his father, Jack Carpenter, tuning, servicing, and rebuilding organs all along the Eastern Shore. When the family moved to Baltimore, Sam went to college, but got to know all the pastors first as customers then as friends.

After college, he tuned organs and pianos throughout Maryland, Delaware, and Pennsylvania. He returned home to live in Saint Michaels after his father gave him responsibility for the Eastern Shore of Maryland territory, where he'd grown up. He was happy there, happy to be home, and glad to have his old friend Grace Albright back in his life. Then the accident happened, and he reluctantly returned to Baltimore.

The repair shop was usually bustling with rebuilding activity, but today it was empty. He made his way past the lunchroom, now filled with a small artificial Christmas tree with wrapped gifts strewn about the base and a sign over the top wishing all employees: Happy Holidays! That room, too, was empty. *Was something wrong?* He walked through the showroom, filled with pianos and smaller organs on display for the consumer marketplace. That was Ollie's idea, but they had sold only two pianos and no organs over the past four years. That room also was empty.

Sam pushed open one of the ornate set of double walnut doors, with large custom-made polished brass organ pipes as door push handles and soon found himself in the executive headquarters area.

He paused as he passed his father's still-vacant office, the nameplate still hanging prominently on the door: Jack Carpenter, CEO. Sam was headed in the direction of the lunch room where he heard voices.

Walking through the shop, he thought back to all the time he had spent here growing up: countless weekends, holidays, and vacations. His father had spent more time in this building than he did at home. His only other place of refuge was the lake house in Saint Michaels, the original home of The Carpenter Organ Tuning Company. To Sam, Saint Michaels always felt like home, his only home, especially after his dad died. Over Sam's objections, the company closed the Saint Michaels location after Jack Carpenter died and instead arranged to send technicians to the Eastern Shore from Baltimore whenever needed. He was greeted with backslaps and familar high fives as he entered the room, looking for a seat.

"Well, well, look who's finally here. Sam Carpenter. Just because your dad's name is on the marquee doesn't mean you can show up late. So glad you could join us," said Oliver. "Find a chair."

"Ollie, I just got the notification fifteen minutes ago and didn't know we were having this meeting, otherwise I would have…"

"Never mind, Sam," interrupted his boss Ollie. "Just take a seat anywhere." As Sam sat down, Ollie looked around the room. Standing next to him was his future son-in-law, Zack Bridges.

"Thanks for coming in," said Ollie. "I know you all have busy schedules, but I wanted to make an announcement. Zack will be coming aboard as our new Vice President of Operations, with a focus on marketing. He represents our future here at Carpenter & Matz. And Zack is also a computer and marketing whiz."

Sam was shocked at the announcement but tried not to show his reaction. He did not want to give Ollie any satisfaction.

Sounds of surprise, along with whispers filled the room, as many near the front discreetly turned to see Sam's reaction. Everyone assumed that Sam would be next in line for the position after Gerry "Bucky" Boyd retired. Bucky was one of the original employees of the Carpenter Organ Tuning Company and served as the overall head of operations. He oversaw scheduling, services, repairs, inventory, and all the hiring. Everybody loved Bucky. The company had suffered its second devasting departure, first Jack Carpenter and now Bucky. Those in attendance looked for a reaction on Sam's face to the announcement but saw none.

"Sam," said Ollie, "I need you back on the Eastern Shore for the next couple of days, maybe for a week or two. I'll be sending over the rest of your team to help later. You know everybody on the Eastern Shore after working with your dad over there all those years. So, it should be a snap. While you're there, I'll want you to work out the bugs with Zack's program to systematize the tuning process using the latest computer technology. Now I'd like to ask Zack to demonstrate." He smiled before turning the podium over to the company's newest employee.

Zack Bridges was tall, with unruly light brown hair, wearing an old torn t-shirt, faded jeans with rips at the knees, and a dark, three-day beard stubble. Those who passed him on the street would have assumed he was a homeless person rather than the newest Vice President at Carpenter & Matz.

He took the stage and held up a cell phone for all to see. "This is the future of piano and organ tuning," he said. "It's a specialized smartphone app I've developed which will listen to the sounds coming from any instrument and immediately tell you what needs to be adjusted. And by how much. It will cut tuning time in half and can even be used by non-skilled employees." He looked around the room at the group of senior expert technicians.

"We will no longer need to send a skilled specialist to handle tunings. People like Sam will come in-house, take phone calls from field personnel, and direct them if they need help. It works for everybody: the customer, the technician, and the company." His face beamed with a broad grin.

One of the senior techs raised his hand. "Now that it will take less time to tune, will we be doing more tunings?"

"This little app will make your job so much easier and—"

"Yeah, that's all great, but will we be doing more tunings per day? We're already stretched to the limit as it is. Working ten-hour days, especially around Christmas and Easter."

Showing his annoyance, Zack responded with a fake smile, "With this tool, your productivity will increase by some thirty percent. And we will have more employees out there doing the work at the same time."

One of the women in accounting raised her hand to ask, "Will we be charging our customers less?"

"No. This is state of the art technology, and customers will be happy to pay for the enhanced service. Besides, we have to have some way to pay for all this new technology." He laughed at his own joke.

George, the field tech for Western Maryland, asked, "No disrespect or anything like that, Mr. Bridges, but have you ever done an organ tuning before?"

"None taken, George. But to answer your question, no, I have not done any actual organ tunings. But I've accompanied many techs on some tunings here in Baltimore. I have also seen many, many YouTube videos, and it seems pretty straightforward."

An undercurrent of chuckles greeted his answer.

Another tech in the back of the room stood and asked, "I'd like to hear what Sam Carpenter has to say about all this. What about it, Sam, what do you think?"

Sam didn't respond at first, thinking of the most positive spin he could put on the situation. He finally said, "I think we need to keep an open mind to anything that will make our jobs easier and provide a better service to our customers. We have to try it and see. Once that happens, then I can give you a better answer. I will say that this sounds like we need to do a shakeout to work out any bugs it may have, but I also think that our customers should come first and that…"

Ollie stood and interrupted him. "Now, having said all that, we are going to try it on a test basis."

Sam had seen many of these apps and tried quite a few, but always found himself going back to the age-old methods he had been trained with: the old tools, the old methodology. It seemed that every so often, someone would come out with an app and say it would save time, save money, and do just as good a job. But they never lived up to their promises.

Sam began again, "As I was saying, we here at Carpenter & Matz are the best. We hire the best, we do constant training of all our staff. I don't think it's wise for our future growth to try to cut corners when it comes to our service. Not if we want to stay in business. My dad, Jack Carpenter, rest his soul, founded this business on the Eastern Shore of Maryland and did no advertising. He built the business one customer at a time on good customer service. Fads and electronic tools come and go, but our customers will be around for another hundred years, and they will be our customers as long as we continue to provide the quality service they have come to expect from Carpenter & Matz."

Ollie appeared miffed but smiled to interrupt again and said, "I think it's safe to say that we all agree with what you just said, Sam, but we must be open to at least trying new ideas. Zack will be going to the Eastern Shore with you to work out any bugs we may encounter before instituting any changes company-wide. A trial run, so to speak. Right, Sam?"

"Yeah, sure, of course," he muttered, then shook his head. *Why didn't they just give me the app to test it out? I can tell in an hour if it works and not waste everybody's time.*

"Thank you all for coming in," Ollie said. "Now I think it's time for everybody to go back to work." He shook Zack's hand as the newest vice president made his way to Sam's side. Zack walked towards him and said, "You want to drive down to the Eastern Shore together? I'm driving down there tomorrow. I can pick you up at your apartment tomorrow, early...say, 11 AM?"

Sam looked at him and said, "No can do. I have a tuning appointment tomorrow morning. Piano tuning. Then some errands to run. Why don't we take two cars? Besides, we're going to need two cars over there anyway. I'll just meet you in Saint Michaels at the Talbot Street Café for coffee or breakfast on Monday. How about seven?"

"Seven?" He gulped. "Make it ten, and you got a deal. I just thought I could pick your brain during the two-hour drive down to the Eastern Shore but...we can talk as we go to our appointments."

"Right, we can talk then," Sam replied. "Is this your first trip to the Eastern Shore?"

"Yes indeed. But you're from that neck of the woods, aren't you, Sam?"

"Yep. Born and raised there until I moved to Baltimore. Worked as an apprentice with my dad from when I was little, up and came back to Saint Michaels after college eight years ago, then moved back to Baltimore three years ago. I think we could have one or maybe two people over there on a full-time basis to handle it all."

"Yeah, I'm sure," came his disinterested reply. Then changing the subject, he asked, "Where do you stay in Saint Michaels?"

"I'm going to stay at my dad's cabin. The old homestead. It's where all this started. I still have the old workshop there in the garage out back and can use that if I need to craft or rebuild anything while I'm down there. Besides, no need to spend the money on a hotel room. What about you?"

"I'm stayin' at the Miles River Inn."

"Zack, you're welcome to stay with me at the cabin if you like. It's a big place, we have three bedrooms."

"Clarisse and I are staying at the Miles River Inn…at Ollie's insistence."

"Clarisse?"

"Yes, Clarisse. My fiancée? Your old girlfriend? Ollie's one and only daughter?" He smiled.

"Yes, of course I remember Clarisse."

"Ollie and I thought she would like the Miles River Inn. Some place comfortable for her."

The Miles River Inn was one of the most exclusive resorts on the east coast, $400 to $700 per night. *Must be nice to have friends in high places*, Sam thought. Either way, he was going to Saint Michaels—he was going home.

"Well, that's a costly place to stay in…" he started to say until noise in the front of the room stopped him.

Ollie raised his voice to get everyone's attention. "One last thing, starting the first of the year we will have a new game room for all employees to enjoy. We're converting the former office of our founder, Jack Carpenter, from an unused executive office to a new game room right next to the lunch room. We'll be breaking through the wall and connecting the two rooms together over the holidays. It should be completed by the time everyone returns after Christmas." He caught Sam's attention and added, "Oh, and Sam, I'll need you to clear out your dad's things in his office before you leave for the Eastern Shore."

Sam was shaken. *I can't believe this. My dad started this company, and I've been with this company since it started. I was here even before Ollie came along. And now look what he's doing. Taking Dad's office? And this is the first I hear of this. I need more than an hour to look through all the things Dad had left in his office. Cool it, Sam. Calm down.*

Afterward, he took Ollie aside and asked him, "Why are you taking over my father's office?"

"Because we need the space and the employees could use a game room. And because I'm your boss, that's why."

"A game room?"

"Yes. That was Zack's idea, and I think it's a good one. They're coming in Monday to start renovations, so see if you can get the office cleared out before then, will ya?"

"Yeah, sure."

Sam spent the rest of the day boxing up his father's office: his personal files, mementos, commendations, awards, and tools. He came across the photo of him and his dad in Saint Michaels at the pier, fishing. Sam was holding up his miniature first fish he'd caught that day. It was his proudest moment. He was nearly brought to tears when he saw that his dad had kept his spelling bee trophy from seventh grade. He found a picture of himself, his mom, and his dad while they were on vacation in Colorado, her in her gingham dress and him in his khakis, standing in front of the Grand Canyon. He remembered that his father had been speechless standing before the awesomeness of the canyon.

He packed the photo of him and his dad as he received his college diploma, and his dad's award of Grand Master Tuner bestowed on him from Wanamaker Organs. He suddenly felt tired and empty as he loaded everything into his SUV. He would go through them again once he got to the cabin. So many memories.

The next morning, he packed what little clothes he would need into two pieces of luggage. Going outside, he felt a chill in the air, a cloudy, overcast December day. He had one more tuning job to do before he left to drive back to his new territory. A grand piano belonging to Dr. Malek Winston and his wife, Coleen.

He parked his car in the basement garage of the condo building, waved to Wilson, the buildings longtime security guard.

"Merry Christmas Sam," said the white haired old man.

"Merry Christmas Wilson," he replied and after grabbing his tuning bag walked to superfast elevator to take him to the penthouse.

Sam looked forward to his regular visits to their penthouse condominium and the opportunity to tune their magnificent Steinway grand piano. Steinway. The name, the sheer size and high glossy shine of the elegant Steinway always took his breath away. Her sleek lines were inviting and intoxicating. He was in love from the first moment he embraced her and taught her to sing such sweet music. And when she did, it was a sound he'd never heard before or since. Steinway had always been his favorite. "Good to see you again, Sam. And Merry Christmas," said the tall doctor, reaching out to shake Sam's hand, then embracing him in a huge bear hug.

"Merry Christmas, Doc, Coleen," he said, smiling to her.

"Merry Christmas, Sam," said Coleen. She was pretty and petite with a fair complexion, short blonde hair, and the most wonderful green eyes he had ever seen. She was also well educated, having attended the Sorbonne in Paris and Harvard graduate school. She spoke four languages and loved to mother him. "Want something to drink? Have you eaten? You look thin. Let me make you up something to eat."

"No, Coleen, I'm fine, really."

Her husband watched her return to the kitchen and said, "She loves to bake for you, Sam, but we never see you much anymore. Feel free to stop in anytime and say hi. Have dinner. We miss having you around."

"Sure, doc. I'll try, really I will. It's been really busy and with Dad gone I…"

He patted Sam's shoulder. "I understand. Just remember, you're always welcome here. Anytime."

"Thanks."

Sam saw Coleen return with a tray filled with Christmas cookies, and after setting it on the table, she smiled and said, "It doesn't feel like Christmastime until the piano is tuned, and I can play it once again. And now our traveling is over; it's good to be home again, at least for a while."

The cookies were delicious, and he soon cleared the plate and downed the glass of eggnog.

"Would you like some more eggnog, Sam?"

"No thanks, Coleen. I'd better get started."

He loved working on the grand master pianos. The Steinway reminded him of an elegant Frenchwoman, aristocratic, fussy, but a delight to work on. Since every instrument had its own personality, he gave each one he worked on their own personal nickname. He called their piano Bardot, after the famous French actress.

The Winstons lived on the top floor of a condominium building which overlooked the downtown inner harbor in Baltimore. The view from their 34th floor never failed to impress him. Standing in front of the floor-to-ceiling glass wall of windows, he could see Fort McHenry far to the south of Baltimore's inner harbor, and to the north, the entire city of Baltimore lay at his feet. It was breathtaking.

Malek and Coleen had bought two adjacent penthouse units on the top floor, then combined them to make one vast living space. She hired a top interior designer to help decorate their new home. It was very impressive, with pearl white Florentine marble floors, and elegantly furnished with classic French provincial furniture. An original French impressionistic art hung on their walls. A classic Monet graced their foyer. A Cezanne hung in their hallway. A Matisse adorned their bedroom. And Sam's favorite, the Degas Ballerina danced on a pedestal near the Steinway.

A splendid Christmas tree filled the corner of the apartment. On it hung various ornaments from their travels abroad, including some from Spain, Morocco, Hong Kong, China, Russia, Venezuela, and many others. Shiny silver and gold streaming metal icicles hung gracefully from the branches, with an angel perched on the very top. Piles of brightly wrapped gifts surrounded the base of the tree. It was a perfect Christmas setting.

The piano commanded the corner of the room, waiting. He set his leather tool bag on the floor and opened the keyboard. Sam slowly unrolled the felt piano tuning kit on the bench, including his old-time tuning lever, a felt mute, a rubber mute, a felt temperament strip, treble mute, and a *papps* mute. Soon he went to work. Taking his time, testing and tuning each note, then one chord at a time, working methodically and intently on the fine musical instrument.

Coleen sat across the room on the sofa. She sneezed once, then twice, saying, "Sam, we so look forward to having you work on our..." She stopped to sneeze once, then again.

"Allergies again?" Sam asked.

"Yes, a very severe one this time, I'm afraid. We're staying in town to have more allergy tests run. I think it's dust." She sneezed again.

Malek joined Sam as he worked. After a few minutes, he lowered his voice and said in a near whisper, "How are things going at work?" He'd always been somewhat of a mentor to Sam, someone he could go to and talk to when he needed help, regarding both personal and business matters. Sam had stayed overnight with them the night his father died. It was one night he wanted a family, one night he did not want to be alone.

"Good, I guess. Except Ollie's making my dad's old office into a game room."

"What a clod. That man has no class."

"Yesterday I had to move all of Dad's personal things and files out of his office. Stowed them in my car." Coleen sneezed again in the background. "And now I'm spending the next week or so on the Eastern Shore in Saint Michaels."

"Going home, are you, lad?" said a chipper Malek. Coleen sneezed again.

"Yes...I guess. It's been three years since I left there and came to the Baltimore office."

"Oh, it can't be that bad. Saint Michaels was home, and I'm sure you do have some fond memories of that place, if I recall."

"Oh yes, I do," he said, pausing long enough to glance towards Malek before retrieving his tuning rod. "And I also..." his voice trailed off, not saying anything more. Silence.

Malek asked him quietly, filling the silence, "Have you heard anything more from Wanamaker?"

"No, sir. I had a couple of telephone interviews a few weeks ago, I think they went very well, and they checked my references, but I haven't heard back from them."

"Tell me again, what's so significant about the Wanamaker job?"

For the first time in a long while, Sam smiled. "Well, for one thing, it's the largest pipe organ of its kind in the world. The organ was installed by John Wanamaker in 1911 in the rear of his department store in Philadelphia. He kept expanding the organ's size over the years until it eventually took over seven floors of the flagship department store. The Wanamaker building is a National Historic Landmark, and now it's also a Macy's department store. People come from all over the world to listen to their wonderful music."

"Wow, I never knew that."

He paused. "What is attractive to me about Wanamaker is they have a full-time staff of four professionals. The job opening is to refill a position for someone who is retiring. They have associates who tune, maintain, and rebuild the organ, and an organist who plays this beautiful instrument on a regular basis. It is still played every day, and they use it to accompany the Philadelphia Philharmonic Symphony." He laughed aloud. "They use it at Christmastime, playing Christmas carols, and work day and night to keep it properly tuned. For an organ tuner, it's heaven, the ultimate job. Nirvana. But the nationwide competition is very steep. I've heard they had over two thousand applicants apply for the one open position. John Marsh is retiring at the end of the year after spending forty-one years tuning at Wanamaker. So, I gave it my best shot. Wish me luck."

"Good luck as always. Let me know if I can do anything at all to help. I'd be happy to place a phone call to some people I know to see if I could put in a good word for you at…"

A look of dread appeared on Sam's face. "No, no. Thank you, sir, but no, please. If I win this, I want to win it on my own merit. If I lose, then so be it. It was meant to be."

"Okay, okay," he said, and grinned at how serious Sam had become. "As you wish. But if you change your mind, let me know."

Sam began to tune the piano again. An hour later, he stopped and said, "Finished, sir. She's all yours."

"Fantastic, Sam," said Malek. "Would you like to test her out, to play something for us? On our Steinway…our Bardot?"

Sam was hesitant at first before sliding onto the piano bench as they took a seat on the sofa. He limbered his hands and fingers to make them more flexible before caressing the Steinway keyboard. Breathing deep, he whispered softly, "Gershwin's Rhapsody in Blue," and began to play. Softly at first, in keeping with the classic he was then transformed as he played the tune. That wonderful melody. He lost track of time and place as he played the exquisite instrument until he was done.

"No, no. Please play more!" they shouted. "Please play some more. That was beautiful."

Embarrassed, he said, "Thank you, but I really must be going."

Malek approached him while reaching inside his jacket and pulled out an envelope. "This is for you, Sam. Merry Christmas. Just our way of saying thank you. Please take it."

"No thank you, sir, both my father and I have always enjoyed our visits here with you and Coleen. It has been an honor and a privilege to service your Steinway, and I count both of you as friends and more…I think of you both as a family. Friends."

"Can you stay for dinner?"

"Sounds great, but I'm afraid I have to head over to the Eastern Shore for a while. Christmastime is one of our busy times, you know?"

"Are you sure? We're having *Coq Au Vin*, Steak Diane, asparagus almandine, champagne potato fluff, and a peach tart for dessert, lathered with homemade whipped cream. *Non?*"

Malek added, "We would love to have you stay, Sam. It's been too long. We can catch up on things."

"I really must leave as soon as I finish here. But can I have a rain check?"

They both smiled. "Of course. Call us."

"Merry Christmas to both of you."

He grabbed his gear and made his way to his car. As he walked away, it began to snow. His footprints were soon visible on the city sidewalk. "Well, Saint Michaels, here I come." He was looking forward to going back to Saint Michaels. He was going home.

# *Chapter Four*

"I'm sorry, Ms. Brown, but I can't offer you an increase on your line of credit against your inventory."

"Please, Mr. Barnett, call me Henrietta," said the woman. She sat in Barnett's office at the bank, snowflakes gently falling outside the nearby window. "Everyone else does."

"Well then, Henrietta, Saint Michaels Bank & Trust Company cannot see its way clear to offer you an increase in your loan secured by your inventory. Inventory that you have depleted, I might add. Your house already has a second mortgage. You are maxed out on your credit cards with us and others. So we would be securing it merely on your signature alone. That is completely outside of our lending guidelines."

"That's why I need the money, Mr. Barnett," said Henrietta. "Since my store, Ye Olde Christmas Shoppe, has only been open since Memorial Day, my vendors require payment up front for any big orders, and Christmas, obviously, is our prime selling season. We sell a lot of Christmas ornaments throughout the year to the tourists who come to visit here in Saint Michaels. But like most retailers, right before Christmas is our busiest time. I need to pay them so I have stock for the upcoming holiday. We are just about sold out and have had a tough time reordering."

She leaned forward in her chair. "They require C.O.D. payment before we can take delivery. We're just about out of inventory, so we have very little to sell in our store."

"I understand what you are saying, Ms. Brown, but the bank does not feel that it is a wise investment for us to make."

She could tell he was feeling a slight discomfort as he repositioned his tie to perfectly align with his shirt collar.

"Mr. Williams promised me when I moved all of my accounts to your bank that I would have no problem in increasing my credit limit when I needed it."

"Well, as you well know, I'm just the assistant manager here," said the banker. "Mr. Williams, the former manager, passed away last month, and my superiors in Baltimore thought it would be a good experience for me to come down from New York to this...place, but Ms. Brown, running a business is hard work, even such a small business as your Christmas store. I think..."

She interrupted him as he began to fidget in his chair. "Mr. Barnett, please do not tell me about hard work. I worked just outside of town at Jackson's crab packing plant for twenty-two years. Every day, six days a week, from sunrise to sunset, I picked crab meat from a thousand blue crabs a day, up until the crab house closed two years ago. Years later, my hands still reek of crabs. Do you know how long it takes to pick crab meat from a thousand crabs, Mr. Barnett? Do you? Well, let me tell you, sir, it..."

He raised his hand politely. "Ms. Brown, Henrietta, please. Your pro forma numbers are great, sales are soaring from month to month, your receivables are right in line, but your payroll is way out of line. And that's a cause of concern for the bank. For instance, Hilda Mae Cooper? What does she do for you?"

"Hilda Mae is an old friend, and in addition to formerly being one of the fastest crab pickers at Jackson's Packing House, she's also the best darn designer on the east coast."

"Designer?"

"Yes sir, designer. She designs all our newest ornaments. You could call her our creative guru, so to speak. She designs our unique, one-of-a-kind Christmas tree ornaments. They have all become bestsellers, outpacing sales of all our other ornaments. I believe your former secretary inquired about placing quite a large order with us. I also heard at the beauty salon that she's thinking of going into the same business that I am, here in Saint Michaels, and that she rented the old barbershop on Talbot Street. Opening soon, so I hear."

He looked startled, then huffed and puffed, his chest rising with each breath. "I don't know anything about that at all. But back to your payroll issues, please, Henrietta. What is Henry Brown doing for you? He's your son, correct?"

"Yes, sir. Proud of that young boy."

"And?"

"Well, young Hank is completing his MBA in finance and is a computer and Internet whiz. In addition to his college courses at Morgan State University, he's been setting up our website so that we can be more global in our sales focus. I'm not exactly sure what all that means, but let me tell you, what he has shown me is quite impressive. We are already receiving online orders, and it was just activated last week. So that's why he's been on my payroll." She smiled. "He's also been interning at a bank branch in Baltimore and graduates next week. Hopefully, he'll be coming back home here to Saint Michaels to live. Mr. Barnett, now you can see why I need that increase in our line of credit."

Barnett stood and held out his hand. "Ms. Brown, you'll have the bank's decision soon. Good day, and thank you for coming in."

Henrietta knew what he meant. It meant no. People had been saying no to her for years. She smiled but kept her silence when she shook his hand. "Thank you, Mr. Barnett. Yesterday can't be soon enough. I will wait to hear back from you."

She knew then she would never get her badly needed loan. Henrietta buttoned up her old topcoat and wrapped the scarf around her neck, the one Hilda Mae had knitted for her some thirteen years ago. The sound of Christmas hymns was coming from the Saint Michaels chocolate store as she passed by. She was not going to let some banker ruin such a beautiful day. She was lost in her own troubles and did not see the scruffy-looking man approach her until he was standing right in front of her.

"Excuse me, ma'am. Can you spare a dollar or two, so I can get me some soup?"

Henrietta stepped back, looking him up and down, her eyebrows raised. Obviously homeless. Old green army surplus topcoat was ripped and torn. Grime smudged his face. Stained dark trousers and shoes missing shoelaces. Three different layers of shirts worked to keep him warm under his topcoat. But those eyes... those eyes bore right through her: peaceful eyes, needy eyes, forgiving eyes.

She opened her purse and pulled out her wallet, fishing for some spare change. Looking at him at the same time, she pulled back, holding it close to her chest. "How do I know you're going to buy soup and not whiskey?"

He smiled a genuine smile. "Because I'm hungry, ma'am, not thirsty." He held out his soiled hand again. He wore gloves without finger coverings.

Henrietta looked back in her purse and handed him two five-dollar bills. "One is for soup…and the other is for honesty. Merry Christmas to you."

"Merry Christmas, ma'am. And thank you." He grinned and walked away.

That sounded so good, she thought: Merry Christmas. Suddenly she felt warmer and felt the cold brush of a snowflake as it whisked past her, brushing gently against her cheek. It was beginning to snow. She began to sing a soft Christmas hymn: *Silent night, holy night, all is calm, all is bright.*

Then she remembered her old friend Hilda Mae back at the shop. She dreaded having to tell her that they didn't get the loan. It was not going to be pretty, but she smiled anyway. Merry Christmas.

When she reached the entrance to the store, she found her old friend Hilda standing with her hands on her hips, tapping the floor with her shoe. "So, did you get the loan? Did you get the money?"

"Good morning and Merry Christmas to you too, Hilda," she said with a grin, shedding her coat. "I just felt a snowflake outside. A white Christmas?"

"Henrietta Brown, you know that we don't get snow here in Saint Michaels and haven't had a white Christmas here in over fifteen years. Too close to the water. Now stop changing the subject. Did we get the money from the bank or not?"

"He said he would let us know in a day or so."

"Humph. That means no. Darn. Girl, I bet you were just too nice to him like you are to most people, and you let him blow you off."

"No, I was quite firm, if I must say so myself. Quite firm."

"So what are we going to do now? No money means no inventory, and no inventory means no sales. No sales means…" Hilda paused, then gulped and sighed. "That's just great. We need that loan to keep going. We have a good business here, but now we could lose everything, our savings, our retirement…our homes." She was nearly in tears, something her best friend had never seen.

Henrietta took off her woolen cap and heavy coat and put her arms around her. "Smell your hands, old friend. Then think of some of the brighter things in life." Before Hilda could answer, she added, "Do you smell the crabs?"

"Yes. Everyday. I can't get that smell from my mind."

"Remember…a thousand crabs a day? Just think of that when adversity knocks on your door. Remember old Mr. Crab. We ain't never goin' back to pickin' crabs, girl. We got my Lil' Henry and your Frankie to think of. You remember those crab pickin' days, old friend? Well, do ya?"

"Yep, I do. Everyday. For me getting away from there makes every day like Christmas. If only I had…"

Henrietta knew her old friend Hilda Mae well. "Frankie?" she whispered.

"Yeah."

"Still no luck trackin' her down?"

"No, but that still doesn't stop me from tryin' to find her, though." A tear formed in the corner of Hilda Mae's eye.

Twice in one day, Henrietta had seen her longtime friend nearly in tears.

"Even if I do somehow find her," said Hilda Mae, "then I have to convince her to come home. To get a fresh start here rather than hangin' around those good for nothin's that she calls friends. I send out five or six letters a week to new leads on her whereabouts. And the addresses from the postcards she's been sendin' me for the past couple of months. And the letters that don't come back marked 'return to sender,' then I send more letters to that address."

"And?"

"Well, so far I've narrowed down her location to somewhere in California, either San Francisco or Los Angeles. She used a return address of some homeless shelter when she sent me a birthday card." Her face had that preoccupied look. Hilda Mae sniffled. "You know, every night when I go to bed, I'm warm and dry—not the least bit hungry. Then I think of her. When it rains, I think of her hungry, sleepin' in some old car, homeless shelter, behind some dumpster, abandoned warehouse or…" She stopped and looked at her old friend. "Be right back. I think I'm gonna go powder my nose."

Sitting on the stool behind the counter, wishing there was some way she could help her old friend, Henrietta watched her walk away. *I gotta be able to help her somehow. It's Christmastime*, she thought, *and the strangest things sometimes do happen. The best things.*

She sat looking around her small Christmas store, pondering her next move. She had worked hard to start this business and make it successful. She had invested everything in making it a success. All her life savings, a second mortgage on her home, cashing out her late husband's pension account, and numerous loans from friends and family, all the while paying for Lil' Henry's college education. And now, just as it was becoming successful, she needed more. Just a little more.

When Hilda Mae returned, she asked, "How much inventory do we have to sell?"

"Not much, not much at all. The garage storage out back is completely empty. Same for the upstairs area. Bare to the bone, so to speak," she said with a laugh, trying to make light of the situation. Hilda reached beneath the counter and pulled out a file. She handed her a sheet outlining the complete inventory, the returns sheet, and expected shipments. Hilda was very efficient. Henrietta perused the records, hoping that by some miracle if she read it a few times more, it would somehow change. "Anything else?"

"Downstairs, all we have are the old boxes from old man Miller's former fishing tackle store."

"Henny, you wanna sell fishing tackle?" She laughed. "If you do, I got plenty of old fishing line weights, casting gear, deep sea lures, you name it. I got it down there just sitting in boxes. And boxes. Heavy boxes at that."

Miller's Block and Tackle, fishing supply store, had been the prior tenant in their space for over eighty years, servicing fishermen in and around the Chesapeake Bay and all along the Eastern Shore. But as the area became less dependent on the fishing, crabbing, and the oyster industry, business slowly dwindled away. When old Silas Miller died, so did his business, and the store stood vacant for five years until Henrietta signed a ten-year lease to realize her dream of opening a Christmas store on the main street of Saint Michaels.

Over the last few years, more upscale residents had moved to nearby housing communities to flee the big east coast cities for the quiet, bucolic hamlet of Saint Michaels. Upscale cars, SUVs, and convertibles replaced the aging farm trucks and tractors on the village streets. The town was slowly becoming the chic place to go, relax, and have a nice meal on the scenic waters as the new residents built huge homes on neighboring waterfront properties.

Suddenly Henrietta had an idea and jumped from her chair. "What about all those ornaments that were damaged when the roof leaked?"

"Well, I've never gotten around to throwing them out. What about them? Sell them? The boxes were all wet and…"

"Yes. Exactly. The outside boxes were all wet, but the ornaments were fine. We'll bring them up here, unbox them, clean 'em up, tag 'em, and hang 'em up for sale on the Christmas trees."

Hilda nodded in agreement. "I don't know about that, Henrietta; besides, it wouldn't be enough inventory until we get the new stuff. We need something different. Something unique to maintain our edge and image. Wait. Wait just a minute. I have an idea." She quickly made her way to the door leading to the basement storage room.

Henrietta sat and waited for her friend until the bell over the front door rang, announcing that a customer had come inside. She turned to see the old homeless man standing there, approaching her, again.

*Oh no. Not again. Just what I need. Another distraction. He's going to ask me for more money. I knew it. Like my mother always told me, no good deed goes unpunished. Humph.* She stood and began walking towards him. "I'm sorry, sir, but we aren't open yet. You'll have to come back later."

"Oh, I'm not a customer."

"Really," she said, standing taller, trying to make her five-foot-two frame appear larger and more formidable.

"No, ma'am. You dropped this outside, and I just wanted to return it to you."

Henrietta looked down at his hand, then back to this stranger's face. He was holding her church envelope containing four twenty-dollar bills. She took the envelope in silence and amazement while she looked at him but could not say a word. "Oh. Thank you, thank you so much. I can't…"

A loud voice behind her distracted her.

"Lookie here, Henny. Look what I found." Hilda Mae stopped for a moment to size up the little old man before going over to the counter and plopped down a brown, dusty cardboard box. "Look at this." She pulled out a white container from inside and held up a multicolored fishing lure used for marlin, tuna, and other deep-sea fish. "This inventory was left over from the old days, from old man Miller. Antiques!"

"Yeah?" answered Henrietta. "So?"

"Glory be, Henny. Do I have to do all the creative thinking around here? Lordy, lo."

She handed her the beautiful rainbow-colored lure with two giant hooks dangling from the belly of the end. "This, my dear, is an antique fishing lure. Beautiful, isn't it?"

"Yeah," she said, still not understanding where her old friend was leading her.

"Let me spell it out for you, girlie girl." She retrieved the lure from her hand, all the while casting a cautious eye on the homeless man, who still stood there patiently behind her best friend.

"We take this beautiful multicolored antique lure, snip the hooks off the bottom, sand it smooth, polish it, and then on the side, we hand-paint the greeting, 'Christmas in Saint Michaels.' Add the year, tag it, and put it up for sale. *Voila!* An instant heirloom. I can even personalize it with the family name if the customer wants. And we have boxes and boxes of them downstairs so we have no additional inventory costs. What do you think?"

Henrietta's eyes were beginning to swell with pride and appreciation as tears formed. "I think it's a wonderful idea. Just wonderful. Do a few in different colors, and we'll hang them on the tree in the front window and see what happens."

"Only one problem. Those are some big heavy boxes, lots of them, at the very rear of the storage room. I don't know if I can carry all of them, with my bad back and all, unless I open them up and bring up a few at a time."

"That'll take forever. We need somebody who can bring them all up...and quick." They both got the idea at the same time, and each turned their attention to the old man. "Well, old man? You want to move some boxes for us and earn twenty dollars?"

Without saying a word, he removed his jacket and wool sailor's hat, then shoved the hat in his pocket. "Yes, ma'am. Just show me the way."

Two hours later, the homeless man had finished his task, and Hilda had completed a dozen of her new personalized fishing ornaments. Henrietta displayed them, hanging from a miniature Christmas tree in the front window of the store. Hilda lifted the tree and moved it to the front window.

Several tourists came into the store while Hilda was decorating a miniature tree with the new ornaments, and two of them bought Hilda's new ornaments as unique Christmas gifts. The first new ornament sold in less than twenty minutes. They knew then that they had a winner on their hands.

## Chapter Five

The next morning, with Sam's SUV loaded to the point that nothing more could fit inside, he climbed aboard and headed east towards Maryland's Eastern Shore. *Home.* The drive was relaxing and settling, bringing back many fond memories as he rode along Route #50 on his way to the Bay Bridge, the historical link to Marylands far distant Eastern Shore.

The bridge stretched four miles over the bountiful Chesapeake Bay. He smiled as he remembered taking out his first sailboat on the broad body of water with his dad. It was only a fifteen-footer, but to Sam, it was a yacht. So proud he was that August afternoon with his father beside him, his hand alone on the tiller with the canvases full of wind as they sailed the Chesapeake Bay.

While the Eastern Shore of Maryland comprises more than a third of the state, it houses less than eight percent of Maryland's population. Ever since its rural beginnings, more than five hundred years before, it had always been an expanse of immense beauty. The area contains lovely vistas, vast cornfields, and small towns filled with a variety of residents, ranging from rugged watermen, and hardworking farmers to landed gentry.

It was a world unto its own on the other side of the immense Chesapeake Bay. A world some said was stuck in time in years gone by, while others said it was a friendly, slower-paced environment, an excellent place to raise a family. The population there had remained at the same level over the last fifteen years until recently, as wealthy families who had built second homes there decided to establish themselves and move there permanently.

The Bay Bridge loomed before him as he entered a new world. He looked down at the white-capped waters below, remembering the many times he and old friends from the Saint Michaels Sailing Club had sailed and raced J-Boats on the Miles River and the Chesapeake Bay. The times on Memorial Day weekends when he joined them to race J/88 sailboats. The sleek bay cruisers full of wind in the sails, gliding smoothly over the waters of the bay. He missed sailing, the glorious independent feeling it gave him. To him there was nothing like it.

But as Sam drove over the Bay Bridge, leaving the big cities behind him, he could feel himself change, looking at life through a different reference point. A slower, healthier point of view. He was going home. Quiet times. The Eastern Shore.

As he traversed the four-mile-long bridge and reached the other side, he soon saw the sign that never failed to bring a smile to his face:

*Welcome to Maryland's Eastern Shore*
*Stretching from the grand Chesapeake Bay to the broad Atlantic*
*Ocean*
*Take your time, drive slowly—we'll leave the light on for you.*

The two-hour drive from the nearby cities of Baltimore or Washington, D.C. was more than just a ride over the Bay Bridge. It was a drive back in time, back to when things were simpler. A time when people knew each other's names, and neighbors waved to each other and talked over the knee-high white picket fences that dotted the town. During the winter offseason, Saint Michaels was a town of no more than a thousand residents, most of whom never locked their doors at night.

On the Eastern Shore, a summer night's preferred entertainment was often a slow walk through town or a sailboat ride on the Miles River with family and friends. Chasing lightning bugs in the summertime was a family affair. And Christmastime was especially delightful. By December, the town had come into its own. The small village had long since shed its usual throng of summer tourists, who had arrived to visit and enjoy the atmosphere, excellent food, and good cheer of the small town. All gone until the next season.

In winter, local folk liked the quiet just fine. With the tourists gone, they could celebrate the holidays the old-fashioned way, with family, friends, and neighbors.

The main artery heading east was Route #50 and narrowed from ten lanes to six lanes to four lanes until just outside of town.

Sam approached the Route #33 turnoff leading south to Saint Michaels until it became a rambling two-lane state road. Driving east, he recalled the vast cornfields and broad sunflower fields. He thought he saw a snowflake bounce off his windshield. *Must be mistaken, we don't get snow on the Eastern Shore.* Just outside the village limits, he was surprised to see many new housing developments. Single homes. Waterfront homes. Apartments. Townhomes. All tastefully done and sited, and now they looked as if they had always been there.

Driving further along, he soon passed a sign which read:

*Welcome to Saint Michaels, Maryland*
*Population 1,029*
*Established 1677*

Home.

He leisurely drove through town, taking it all in. Not much had changed. The bakery and the hardware store were busy. The general store and the beauty parlor were abuzz with activity. He drove past the café, the barbershop, the post office, the shipyard store, the antique stores, Doc's pharmacy...they all remained the same. Nothing ever changed in Saint Michaels. But then he noticed something new: a Christmas store, Ye Olde Christmas Shoppe. A new store on the main thoroughfare in town. He made a mental note to visit it during his stay.

Slowing his drive, he passed the first of the three churches in town, Saint Michaels Church. It was their oldest church and the town's namesake. It stood tall and proud with its white steeple and silent church bell tower; the building was clad in gray stone, with Indian red brick rounding the windows and doors. Two small cemetery plots flanked each side of the entrance walkway. He slowed his car to see if anyone was there walking about. Perhaps Grace? She lived there with her father, the Reverend Bill Albright. Deserted. It was then he realized how much he missed her. Talking with her. Seeing her.

Disappointed, he turned off his satellite radio and tuned into the local AM radio station, WKSM, just as the last refrain of "Jingle Bells" finished.

"Good morning, Saint Michaels, Cambridge, Easton, and everybody else waking up on the Eastern Shore. Merry Christmas! This is Bobbie Rich here at WKSM, letting you know that if you're still searching for that perfect Christmas gift for someone special, you may want to check out Hamilton's Jewelry for fine jewelry, antiques, and estate pieces. And for Christmas decorations, you must visit the new store on Talbot Street, Ye Olde Christmas Shoppe. Check it out, you won't be disappointed. And now for all the Eastern Shore news and weather. The city council is still wrestling with how to handle the problem from the fire at the local city-owned storage building. It looks like a resolution is on the way. Stay tuned. In other news, Grace Albright is looking for more carolers to join her group at Saint Michaels Church." At the mention of her name, he turned up the volume to listen. "Bring your good cheer and your voice for auditions. Also, don't forget to join in the festivities at the bonfire late this week. Pray for snow, and let's make this a really special Christmas this year. If you…" Sam stopped in front of the café, pulled into a parking spot, and turned off the ignition. *I sure could go for a piece of freshly baked pie*, he thought. *It's good to be home.*

The diner looked and smelled the same. The menu still offered home-baked bread and muffins, local farm fresh eggs, toast, homemade jam, and coffee—nothing here ever changed.

He heard a familiar voice from behind the counter. "Well, lookie here," said the tall, broad-boned older woman who ran the main street restaurant. "Look what the cat dragged in. As I live and breathe, if it ain't Samuel Jason Carpenter. Welcome home, Sammy." She set down the coffee carafe she was carrying to throw her arms around him.

"Hi, Molly," he said with a boyish grin.

She never hid the fact that he was one of her favorites. "You know, I was just thinking about you as I was takin' some pies from the oven. Fresh apple and my favorite, Impossible Coconut Pie. What's your poison?"

He always felt like a little kid around her, like he was ten years old again. "I gotta go with the apple pie."

"Have a seat and make yourself comfortable," she told him, as she pushed a dangling wisp of gray hair away from her face, tucking it back behind her ear. "Lunchtime. Want some homemade chili? Cheeseburger?"

"Just pie, thank you."

She came back ten minutes later with a plate of French fries, a cheeseburger, three pickles, and another with a slice of fresh pie. "You looked hungry," she pleaded sheepishly. She returned five minutes later with a glass of milk and a cup of coffee for herself as she slid into the booth across from him.

As he began to devour his burger and fries, realizing he was hungrier than he'd thought.

She sat, watching. "I love to see a man who loves to eat. So how ya been?"

"Good."

"And how's everything at work?"

"Good." He finished the last of the burger and began to nibble on the fries.

"Sam Carpenter, you'll never change. You sure are a talkative cuss. I can hardly get a word in edgewise if you know what I mean."

He laughed with her, then slid the plate holding the warm slice of pie closer in front of him and began to eat. Halfway through, he asked her, "Anything interesting going on?"

"Here? In Saint Michaels? Never." She paused for a moment, aimlessly stirring her coffee, then asked, "Have you seen her?"

"Who?"

Her face puffed in annoyance. "You know darn well who I'm talkin' about. Grace Albright, that's who."

"No," he whispered.

"Grace knows we speak from time to time, and since you moved away, she comes in to talk. Still as cute as a button. But her dad helps her pick out some of her clothes, dresses her, and fixes her hair. Just needs more of a woman's touch to help her. Shame, she's so pretty." She stopped then lowered her voice. "She asks about you every time I see her. Always wants to know how ya doin' and all. Says to say hi."

He stopped eating his pie to ask, "You never told me that."

The look on his face told her she had struck a tender nerve. "What's the point? You being there in Baltimore and her bein' here. But now, well, you're here, and she's here, so…" She paused. "You should go see her. Say hello."

"Well, her dad may have something to say about that."

"Reverend Bill? He's full of bluff and hot air. Sammy, he's like any other father. All he wants is for his daughter to be happy, that's all. I'm sure he'll come around someday. He can't still be angry with you. He's a man of the cloth and not supposed to hold a grudge. But if I were you, I wouldn't wait too long. Like I said, she's a real pretty lady, smart, funny, and some ole farm boy's liable to come by, make her smile, say sweet things in her ear and snatch her up lickety-split—if you know what I mean."

He resumed eating his pie. "Maybe I'll stop by later and see her and say hello. For old times' sake, us being old friends and all. Just to say hi. Her father can't object to that, now can he?"

"Nope. Want some coffee?"

"No thanks. I gotta get on home and chase out any critters who might be using the old lake house as home."

"Moving back to Saint Michaels, are ya?"

"Nope, just here for a visit. Business. Got some tuning jobs to do, that's all."

"How long you stayin'?"

"Few days to a few weeks, depending on how much work they give me while I'm here. I'll just take the check, Molly."

"You got it. Give me a minute. Be right back."

Sam sat waiting for her in his booth, looking out onto the street, but was distracted by a disturbance coming from the table behind him: a younger waitress waiting on an older man, a homeless-looking sort. He had never seen the waitress before.

She stepped back from the table and nearly shouted, "I'm sorry, sir, I can't serve you. Unless I can see your money up front, on the table. You'd better be quick about it. And we have a dishwashing machine here and don't need anyone washing the dishes to pay for their meals. So maybe you better leave before I have to call the sheriff."

Sam stood and laid a crisp new twenty-dollar bill on the table in front of the old man, then turned to the waitress. "This should cover anything he wants to order, including a tip…if you act real nice to him."

The old man smiled. "Thank you, son. Thank you very much."

"No problem," Sam said as he walked away, heading for the cash register. He loosened his coat around him, feeling warm. Molly greeted him carrying two large bags, filling both of her hands.

"What's this?" he asked.

"Just some provisions to get you started. Detergent, coffee, milk, bread, eggs, frozen waffles, syrup, things like that."

"You're a good lady, Molly. The best." She was the town chatterbox. If you wanted to know anything at all, you didn't bother to read the Saint Michaels Town Crier, you just stopped by the diner, had a cup of coffee, and chatted with Molly.

"Now, don't make an old woman cry."

"You ain't that old, Molly."

"You're a sweet boy, Sam, but I found a bunch more gray hairs the other day. Not a good sign. And oh, by the way, lunch is on me. Merry Christmas. See you around later. Don't be a stranger, ya hear?"

"Yes'm." Still, Sam left her a generous tip. She was a kind lady.

It felt like snow in the air as he walked outside and glanced at his watch. "Just enough time to drop these grocery things off at the house before they go bad," he mumbled to himself. "Maybe stop by the church for a visit. Just a visit. That's all."

A snowflake glanced against his cheek. Then another. *Snow in Saint Michaels? At Christmas?* That would be a first in many, many years. One could only hope.

After he found his car, Sam drove off towards the family homestead. He passed the town's only fine dining restaurant, #208 Talbot, and saw a line outside waiting to get inside. A little while later, he saw a discreet sign for the entrance to the exclusive Miles River Inn, set back on a gravel road much closer to the river. A few yachts filled their private docks. Looking at their size, he surmised the owners were likely visitors from Washington, Baltimore, or Richmond.

He passed a roadside Christmas tree stand and pulled over on the gravel parking lot. The weathered sign out front proclaimed, "Sanders Fresh Produce." During the summer, the stand sold freshly picked corn, cucumbers, and fresh watermelons. In the fall the stand sold pumpkins of all shapes and sizes. Around Christmastime, old man Sanders sold Christmas trees, pine wreaths, oversized homemade candles, and other Christmas decorations. He still wore his trademark winter uniform of blue coveralls, red flannel shirt and green plaid hat.

"Merry Christmas, Mr. Sanders," said Sam, looking around the lot.

"Merry Christmas, Sam. Good to see you. Been quite a spell."

"Yes, sir, it has."

"You lookin' for a tree?" said the old man.

"Yep."

"Sounds good. Follow me. One thing I got a lot of is Christmas trees. The best deals are the ones in the back, down this row here. Give you a good price on 'em, too," he said, as he led Sam to the rear of his yard. Sam had worked the Christmas tree lot with him for three years when he was in high school.

He walked the lot for over thirty minutes before settling on a tall blue spruce tree, a huge wreath, some oversized candles, dangling cranberry vines, two potted poinsettias plants, a few sprigs of mistletoe, and fifteen feet of garland. Old man Sanders helped him load it into his SUV and thanked him for stopping by. Sam knew the old farmer would be there until he sold every last Christmas tree, just like he always did. Christmas would not be Christmas without old man Sanders and his tree lot.

Sam turned the steering wheel back onto the road and headed down Tilghman Island Road, with the Miles River slowly lumbering along to his right. He saw seagulls diving and fighting over food as they gracefully glided over the water's edge.

He slowed the car the closer he got to home and stopped at the top of the hill on the gravel driveway. The faded name, "Carpenter," was still visible on the side of the green mailbox. It felt like centuries since he had been home last as he drove down the long tree-shrouded driveway. The leaves from the sycamore trees were gone, but the massive sentinels still stood tall to the wind.

A group of startled deer, unaccustomed to having human company in their domain, ran across his path. The farmhouse and the old converted barn, which was formerly his father's first office and workshop for Carpenter Organ Tuning, was located at the end of the long, winding stone driveway. It was just behind the cabin. He saw it up ahead, just the way he had left it a few years before.

The hand-crafted cabin was a three-bedroom house overlooking the Miles River. One of the bedrooms had been converted to an office. On the front porch deck, the old swing moved quietly in the gentle breeze, next to a neglected flower box. When his mom was alive, she would plant petunias in them every summer, but after she passed away, it fell into disuse, his father not wanting any more memories to remind him of what he once had.

Sam grabbed his luggage and made his way up the wooden porch steps, lifting the welcome mat to retrieve the key and unlock the front door. No need, he remembered as he soon discovered, the door was unlocked.

The cabin seemed surreal in the dark quiet, the furniture still covered in spooky, ghost-like white sheets. He stood at the door and saw past visions of his mom and dad, dancing barefoot to some unheard tune around the kitchen table, while freshly baked loaves of bread cooled on the countertop in the kitchen. Sam smiled as he recalled sitting next to his mother at that very same table, as they shucked corn and snapped bean pods before tossing them into a big kettle of nearby saltwater. When they finished, they would sit together on the swing on the back porch and watch the fishing boats return from a day on the water. She would dry her hands on her apron, then pour them each a glass of freshly squeezed lemonade and sing a tune. How she loved to laugh, sing, and dance. Sam could still hear her raspy voice singing an old Joni Mitchell, Taylor Swift, or Paul McCartney song.

But Christmastime was always her favorite. Never having money for what she always termed as store-bought frivolities, she would make her own candles, garlands, gifts, and pinecones for the fireplace. She would soak the cones overnight in a bucket of water, then add a unique mixture, depending on the color she wanted. Water and salt for a blue color, boric acid for yellow flames, and Epsom salts for a red glow. After they dried, his dad would dim the lights, and the family would watch as the different colored flames flickered in the fireplace.

Most times, his mom sat on the couch between the two men in her life, and she was in heaven. All she would ever do was smile and always repeat, again and again, "I am the luckiest woman alive." Sometimes Grace would visit and join them on the floor or couch, no one saying a word, just watching the flames sparkle and snap in the night flames.

He set his luggage down by the door. "I'm home," he whispered to the empty house, standing in the dark just inside the landing. He made no effort to move. Instead he waited for a welcoming sign to allow him to enter. Once his eyes grew accustomed to the dark, he saw his father's homemade oak table off to the right. To him, the table was the heart of the house. His father's table was the place they would share their meals, talk about their day, play games, and at Christmastime, make handmade candles, string popcorn, and cranberry garlands, and sing Christmas carols. And laugh. And dance. And be a family.

The area in front of the fireplace was reserved for his father telling scary stories to him and Gracie, roasting marshmallows, and sprinkling the hearty flaming logs with fairy dust to turn the flames blue and gold. Grace would hold on tight to his arm, afraid for her life, but loving every minute of it.

In the shadows, he remained motionless at the front door, waiting for permission to enter. The wind blew the door shut behind him. He smiled and took it as a sign. "Thanks, Mom. Thanks, Dad. I love you too."

Sam turned on the electric at the panel, then the refrigerator, water supply, propane tank, water pump, and hot water heater. He soon heard the water rush through the ancient pipes. The water heater shuddered its resistance as it began to heat the inflow of cold liquid. The house was full of noises, a cacophony of sounds waking a long-slumbering home.

Unlocking, then removing the heavy outdoor shutters, he opened the windows to let the air and light bathe the inside of the cabin. Fresh air made everything feel good again. He breathed deep, then again. A hint of his mom's violet perfume caught him off guard.

An hour later, Sam had finished unloading the car, with the files, the boxes, and Christmas tree, while restocking the refrigerator with the things Molly had given him. The big blue spruce Christmas tree filled the corner of the cabin, and the smell of fresh pine filled the air. He wrapped the garland loosely around the banister leading upstairs as he attached one wreath to the front door and placed the smaller one on the kitchen table, interspersed with the dried cranberry garland. It was already feeling more like home. He set the big red candle at the center of the wreath and hung the last of the garland from the mantel over the fireplace. It's good to be home. He tacked the family's four stockings to the thick roughhewn log mantel: Mom, Dad, Sam, and of course, Gracie. It was good to be home.

When he was finished unpacking, he went to the back porch, where he could see the river's edge at the bottom of the small hill and his father's old workshop off to the left in the shadows. Walking down the small lane, his eyes began to tear as he passed the tire swinging loosely in the wind coming off the river. Pushing open the unlocked door to the old workshop, Sam searched for the light switch on the wall. The lights begrudgingly flickered on, and he soon felt his father's presence all around him, smelled faint whiffs of his old aftershave and traces of the smoke from his cherry pipe tobacco. This made him shiver, or perhaps it was the cold winter weather, cooling the day as the sun went down.

Tools still hung on the wall above the fifteen-foot workbench. Shadow outlines on the wall showed where every tool belonged. Nothing was missing. Nothing was out of place. It remained just the way his father always said it should be. He ran his fingers along the uneven and rough surface of the workbench they both had made so many years earlier. A three foot, handmade stool sat off to the side, made of cherry and hand-polished to a high gloss. It was a unique stool, made at his father's insistence. The stool was made just for Grace to sit on and watch them, as they worked on fashioning organ pieces while joking and laughing.

Old leather hides hung by size and thickness in stalls, which dotted the barn, along with pieces of wood replacements, old organ pipes, leather straps, and replacement motors. Everything there was just as he had left it. Everything was there except for…his father. It was too much for him. "I'll be back, Dad," he whispered. "I'm going to see an old friend."

# Chapter Six

Grace Albright's favorite place to sing was in church. Early, when no one was around to listen or bother her. If she stood in front of the altar, at the front of the church, she found perfect acoustics. Every day, she would leave the rectory very early in the morning and make her pilgrimage to the church to sing. She sang ballads. Hymns. Christmas carols. And her favorite, opera. Puccini. Halfway through her early morning chorales in the darkened church, she heard a noise, and then again.

She stopped and listened in silence before asking aloud, "Hello? Anyone there?"

After a few moments, she heard the creak of an ancient oak pew off to the left, and the steady sound of a man's footsteps on the terrazzo floor approach her. From the length of his stride and the heft of his steps, she could tell he was big and tall.

"Hello?" she asked again, and for the first time, she felt fear. Instinctively she reached for her cane for protection. Afraid? In church?

"Good morning," the man replied. "I'm sorry, I didn't mean to startle you." His voice was calm and educated. "My name is Justin Reynolds. I'm a principal partner in the talent firm of Reynolds and Geyser in New York."

*New York?* she thought. *What's he doing here in Saint Michaels?*

"I'm sorry," he said, "I didn't mean to surprise you."

"I'm fine." Relieved, she stuck out her hand. "I'm Grace Albright. I usually have the church to myself this early in the morning. I like to practice before my choral class." She paused. "I didn't realize there was anyone else here."

His hand felt warm, clean, and slightly moist, with remnants of old calluses long since gone. "I know who you are. I saw your name on the bulletin board out in front of the church. I've been staying at the Miles River Inn for the last week for a business conference, and I jog every morning into town. One day last week it was raining, so I ducked in here to stay dry and...I heard you sing."

"That's a long jog," she said, trying to change the subject.

"Keeps me fit," he laughed, then paused. "Can I get right to the point, Ms. Albright?"

"Please do."

"I have been jogging around here for the last week, and for the past three days, I have stopped here and listened to you sing. You have a glorious voice, Miss Albright. It is very special, a natural talent. A gift."

"Please call me Grace, especially if you're going to be handing out such nice compliments."

She could hear him chuckle. A warm and kind voice. A trusted voice.

"Ms. Albright...Grace, have you ever entertained the thought of singing professionally?"

She laughed. "Years ago, I thought about it, but now I have so much to do that—"

He interrupted her. "Grace, your voice is more than glorious, it is exquisite. Special. One of a kind, very distinctive. I've been in this business for over twenty-five years, and I know what I'm talking about. If you're interested, I would like to offer the services of my firm to manage your career. I would suggest some vocal training to help you along but, in the end, I think you would do very well. Three times a year, we have vocal training programs to help assist and accelerate a singer's development. Here's my card. Think about it, talk to your family, and if you're interested, please call me. My business here in Saint Michaels is over soon, and I leave Christmas Eve to go back to New York City." He handed his business card.

"Let me give you my cell phone number, Mr. Reynolds," replied Grace, "in case you need to reach me directly. But you can usually find me here at the church. Or the rectory. It is right next door. My dad's the pastor. His name is Bill, Bill Albright, rather Reverend Bill Albright. I can't wait to tell him. You have really made my day." She stopped long enough to say, "I'm sorry...I ramble when I get excited, Mr. Reynolds." Grace could hardly contain herself. It was like winning the lottery, only better.

"Sure, but please call me Justin. Now I'll let you go back to your singing, and I'll continue my jog. So long, for now, but please think about it. Merry Christmas, Grace."

"Merry Christmas…" She had already forgotten his name, and his company. He said he worked in New York, but where? She was so excited about everything he told her that she'd forgotten his name. She panicked and went to call out to him, but then remembered: Justin Reynolds, Reynolds & Geyser, New York. Reassured, she tucked the card away, deep inside her pocket. *Singing, professionally? Every day. And getting paid for it? Heavenly.* She had a lot to think about.

The conversation she had with him stayed with her the whole morning, through her English, History, Geography, and Reading classes. She could not shake his words from her mind. *"Have you ever entertained the thought of singing professionally? Your voice is exquisite."* Holy cow! She suddenly wished her old friend Sam was there to talk about it. To share. To discuss.

Just before lunch, she returned to the church for choir lessons with her young group. "Okay, class, you're doing extremely well. Very much improved. I can hear the difference just since our last class. Ready for 'Silent Night?'"

They murmured their agreement, but before they began to sing, she heard the rear church door swing open and a blast of cold air rush inside. Footsteps. Coming towards her. Familiar. *Is it Mr. Reynolds? Justin? The talent agent. Had he forgotten something from this morning?*

*No. This sound was different. Younger. Faster-paced steps. Must be a passerby who stopped by to listen to the choir practice.* Then it stopped. She listened. The creak of a pew echoed throughout the silent church. The weight was different from what she had heard earlier, based on the creak from the bench. Lighter.

Turning her attention back to her class when they finished singing, she said, "Well done, class. I'll see you all here tomorrow." Some of the girls chattered with each other as they made their way to their next class and the church began to empty.

It was then she heard the noise again. Creak. Someone was walking towards her; long strides, must be tall. Fresh soap scent. Something familiar. Scented aftershave. She could tell he was getting nearer, steps getting louder. Her hand searched beside her in the pew for her walking cane. She trembled for an unknown reason, then again. "Hello?" she said, standing. Silence. After a few moments, she repeated, "Hello?"

"Hi, Gracie," he said softly.

She recognized the voice immediately. It was Sam!

"Sammy? Sam, is that you?"

"Yes." He walked closer to her and was soon standing directly in front of her.

"I was just thinking about you and what do you know, here you are."

"Is that so? Your wish is my command."

"Hah!" She laughed. He could always make her laugh. Even as kids, he knew just what to say, what to do to make things better. She was so glad he was home. She fought back the tears as she told him, "Oh Sam, I've missed you. Welcome home. Don't ever stay away so long again. You hear me?"

"Yes," he said, "I've missed you too." He took another step nearer to her. She could hear his breathing, smell his spiced aftershave. They both stood there in awkward silence until Grace said, "Well, is this how you greet an old friend that you haven't seen in years? Come here and give me a hug, a big hug. I don't have poison ivy."

He laughed and hugged her, longer than usual. She felt different, he thought...or maybe it was him. Strange. He stepped away from her and said, "I didn't want to jump up and surprise you with a hug. Like the time..."

"... you had poison ivy, and I came to visit you and..."

"... I wanted you to hug me hello."

She laughed—they could always finish each other sentences, like an old married couple. "I was afraid I would catch the poison ivy."

"It is terrific to see you again, Grace. I was listening to you sing in the back. You sounded wonderful."

"You know I love to sing. Oh, big news. A man just stopped by this morning and introduced himself to me! He's a talent agent. His name is Justin Reynolds. He's from New York. He wants to manage my career. Sing professionally. Travel the world." She stopped talking long enough to ask, "Am I rambling again?"

"Yes," he said with a laugh. "Grace, that's great news. No, it is wonderful news. I always said you had a special voice. Would you have to leave Saint Michaels?"

"I guess. I don't know. This just happened and...I have a lot to think about before I call him." She paused. "Come closer. Are you back for good?"

He walked closer to her and was now standing directly in front of her.

"No. Only two weeks."

"Oh," she said, her disappointment obvious. She reached out and hugged him again. She raised her hands to his face, softly touching him, slowly tracing the outline of his face with her fingertips. "It really is you," she sighed as she stepped away, leaving her hands on his face. She heard him removing a cap from his head.

"Yes, of course. Who else would want to be Sam Carpenter?" Her hands felt tender to his face.

She laughed again, but her hands stayed on his face, exploring the contours, his eyebrows, and his cheeks. Her fingertips brushed through his hair. He had a good face, a kind face, and oh, how she so wished she could see his face again. In that instant, she realized how much she had missed him. Good old Sam. For some reason, her hands began to quiver.

Breaking the silence, he said, "And your choir sounded magnificent. Like a finely-tuned instrument."

It was so good to see her again. He had missed her, and suddenly realized that she was the one he was looking forward to seeing the most here in Saint Michaels. He felt something he did not expect. His feelings for Grace had changed—he didn't know why, but they had changed from the moment he saw her when he walked inside the church. *She looked so good and...wait. Hey, cool it. This is Gracie. Best friend, Gracie, from kindergarten. Remember?*

"Thanks," she said. "I'm getting them ready for a special Christmas Eve performance...for the bishop."

"The bishop?"

"Yes, he's coming into town for a Christmas Eve service to see if we have any hope of sustaining a parish." She paused for a moment, nearly in tears. "My father thinks they may close us down. Everything."

"Close down Saint Michaels? The church?"

"Yes. It could happen unless we do something to increase attendance at the church. And they would probably also close the school."

"The school? No. Well, maybe I could help," he said. "If your dad would let me, I could tune the old church organ and maybe even get the bells in the tower working again. I bet they would sound fantastic. Maybe that would get more people to come to the church to hear them," he told her excitedly. "Even if it's just out of curiosity to hear both of them play."

One of the things she always loved about Sam was his enthusiasm. She moved closer to him. "Sam, that would be great. Now we just have to get

Dad to agree," she whispered. "You know, I can't believe how much I've missed you. And you here, now, brings back so many memories. Remember when we used to chase lightning bugs in the summer and you would always fill up the jar and..."

"And when it was full you would open the lid and let them all out." They both laughed as he continued. "Remember when you would come to the cabin and help my mom set the table for dinner and me, and my dad would be working in the shop out back and..."

"I would bring your dad a beer and you a root beer. And after dinner, your dad would turn out the lights and..."

"Tell us those creepy horror stories in front of the fireplace about creepy monsters hiding in the river and..."

"They would come to steal you out of bed and take you away."

"Remember when I had poison ivy all over my arms and legs and I was supposed to take you to the dance at school and Maurice Rauscher had to step in and take you?"

"Ewww, creepy Maurice. I was so angry with you, but he was very gallant at first. Then he got so angry with me because the whole night all I talked about was you and how we were soulmates."

She stopped for a moment then said, "You know even though we've known each other since kids, I always had a crush on you."

"Like a big brother, I guess," he laughed.

She was quiet for a moment and turned solemn, "But seriously, I have always wanted to tell you..."

"Grace?" shouted a voice in the distance, echoing off the walls of the church: her father. "Grace, your class is waiting for you to..."

"I'm over here, Daddy! With Sam, Sam Carpenter. He's come back home."

"I see," he said, as he approached them.

"Hello, Reverend Albright," Sam said, extending his hand. "So good to see you again."

"Hello, Sam," he said, shaking his hand, his voice as cold as a winter frost.

"Well, I just thought I would stop by and say hello. I told Grace that I would be happy to tune Big Ben for you."

"Big Ben?"

"Yes sir," Sam said, turning to point at the massive organ platform towering over them at the rear of the church. "You see, I give all church organs nicknames."

"Hmm, Big Ben?"

"Yes, sir. Because he's a big, massive baritone that needs a big name. I would be happy to tune him for you."

"We can't afford it, Sam," he replied tersely.

"No problem, sir, I understand. But I would be happy to perform an initial evaluation for you. No charge. We could see what it needs and then take it from there. See what it would cost. I would do it on my own time, at no charge to you or to the church." He knew he was repeating himself, but he really wanted to help. "I can even look at the bells you have in the tower. I've heard from some of the old-timers in town that in their day, the bells sounded wonderful."

The reverend's tone did not soften as he responded, "Thank you, Sam. But we still can't afford it. Grace, you have a class waiting for you at the school. Good day, Sam. Good to see you again. Goodbye." Then, taking Grace by the arm, they walked away.

Sam shouted after them, "Grace, I'll call you. I'm only in town for a little while. I'm staying at the cabin if you want to talk." The sound of the door slamming shut drowned out his last comment.

"Well, that went pretty good, if I do say so myself," he said aloud to no one in particular, always the eternal optimist.

He placed his wool cap back on his head, and as he left, he noticed an old man trying to stay warm at the back of the church. It was the same homeless man he had seen at the diner. The man smiled and nodded his head. "Merry Christmas," he said.

"Merry Christmas," Sam replied, and walked out to a much colder winter day. *Now it is starting to feel like Christmas in Saint Michaels*, he thought, as he made his way to his car. He felt good for some reason. A snowflake rolled across his face, another one brushed his ear. Time to go home to the cabin.

# Chapter Seven

Sam drove through town, stopping at Jameson's General Store for additional supplies that he would need for his stay.

The store was outfitted with garland hanging from the walls, mistletoe over the entrance, and Christmas music over the intercom.

Leaving town, he rode past the stores, past the numerous B&Bs at the edge of town, with the Miles River off to his right. He drove past the barren cornfields ringed with tall oaks, sycamores, and poplar trees. The gravel crunching beneath the wheels of his SUV was a familiar sound as he drove back down the hill to his driveway. He stopped in front of the old cabin, filled with so many memories.

Opening the cabin by himself felt funny, almost strange. His dad had always been there to joke with him, kid him, and go over the schedule for the following day. He would review the number of churches and their location and organize the tools and supplies they would need for the day.

His dad, Jack Carpenter, had never attended school beyond the eighth grade, but he knew all the answers to any questions that Sam would ever ask. His mom had been gone some twenty-two years, the result of a careless drunken driver on a late Saturday night. In heaven, Sam always thought, looking skyward to the stars. He still felt that the bright shiny one just below the Big Dipper had to be her. His dad never spoke to him about it, he always just looked away whenever Sam would ask about her. Sam knew he missed her, but rarely would open up and talk about her.

But sometimes, usually around her birthday, when his dad was missing her the most, the pain seemed to ease, and he would talk about his Janey. "She was the best woman in the world," he would always say, as they sat at the end of the boat dock at the back of their property, their feet dangling in the river water below. "She had to be, to put up with a cuss like me."

Then he would sit back and talk about the old days. Even though Sam had heard the same stories many times before, he loved to listen to his dad talk about his mom. The time they met at a dance one night, her love of country music, their wedding at the American Legion Hall, fishing along the Miles River, the traveling he had to do, including the extended apprenticeship programs he went on, which sometimes lasted for months. He would stop, and a wistful smile would appear when he said, "But as soon as she heard my truck coming down the gravel driveway, she'd be heating up my supper in the oven. She never complained, about anything. Not once. Your friend Gracie has that same style," he would always say. "Samuel, that's one fish you never want to let get away." His dad liked Grace, always felt comfortable with her. "But she's a stubborn cuss," he would always say, then laugh, "just like me."

Sam stopped and sat down on the back steps to watch a pair of fishing boats glide by on their return to Saint Michaels harbor. It was a beautiful, crisp winter day. He missed sailing on the Miles River with his friends, the cool breeze, the salty spray in his face and hair. Back in Baltimore, there was never any time for it. He missed his dad. He missed his mom...and he missed Gracie.

# Chapter Eight

The official hours of Ye Olde Christmas Shop were ten o'clock until seven, but the two co-owners were always there early and stayed well past closing time. Anything to keep busy and help the business succeed. Business had been brisk, but the lack of funds for inventory was beginning to take its toll.

"Any word from Klaus Christmas Supplies?" Henrietta asked, while she straightened what little inventory she had to make the shelves appear fuller.

"No," responded Hilda.

"What about Berger's?"

"No."

"Did you call to check with them?

"Yes. Three times."

"And Easton Supply?"

"No."

"What about Groper's Holiday Supplies?"

"Most want CBD. You know, CBD—Cash Before Delivery. Including Steve at Groper's."

Hilda paused for a minute. "Henny, we need to talk. I have something I need to tell you. I'm afraid I've done something you'll be angry about, but listen to me all the way through and then you can yell all you want, but…"

With the loud squeal of airbrakes, a big delivery truck stopped and parked in front of the store, partially blocking the street. The jovial driver was a big man, with a salt and pepper beard. He wore a red and green flannel shirt with a faded jean jacket and scuffed leather work boots. Different tattoos covered his hands. "Mornin', ma'am," he said. "Got a delivery here for…" He glanced down at his clipboard, thumbing through his sheets before continuing, "a Hilda Mae Cooper from Groper's Christmas Supply store. Got eighteen boxes. Where do you want 'em?"

Looking around the small Christmas store, his smile grew as he waited for a response.

"I don't understand," stuttered Henrietta, turning to her old friend.

"That's what I started to tell you. I bought all this on my credit card, so we could have something on the shelves to sell." Hilda turned to the driver. "Just stack them right here by the shelves."

"Hilda Mae Cooper, you shouldn't have done this."

"We're in this together, remember? Good or bad. Well, dahlin', this is the bad."

"You're such a good friend." She hugged her old friend Hilda, while the truck driver's steady cavalcade of boxes began to fill the small storefront.

"It's enough to keep us going for a week or so, but we're going to need a lot more," said Hilda. "A lot more. But it's a good start."

He needed to stack some of the boxes on the counter, causing Henrietta to move a small Christmas tree out of the way to a ledge near the front of the store. She set it on a table behind a wooden plaque of the American flag, which read: WE THANK YOU FOR YOUR SERVICE. The tree looked bare. "Remind me and I'll put some ornaments on it later," said Henrietta aloud, to no one in particular.

Soon there was only a narrow pathway from the front door to the back counter, bounded on each side by stacks of boxes.

"That's it, ma'am. That's all of it," said the beefy driver.

She turned to the driver and noticed he was admiring the small, unadorned Christmas tree, and the American flag at its base with the tribute plaque in front of it. Standing still, not moving.

She walked up behind him. "Are you a vet?" she asked him quietly.

"Yes ma'am, and proud of it."

"Merry Christmas. And just like the sign here says, we thank you for your service."

"You're welcome, ma'am," he replied. "It was my honor and privilege. But you know, ma'am, that tree there looks so bare, with only the flag at the bottom. Just doesn't look right for some reason." His eyes remained transfixed on the flag, the sign, and the tree. A tear came to his eye, and then without saying a word, he reached around his neck, removed a chain holding his cherished army dog tags, and hung them from the tree. He raised his hand and saluted the flag plaque with a wistful look.

"Now it's perfect," he said. Then with a chuckle, he added, "What a great idea, a Christmas tree tribute for vets. I love it. Keep the dog tags for as long as you need them. I'll pick 'em up from you after the holidays. Have a good day and a Merry Christmas." He left, leaving the two old friends quietly looking at one another.

Each smiled a twinkling smile. "Makes you feel proud and patriotic. Come on, we got boxes to unpack." As they turned their attention to the boxes, the silver bell over the front door rang again, and Sherry, their express carrier driver, came inside. Always in a hurry to maintain her schedule, she rushed past the tree, then quickly scanned the package she was delivering and shouted goodbye in what appeared to be one continuous motion. But the young mail carrier stopped and turned around just past the tree, eyeing the truck driver's dog tags, the flag, and the memorial plaque.

"Is this new?" she asked softly. "An honor tree…a tribute to vets?"

"Yes," said Hilda quietly. "It was just dedicated today."

The mail carrier, too, reached around her neck and added her dog tags to the tree. "Merry Christmas, Hilda, Henrietta," she said with a smile, humming the Christmas song, Silent Night as she left the store. "See you later."

The two women stood and looked in wonder at the new tribute tree. "We need to figure out a way for everyone, vets or not, to pay tribute to those friends or family in the military," Hilda wondered aloud. "Let me look into it." She made a dash to the computer in the rear of the store.

"Let's not forget the POWs," shouted Henrietta after her.

"Of course not."

# Chapter Nine

The sun rose over the harbor of Saint Michaels, but Sam was up before dawn, dressed and drinking coffee from his dad's old coffee mug emblazoned with the red and gold Wanamaker logo. Years ago, Jack Carpenter had spent three months at Wanamaker's as an apprentice, working day and night to perfect the organ tuning trade. He had often said it was the best training program he had ever experienced. He returned years later for more training, and ultimately was awarded a master tuner certificate. It was one of his most cherished possessions.

Sam sat on the back-porch steps of the old cabin to sip his coffee and watch the day begin. The sun moved over the horizon, colors of blue, pink, and orange flashes of light spreading high in the sky. Oystermen chugged out the Miles River harbor in their sleek skipjacks, heading towards Kent Island in search of oysters. Their eighteen-foot long oyster tongs were securely fastened to the inside of the boat, waiting for the captain to anchor in shallow water. Then they would troll for their precious cargo using the back-breaking tongs. Egrets flew by gracefully and majestically, trailing behind a formation of white and golden-tinged pelicans.

The night before, Sam had stayed up late, unloading all of his gear and his dad's personal files and bags of tools in the spare bedroom. The gritty tools smelled of his dad—leather, steel, iron, grease, everything a good organ tuner needs to do a proper job.

Shortly before ten A.M., he packed his Jeep with the things he would need for tuning and headed into town to keep his morning appointment with Zack. He parked the car in front of Saint Michaels Hardware Store, got out, and walked towards the diner, browsing the storefronts as he passed by them. He walked past Saint Michaels Realty, with small postcard-sized pictures of properties for sale. He noted they were promoting everything from small harborside cabins, like his, to massive mansions with pools, tennis courts, and their own private dockage on the river.

He passed Jameson's General Store, which appeared to still have the same pair of chinos on display from some four years earlier—or at least they looked like the same ones. But the store featured the most extensive selection of boat shoes and duck shoes in town, *de rigueur* for all of Saint Michaels residents. Walking past the longtime ice cream and chocolate shop, he thought it was too early for McCafferty's homemade hot fudge and ice cream, but it never failed to make his mouth water as he walked by.

The store he noticed earlier, Ye Olde Christmas Shoppe on Talbot Street, was open early. Sam peered through the window and, on a whim, walked inside. It had the proper smell of Christmas ornaments, combined with fresh pine and mistletoe dangling about the store. Boxes lined the floor of the small Christmas store.

"Well, I'll be, if it ain't young Sam Carpenter," a voice rang out from the back.

Hilda Mae rushed to him, hugged him, and lifted his tall frame, all six feet three, off the floor. "Boy, are you a sight for sore eyes!" Then she mellowed and said solemnly, "I was so sad to hear about your daddy passin'. He was a good man. First your momma, then your father. Such a shame good people die so young."

"Thanks, Hilda Mae. I appreciate it." Then, changing the subject, he looked around the new store, with its nearly empty shelves but boxes lining the floor. "Very nice. Very nice indeed. But I think you could use a few more items on the shelf, don't you think?"

"I think you are absolutely right, young man," a voice boomed loudly behind him, "just as soon as we finish unpacking and pricing the rest of these boxes they delivered yesterday." a voice boomed loudly behind him. It was Henrietta. She also gave him a good-sized welcoming bear hug. "Welcome home, Sam. You been missed, baby boy," she said with an understanding smile.

There had always been a special bond between Sam and Henrietta. Years before working at the crab picking house, when Sam was born, Henrietta had worked as a county midwife on the lower Eastern Shore. While making one of her regular visits at the Carpenter home one weekend, his mom had gone into labor. Henrietta soon discovered that the umbilical cord was wrapped tightly around the baby's neck, choking him. She immediately knew what to do and saved both of their lives. He never forgot what she had done for him and his family. She had a special place in his heart, and he would do anything for her.

"I've missed being here. I don't know what made me stay away so long."

"Never mind now, you're here and home for…how long?"

"Well, I'm just here for a few days to a week or so. Just to make the circuit and tune church organs for some of our customers over here. I was just on my way to the café to have some breakfast and meet up with a coworker, but I saw your door was open and thought I would stop by and take a look."

She gave him a warm smile, then turned around to face the shelves. "Once Mister Barnett at the bank comes through with our line of credit, we can fully restock our shelves. And fill up our empty warehouse out back too. So say some prayers."

"Sure will, but in the meantime, I'd like to buy one of your fancy fishing lure Christmas tree ornaments. It'll make a perfect remembrance for this Christmas. I'm going to be decorating my Christmas tree tonight at the cabin."

"Thank you, Sam. You know what they say, don't you?"

"No, what's that?"

"That you need to buy at least one new Christmas tree ornament every year to celebrate properly."

He laughed and said, "I agree. I have one for every year going back eight years." They say it's good luck." He glanced at his watch. "Sorry, but I gotta go. See you later."

"Don't be a stranger now, ya hear?" responded Hilda. After paying, he headed towards the café singing a Christmas tune. A flurry of snow pushed by the wind swept along the streets, over the curbs, and down the sidewalk.

When Sam arrived at the diner, he noticed that Zack had not yet arrived and grabbed a seat at a booth near the front of the restaurant.

A cheerful Molly approached him with a steaming hot coffeepot. "Mornin' Sam," she said with a smile. "The usual Monday morning breakfast?"

"Yep." She brought him his coffee and toasted English muffin with marmalade. *Some things never change,* he mused. It was as if he had never left three years ago. Fifteen minutes later Zack arrived and waved at Molly for service.

Zack proudly held out a computer spreadsheet which contained their schedule for the day. "Got our route for today all laid out for us, right here," he said, then folded it and put it back into his jacket pocket. "Whenever you're ready to take a look at it."

"Okay but let finish my coffee first, but I'm sure that Heather did her usual great job of scheduling out our day."

"She didn't do it," he said with a huge, proud grin and ordered his breakfast.

Sam gulped. "Who did?" He was afraid of what he was going to hear next. He had trained Heather himself in all the intricacies of laying out a schedule: the timing, the age of the organ the location, the last time it was serviced. That all went into how much time to allot for a service call.

"I did. Piece of cake."

Sam anxiously watched Zack eat the last of his muffin and drink the remaining remnants of his coffee before leaving money for the bill. Glancing at his watch Sam asked, "Ready?"

"Yep. Let's go."

"Where's our first stop?"

"Cambridge, Saint Paul's Church on Maryland Avenue. At eleven fifteen."

"You're kidding, right? Come on, let's go. We're going to be late."

At the front door of the diner, a tall, broad-shouldered man walked inside. A light dusting of snow covered his grey wool topcoat. Sam's face lit up with a smile at seeing an old friend. "Hiya Charlie," he said, shaking his hand.

"Hey, Sam, good to see you again," said the tall man, flashing an effervescent smile, the smile of a true politician. "I heard you were in town. Welcome home." He had a middle-aged paunch above his belt, and long swirls of perfectly placed wisps of grey hair strategically placed on his head to cover his ever-expanding bald spot.

"Zack," said Sam, "meet Charlie Wilson, the mayor of Saint Michaels."

Charlie reached over and shook Zack's hand. "Welcome to Saint Michaels, Zack. A great place to live and raise a family, if you're so inclined."

"I'm not married, sir…yet."

"Well, when you do decide to settle down and have a family, come on down and move to Saint Michaels. You'll love it. Maybe we can even offer you a white Christmas, hopefully someday. Well, keep it in mind. You'll love it here in Saint Michaels. Pretty much stays the same year after year. It has that small town feel that no one ever tires of, right, Sam?"

"Yes, sir. But I wanted to ask you, I was amazed, I didn't see a lot of the usual Christmas decorations when I was walking around town. That's unusual for Saint Michaels. What's up?"

Charlie made a pained face. "Oh, it's terrible. Everybody feels so bad. This town loves Christmas, but we're a little behind this year. Our warehouse in Easton burnt down. Where we stored all the town's Christmas decorations. Now we gotta order some new stuff, somewhere, from somebody, somehow." He shook his head in desperation. "It may be too late in the season to get replacements. Really crazy. Gotta go. Nice to meet you, Zack. Take care, Sam."

Sam stopped him, grabbed his elbow, and said, "Hey, Charlie, why don't you stop by and see Henrietta Brown at Ye Olde Christmas Shoppe? She knows all about that kind of Christmas stuff. That's what she does all the time. She'll be able to tell you who to order it from and how to get it quickly. Maybe even order it for you. Besides, she just got a huge shipment of Christmas supplies in today."

"Really? Hey, great idea. Thanks, Sam."

The two of them watched him walk away. "Seems like a really nice guy," said Zack.

"Yeah, he is. Charlie owns the Saint Michaels Hardware Store down off Willow Street. Been mayor of Saint Michaels here for as long as I can remember."

After leaving the diner, they got in the red Jeep, and Sam drove onto Talbot Street and headed south towards Cambridge. On the edge of town, he slowed the car as he drove past a sign which read "Saint Michaels Quarry Swim Club." A large sign hung diagonally across the rusted front entrance to the gate: PERMANENTLY CLOSED. He breathed in deep—so many memories—then pressed on the gas pedal and sped off down the road. It was getting colder and beginning to snow, hard enough that Sam had to use the wipers to see where he was going. Snow? Winter is here, he thought with a smile.

"How many churches are we scheduled to service today?" he asked Zack, as he drove south on the two-lane Route #33, past the broad, dormant cornfields, towards the town of Cambridge.

Zack reached inside his briefcase and, again, retrieved his computerized scheduling sheet. "Wait a minute, let me check and see." He began counting the service calls, and when he was done, he looked to Sam to say, "Nine today and ten tomorrow."

"Nine? How on earth are we going to do *nine* calls in one day?"

He stuttered in embarrassment, "Too many? I can help. We can do it together. Can't we, Sam?"

Sam had a decision to make. He paused, then said, "No, Zack, we can't do nine calls in one day and expect to do a good job. You can do four, maybe squeeze in five in a day, depending on how complex the tune really is. But I've never rushed through a customer service call in my life and I'm not about to start now. You never know what you're going to be faced with when you walk into a church. And usually, the older the organ, the longer it takes to tune. These are longtime customers. If I find I have time left over at the end of the day, then I can always call the next customer and see if they'll let me come by early and fit an extra one in for that day. But never nine."

Sam had found over the years that everybody had shortcuts, but in the end, the old way worked the best—it just took the longest.

"Sam, with this new app we can get so much more done. That's progress, like it or not."

"Zack, if the organ doesn't sound right after we get finished with it, the customer will call us back to fix it. A retune. At no charge to them. That's a waste of time and money, and we could possibly lose a customer. Understand what I'm saying?"

Zack hung his head. "Yeah, I kinda figured that, but Ollie was so insistent on trying to help me fit in at the company. Sorry, but this is all so new to me."

"Okay, okay, Saint Paul's Church is first. Then where?"

"Then Seaford, then Georgetown, then..."

Sam pulled into the parking lot of a local donut shop and parked the car. "Can I see the schedule?"

"Sure," replied Zack, happy to hand off the problem to Sam.

"Hmm," said Sam, as he breezed through the list. He returned to the first page and looked at Zack. "Look, Zack, nobody expects you to know it all, so don't be afraid to reach out and ask for help. Heather may be young, but she's been doing the scheduling for the company for the last three years. She's very good at what she does, and she knows what she's doing. Some of these tuning jobs are routine, but others on this list are a little more complicated, and they'll take a lot more time. She knows which ones are which. Got it?"

"Yeah," responded Zack, but kept quiet as Sam made his point.

Sam paused. "Some of these older pipe organs are on their last legs, and we may have to recommend to the pastor that they do an overhaul over the slow summer period. Summer is everybody's slow time. Theirs and ours."

"I really screwed up, didn't I?"

"No, Zack, it's just new to you, that's all." Sam reread the printout and said with a frown, "Hmm."

"What's wrong?"

"Well, I know this is new and all to you, but…"

"But what? What's wrong?" Zack asked, grabbing the sheet from his hands. He looked it over closely before handing it back to Sam. "What's the problem?"

"Well, you also have us going from here to Cambridge, to Easton, to Centerville, to Salisbury, to Ocean City, to Wattsville. There's no rhyme or reason to this schedule. We're crisscrossing all over the Eastern Shore rather than clumping the customers' service calls together. This takes up a lot of extra time. Heather knows which ones take more time, and she'll also try to group the jobs geographically to make the best use of time. For instance, we have eight customers in Cambridge alone. We could spend a day or two there and get a whole lot done."

"Right."

"And that's just this morning's calls. Besides, we didn't start today until 11 am…after breakfast. Half of our workday is already gone. I usually begin my work between seven and eight." He watched as he saw Zack's body language become rigid and defensive.

"Listen, Zack," Sam said as his voice softened. "I know you're new to the business, and it'll take a while for you to learn it all. No one can expect you to learn it overnight."

"But I'm going to be the new Vice President of Operations, I gotta know it all. It's my job."

"No, you don't, Zack. Just take your time. And don't be afraid to ask people for help. You don't need to know it all. Others want you to succeed, just as badly as you do."

He shook his head. "I disagree. Everybody else wanted you to get this job."

"Yeah, but not everybody gets what they want. You have to do what's best for the company." Sam let out a deep breath as he studied the paperwork. "You know, I originally thought that I wanted the job, but then the more I thought about it, the more I knew that I love doing what I'm doing. I like working with our customers, tuning organs. Making them the best they can be. That's what I love to do."

"Is that why you applied for a job at Wanamaker's?"

Surprise crossed Sam's face. "How did you know?"

"Sam, the church organ tuner community is a tiny and tight-knit group." Zack laughed. "I may be new to the business, but I'm not stupid. I do know that everybody in the world has applied for the job there. I don't blame you."

"I love my current job, but the opportunity to work at Wanamaker's is something I could not let pass me by. It's a once in a lifetime opportunity. My dad did his apprenticeship there, so they consider me a legacy candidate, and I get some preference. It may help, I don't know, but it's always been my dream job ever since."

"Sam, I don't blame you. Have you heard anything back from them yet?"

"No. Just two phone interviews. I can only hope that I make it to the next step."

Returning to their work for that day, he asked, "What about this schedule?"

"Like I said, you have us doing a five-hour drive going from one end of the territory to another. With no time allocated for lunch or to do any tuning. It doesn't work."

"Oh," said Zack as he looked over his masterpiece. He had spent a lot of time and effort in preparing the schedule for that day, and now it was all wrong.

"Don't get discouraged."

"It's dawning on me now. There's a lot more to this than I thought there would be. Most of my work was in the office, working on the computers.

Advertising. Marketing. Computers." He appeared overwhelmed and discouraged.

"Zack, we charge $500 per job, on average. That's a lot of money, twice a year, for these churches to spend. Some of these other churches have been our customers for twenty years or longer. They trust us."

"Got it." He swallowed hard. "But what do we do with all of these customers I've booked us for today? They're expecting us to come today. Can you fix it?"

"No problem. I'll call them and just explain what happened and reconfigure the schedule. They'll understand and appreciate the honesty. These are more than just customers, many times they're friends. Some of the local pastors will invite you to stay for dinner after the job is done. You have dinner, listen to some music, or play some chess."

He studied the scheduling sheet. "I just need some time to make a couple phone calls for our calls today, then I'll call Heather and have her take care of tomorrow's calls. I can fix it, no worry. Tell you what, why don't you run inside and grab us some fresh coffee, and while you're inside, I'll reschedule some of these customers, reach out to Heather, and have her handle the rest. Okay?"

"Sure," he said with a nervous grin, and opened the car door. "Hey, Sam…Ollie doesn't need to know about this screw-up, does he?"

Sam chuckled. "Naw, don't worry about it. My lips are sealed. Oh, and make mine a latte."

When Zack returned with the coffees, Sam was just finishing his last phone call. "Yeah, Heather," he said, "that would be great. We can fit them in our schedule and be back on a regular timetable. Good job. Thanks, I really appreciate it." He smiled a welcoming grin.

Zack handed him a fresh steaming latte as Sam nodded his thank you and finished his phone call. "…and Heather, just keep these scheduling changes between us, will ya? Please? No need for anyone else to know about it." He smiled and nodded again. "Thanks, I knew I could count on you. Call me if you need me or if there are any other changes. So long."

He turned to Zack and said, "All done. Usually, we schedule a team of techs to work the region and have these all done in a few days. But that's Ollie's call, I guess, not mine. I took care of our calls for today, and Heather will take care of the rest starting tomorrow. So, we have five organ tune-ups for the rest of today and four for tomorrow. Even most of those

I scheduled for today are minimal jobs, but I can tell you that today is going to be a long, long day, so we better get a move on."

Zack made a face as he squirmed in his seat.

"What's wrong?"

He was silent at first, then asked, "How late?"

"I don't know. I'm guessing six, seven o'clock tonight. Maybe later, maybe earlier. It all depends. Why do you ask?"

"It's just that I have a dinner reservation tonight. With Clarisse."

"Oh," said Sam. He paused, then said, "We'll have to see how many we finish and where we are with the schedule later. But to make it work correctly, it usually takes two people to do an organ tuning. One to use the keyboard console and pull or set the stops, while the other does the actual tuning inside the chamber room. Many times, in a pinch I can have one of the clergies work the keyboard while I tune. But if you gotta leave, you can always have a ride service pick you up and take you back to the inn. Let's just wait and see where we are, okay?"

"Sure, Sam."

Young Zack smiled; seemed that he now saw Sam in a whole new light.

# Chapter Ten

Early in the morning, during the hectic Easter and Christmas seasons, the Reverend Bill Albright liked to sit in the church, quiet and alone, when he had it all to himself. This was when he could have an uninterrupted personal conversation with his creator without distractions. Today he had a lot on his mind and a lot to talk to about. The possible school and church closing. Mrs. Schoeman's losing battle with her chronic illness. The recent passing of Harry Grevis, a long-time parishioner. Grace moving out to an apartment. Sam Carpenter returning. The bishop coming to visit. Tending to his flock. And then all the other added duties that fell onto his shoulders at Christmastime. It was a lot. He smiled as he remembered telling Grace about some of the issues he was concerned with and her response – "Well Dad, that's why they pay you the big bucks." He chuckled to himself.

When he closed his eyes to ask for help and guidance, he was alone, but when he reopened them, he found he had company. A man in a green army overcoat was kneeling two pews off to the side in front of him, intently praying with his hands folded, his lips moving, and his eyes closed.

Bill Albright gave the visitor a quick once-over, including his stained pants, tattered topcoat, and multiple layers of clothes, like those worn by most of the homeless people who lived under the railroad bridge down by the river.

The man continued to pray as the reverend observed him, wondering. A local? Had he slept here in the church? Was he the noise that Grace had spoken about?

During his walk to the church outside earlier, it had felt like snow in the air. For December, it wasn't that cold, but it was getting colder every day. If one homeless person came inside and slept, then more were sure to follow. He stood, and the creaking of the pew seemed to alert the kneeling man, who seemed lost in prayer.

The Reverend walked to the pew behind the man and knelt.

The man sat back, keeping his hands in his pockets to stay warm. "Beautiful church you have here, Reverend," he whispered.

"Thank you," Bill responded, his hands still clasped together. The pastor thought that the man had a kind smile.

"Almost like a temple. But you knew that, didn't you, Reverend?"

"I guess I did. Are you new here in town?"

Ignoring his question, he responded, "You know people are like temples too, are they not?"

The reverend squinted to get a better view of the man just inches away from him, looking beyond the matted brown hair and tattered overcoat. "That's what the Bible says."

"That's a good book. One of my favorites. But always remember, people are important too. I think it was brother Matthew who said, 'Why can people see the speck in their brother's eye but can't see the log in their own eye?'" He smiled, and Bill could see him clearer now. "Matthew always did have a way with words."

The man shifted his stance and turned towards the preacher. "People you love will always be there for you. The good book says that envy and hate will eat away at your insides until they destroy you, like an acid. They poison the soul. But you can release yourself from their grasp. All you must do is believe. Trust those you love, your family, your friends, and others. Love your enemies, and those you disagree with, for they are also the children of God. Forgiveness is the only divine act that we, too, can achieve. Right, Father?"

The reverend gasped. *What was he saying? How did he know all of this about him? About his feelings against Sam? Who was this man?* He swallowed hard and confessed, "I try."

"You must try harder, or not even bother making an effort. Try until it hurts." The man stood, bowed his head towards the altar, and quietly went to leave.

"Thank you. I hope to see you again here," the reverend said.

"Of course you will. I'm always here," he said as he walked away. "Merry Christmas," he added.

"Merry Christmas, ah…" Bill responded quietly. He stayed for over an hour to pray and think, now alone in the vast church, feeling fulfilled. Thinking about what the man had told him, he suddenly had an urgent feeling to talk to his daughter. *Grace? I must see Grace, now,* he thought, as he bowed his head, leaving the church, and walking faster towards home to the adjacent rectory building, where he found her having breakfast.

"Good morning, pumpkin. How ya doin'?" he asked with a smile, joining her in the kitchen as he made his usual pot of tea. He noticed his daughter was up early again and dressed. "What's on your calendar today?"

"I have a long break in classes today," Grace replied, "and thought I would take an extended lunch break and walk into town to hang some of these posters you made for me. I'll try the bakery, the café, the hairdresser, the hardware store, the barbershop, and some of the other stores. Maybe we can get more people to join our choir. And then maybe…" She was silent for a moment, then asked quietly, "Dad, can we talk?"

He stopped sipping his tea and sat down. "What's up?"

"I have something I want to talk to you about."

He interrupted her by saying, "Please, before you start, I would like to say something. I was in church and gave a lot of thought to a lot of different things and people. I also did a lot of…soul-searching about what you said about moving back in with Karen. And many other things. Perhaps you're right. Maybe it's time. Time for you to be on your own again. I know that Karen is a good person, and between school during the week and church on the weekend, I'll still see you just about every day anyway. So, it'll be like you still live here anyway."

"Thanks, Dad. But…"

"And another thing. About Sam, Sam Carpenter." He breathed deep, sounding relieved. "I've been holding a grudge against him for all these years. I've blamed him for causing your blindness. It's not Christian-like for me to hold a grudge like that for so long. So, you can call him and tell him it's okay for him to stop by, or I can drive you to visit him if you prefer. I always liked him before and…"

"Thanks, Dad," she said. She had been waiting for years to hear those words from him.

"Well, now that we have that out of the way, what do you say I make us up a Greek lamb casserole for dinner tonight? Maybe add a little ouzo for some zest and…"

"Dad, I still have something else I need to talk to you about." She reached out her hand in his direction, searching for him, as he took hold of it. "A man approached me in church the other day. A talent agent. He had been coming in during the early mornings to listen to me sing. He feels I have a natural talent, a gift."

Her father lowered himself into a chair beside her. He had an uneasy feeling in his stomach, it made him feel queasy. "I see," he said. "You take after your mother." He swallowed, and for once he was glad that she could not see his face. It was filled with fear, for he knew where the conversation was heading. "I've always said that you have a glorious voice, Grace. So pure, so sweet, yet so strong." He waited.

Grace gripped his hand tight and pulled him closer. "He wants to represent me as a professional singer and come to work for him, singing. He's a partner in a talent agency in New York City, and he thinks I can make it as a professional singer if I really want to be. I can't believe it. My wildest dreams coming true. I love to sing, and to do it professionally...well, that is heaven. Justin, that's his name, Justin Reynolds, said I would still have to take vocal training for a while, but that in a few months I could be singing with a group or maybe even singing solo. I can't believe it."

"Yes." The Reverend Bill Albright listened to his daughter pour out her heart to him. At that point, her life was in his hands; he could crush her dreams, or nurture and encourage her. She had overcome a lot. Losing her mother at a young age. Losing her sight. And losing contact with her best friend Sam, the only other person on Earth she cared about. "That's a lot to take in at one sitting, Grace. But tell me, what are your thoughts about it?"

She took in a deep breath. "It's scary, Dad, but exciting at the same time. I'm giving some serious thought to it, but I wanted to talk to you first. I wanted to get your input."

"It's a big step, but if that's what you decide to do, you have my full support."

"I would miss you and miss Saint Michaels and everybody else here."

"I know, and I would miss you too, more than you would ever know, but it sounds like a great opportunity. Go for it."

She hugged him tight and said, "Thanks, Dad. I know I can always count on you."

"Yes, of course," he said, trying to sound as supportive as he could muster, but already missing her.

# Chapter Eleven

Henrietta Brown held the phone away from her ear so that Hilda Mae could hear what her son was saying. "Mom, I just have one more exam for my MBA, then I'm done. I can't wait to see you—both of you. Hi, Hilda, I know you must be on the line too. Do you miss me?"

Hilda put her hands on her hips and said indignantly, "Young Henry, don't you be mouthing off now, ya hear? I just happened to walk by and hear your sweet voice on the phone talking to your momma. But of course we miss you. It'll be wonderful, I…we are so proud of you. A college graduate in our family with an MBA! Well, I'll be…you know, the buttons are just popping off my sweater, I'm so proud of you."

"Yes, and I owe it all to you, both of you." He lowered his voice to ask, "Have you heard anything back from Barnett at the bank?"

Once again Hilda jumped into the conversation. "That Judas. Don't you be talking to me about no bank now. We don't need him or his money. Just you never mind 'bout him, ya hear? You just worry about school, and 'bout comin' on home here, you hear me?"

"Yes, I do, Aunt Hilda. I love you, both of you. You make a fella proud. You want me to talk to my contacts here?"

His mother responded immediately, "No, we'll be just fine. You just worry about school, and nothin' but school, okay?"

"Okay. I gotta go now. See you both soon."

"Bye, Hank," said his mother, hanging up the phone and slumping into a nearby chair. "Lordy, if we don't get that money soon we're…"

Hilda gave her a reassuring hug. "Have faith, Henny. Have faith. Say a prayer to the good Lord. Come on now, let's straighten up, dust up, and get this place presentable for our customers."

Henrietta had to laugh. Her old friend never rested or gave up, never. She stood up, moved some of the boxes around the counter, and looked out the window, just in time to see her tight-fisted banker Barnett walk by the front of the store. He smiled but kept on walking, speeding up as he went by the door. She wondered to herself, doesn't he know that it's Christmastime, a time for giving? A time for helping those in need? "Mornin' Mr. Barnett," she said, and smiled, grudgingly remembering it was Christmastime after all. "Merry Christmas."

As Barnett walked across the street to the park, he soon found his favorite bench to have his lunch. He was from Minnesota and preferred the cold air to the hot, humid Maryland summers, and this was one of the few places he liked in the small village of Saint Michaels. He missed the big cities of Washington and New York, and especially missed Minneapolis. Not too much longer, he told himself and his wife: his very pregnant wife. *They'll promote me to somewhere else. I hope. They said a replacement would be here soon. Not soon enough,* he thought.

The weather was turning colder, but on that bright day, he felt the warmth of the winter sun on his back. He loved to sit on the bench, look out over Saint Michaels harbor, and watch the fishing boats chug back into port loaded with the day's catch.

He peeked inside his brown paper bag and retrieved the sandwich that his wife had packed for him, sealed tight inside a zip-lock plastic bag. He was hungry. When he looked up from his lunch, he realized he was not alone. A homeless-looking man in stained clothes, torn wool topcoat, and dirty hands sat down at the other end of the bench and proceeded to feed the pigeons.

*Just what I need, pigeons.*

The man was content to toss a few seeds to each bird, ensuring that each one received something to eat. He was engrossed in his noonday activity, smiling as he watched each bird hustle to secure its own food.

After nearly ten minutes of watching this activity, Barnett was annoyed. He scolded him, "You know, you're not supposed to feed the pigeons here."

"Why?"

"Because."

"Oh, that's a great reason," the man responded while throwing more seeds on the ground, followed by more into the air.

"Well, we don't want them here in the park."

"Why not?"

"Because they're pigeons, that's why. They're dirty birds."

"Dirty birds? How can a bird be dirty?"

Perturbed, he repeated, "We don't want them in the park?"

"Where are they supposed to eat?" he said with a slight grin. "In your dining room?"

"No, don't be absurd. It's just when you have one pigeon come to eat, the next thing you know you have ten, twenty, or more."

"They're hungry, just like you. They want something to eat. Just like you and your family."

For some reason, Barnett felt a twinge of guilt as he continued to munch on his sandwich. "They're noisy and disturbing my lunch," he finally declared aloud to himself.

"Like a crying baby? Now you want to get rid of not only helpless pigeons but also defenseless hungry babies. You'll make a great father someday." His words hung in the air, refusing to go away.

The old homeless man threw out an even larger amount of feed for the ever-growing crowd of birds. "You have to help those who come to you for aid. Where else can they go? How do you say no to a child? To a helpless animal? To an old woman?"

Barnett felt his eyes bore right through him. Brown eyes, sweet brown eyes, the shade of fresh maple syrup. He shivered not from the cold but from the man's pure revelation.

The man continued, "We only come through this life once, make the best of it…for the best is yet to come." Standing, he brushed the crumbs off his green overcoat onto the ground as the remaining pigeons scrambled to retrieve what fell from his lap. Then he smiled, his whole face embracing the laughter he felt.

As the old man walked away, Barnett felt better, warmer, and shouted after him, "Merry Christmas!" The old man raised his hand above his head but did not turn around as he walked away. Barnett shouted again, only louder, "Merry Christmas!"

The old man stopped, turned, and smiled, "And Merry Christmas to you and your family. Especially your new son."

*Son? What?* Barnett rushed back towards the bank, without appearing to be running. He wanted to call home and talk to his wife. He rushed past the Christmas store, then stopped and stuck his head inside.

"Oh, Ms. Brown, Henrietta. I'll be sending you a letter in the mail later today, but I wanted to let you know—the line of credit you applied for...I approved it. Merry Christmas!"

A stunned Henrietta Brown could only admire his words and say, "And Merry Christmas to you too, Mr. Barnett!"

# *Chapter Twelve*

The drive from Saint Michaels to Cambridge was a short one, a mere forty-five minutes. Sam was lost in thought, thinking about his dad, about Christmas, Wanamaker's, and of course—Grace. It had been good to see her again at the church, and he had not realized until then how much he missed her. Her laugh, her funny ways, and her warmth.

They drove in silence until Zack asked him, "If you don't mind me asking, what's with the Quarry Swim Club?"

"It's a long story."

"I got plenty of time if you don't mind sharing."

"Well…" he started to say, then stopped.

"Just curious, Sam, that's all. I overheard somebody in the café talking about it, and when I asked them, they said to speak to you. But if you prefer not to say anything that's okay, I'll understand."

At the next stop sign, Sam turned his head to look at Zack before turning away. "For years it was a local watering hole where the whole gang from college and the neighborhood went to go swimming. About three years ago, one August night, Grace Albright and I went swimming there."

He paused, then smiled. "Grace has always been my best friend, ever since we were kids. But just friends. As kids growing up we went to different schools, but during the summer, when I wasn't workin' for my dad, we did everything together: swimming, fishing, exploring the river—you know, like Tom Sawyer and Huckleberry Finn." His eyes became misty.

"That day," he continued, "we swam in the quarry and then relaxed on a blanket by the water's edge, joking and laughing like we always did, and she fell asleep on the blanket. When she woke up…"

He could not say the words. He began to breathe faster, but his words would not come out, until he finally said, "…she was blind. Now her father blames me for it, and everything else, and forbids me to even talk to her."

"But what about you? You didn't go blind?"

"No, and I still feel guilty about it. I mean, it happened to Grace, her of all people, but not me, I'm fine… but she's blind. Her whole life has changed. The doctors at the local hospital were puzzled. So were all the eye specialists. They seem to think it was something in the water that caused it. But all the others who went swimming there were fine. It only affected Grace. And now her dad blames me, he hates me. He took her to all kinds of doctors and specialists, but nobody could ever find the cause of it." He paused, then looked at Zack as they pulled into the church's parking lot. "Now you see why I don't like to talk about it, but since you asked, that's the deal with the swim club and…that's why they closed it. Okay?"

"Sure, okay," he stuttered.

Once on the church's parking lot, Sam grabbed his leather bag of tools and gloves, saying, "Come on, Zack, we got a long day ahead of us. Let's go tune the church's organ." Try as he might, he could not get her out of his head. Grace. Seeing her again had made him think of her more often. His feelings were changing since he saw her. Strong feelings. Warm feelings. More than friends. *What's going on here? This is Gracie. Remember?* He had to talk to her…again.

"Ready?" asked Zack, interrupting his thoughts.

"Yeah. Let's go."

The old church was in need of repair—a new roof, sidewalk, and a new boiler—but one thing that the local pastor, and his congregation, always insisted upon was to have the organ tuned on a regular basis. After checking in at the office to let them know they were there, they made their way to the pipe organ. It was a Schlosberg, a fine old organ of German design, made in Dresden over fifty years ago.

Sam stopped to admire the age-old pipes before proceeding to tune the large pipes first. As he went to tune the others, Zack said, "Sam, I can take it from here, and we'll be done in no time. Okay? Let me show you."

Reluctantly Sam agreed, exiting the cramped chamber area behind the organ. He watched Zack open the app and disappear from sight, back behind the organ. He heard the pipes bellow from the rushing wind, and he had to admit they sounded good…so far. But the further down the range that Zack worked, the more Sam could tell something was amiss. The pipes began to sound tiny, flat, while others offered no depth.

"Zack, wait a minute," he said. "I think maybe you should…"

"Be done in a few minutes," came a voice deep inside the instrument. Ten minutes later he emerged with a triumphant smile on his face. "Test it out," he bragged. "Ten minutes and I'm done. Now you're going to really hear something."

He was right. Sam sat at the console and began to play the old organ, and while the deep mellow tones of the longer base pipes rang out loud and clear, the mid-tones and smaller pipes sounded like fingernails on a chalkboard. They both shuddered at the sound, and Sam was glad that the pastor was nowhere to be seen. Without saying a word, Sam returned to the confined room behind the organ and began to retune it. Two hours later he reemerged.

"You want to play it? Test it?" he asked.

"No, you go ahead," Zack responded sheepishly.

Without saying a word, Sam sat on the bench and began to play. The sound was heavenly, full of range and depth.

Dejected, Zack said, "I guess my app needs some more work."

"It sounds like it, but we can test it out on the next couple of churches we visit. If you want."

"Yeah," he responded with a smile. "That would be great. Thanks, Sam."

Zack tried numerous times to use his app at the next few churches they visited, with the same result. In the end, he decided that Sam's way was best, and he had to admit the organs did indeed sound wonderful.

# Chapter Thirteen

"Mornin' Henrietta," said the cheerful voice of the village's longtime mayor, as he entered their store.

"Howdy, Mr. Mayor. Good to see you again. Merry Christmas."

The mayor walked around the small store as Henrietta and Hilda were putting away the last of the boxes from the delivery truck. "Morning, Charlie. Merry Christmas," said Hilda Mae.

He stopped at the small Christmas tree at the front of the store and stood admiring it, the American flag plaque and the dog tags which hung from the branches. "What's this?"

She walked alongside her old friend, dusting the counter and boxes. "In honor of our veterans. A few vets have come in and hung their dog tags on the branches and signed the logbook. Kind of a spontaneous sort of thing, if you know what I mean?"

"Yep, I sure do."

"So, we decided we're creating different colored paper ornaments in the shape of dog tags to hang on the tree. Customers can write the name of their respected veteran on the tag and hang it on the tree. They can add a small cash donation in the jar here, which we'll turn over to Saint Michaels Veterans Association to help in their work with needy vets."

She stood next to him, admiring the tree. "Sure is pretty, if you know what I mean."

"Yep, sure do."

She started to walk away, but he stopped her and said, "Henrietta, I need a favor—a Christmas favor, so to speak."

"What can I do for you, Charlie?" she responded, as she set aside her duster on the shelf.

"Well, as you may or may not know, a few months back the city's warehouse caught fire. It was down on Maple?"

"Yep, I remember. A big fire. You could see the smoke for miles around. Burned the warehouse straight down to the ground. Pity."

"Well, let me be straight with you, Henrietta." He shoved his hands deep inside his pants pockets and looked down at the floor. Taking a deep breath, he said, "You see, that warehouse contained all of the city's holiday decorations, Fourth of July, Labor Day, Memorial Day, Saint Michael's Day, and most important, all of our Christmas decorations. Burned them all right up." His face looked dejected and she took pity on her old friend.

"We got nothin' we can put up for Christmas, and people been callin' askin' about it day and night at city hall. Blaming me for not puttin' up any decorations. They like their Christmas decorations up on the streetlights. Their wreaths. Their lights. So Christmassy. And the merchants have been callin' as well, buggin' me. Seems they all like 'em quite a bit. A lot of rumblin' goin' on."

"Charlie," she said, touching his arm, "Saint Michaels doesn't need Christmas decorations around town to celebrate Christmas. Our folks here are full of Christmas spirit. I see it all the time. Now don't get me wrong, I love the decorations too, especially in my business, if you know what I mean, but people will still celebrate Christmas all the same."

He smiled at his old friend. "I agree one hundred percent, Henny. But to be truthful with you, I think it adds to the Christmas spirit." Charlie pulled his hands from his pockets and stood straight up. "Listen, Henny, I got an election comin' up next year…and well, it don't seem right for this town not to have its decorations. So, I'm askin' ya what you can do to help me, and the fine citizens of Saint Michaels get their Christmas decorations up? And quick like, too."

"Hmm." She put her hand to her face, massaging her chin, sizing him up. *Was she talking to her old friend Chuck, or was she talking to some smooth-talkin' politician, Charlie Wilson?* Her business depended on that answer. He had always been straight with her. She trusted him.

"Chuck, let me be honest with you," she said. "I run a tight ship here. We're a real small operation, and to be truthful, I can't afford to wait six months to be paid back by city hall for the things I buy for them. I'm sorry. But I can't help you."

"Henny, I need your help. I can walk the purchase order paperwork through to get your money in a hurry. Maybe even a small advance like a down payment. You know, to help you out, so to speak."

"That would help. But Chuck, you know those Christmas supply folks. Well, they demand CBD."

"CBD?"

"Yeah, you know, CBD—Cash Before Delivery. Payment, money in advance?"

"Oh. Hmm."

"I have a new line of credit, but your purchase is probably going to exceed even that. Whatever you can do to speed up payment would be appreciated."

"I might be able to do something to help you out, but…"

"But what, Charlie?"

A shadow of doubt and defeat crossed his face. "I don't know, Henny. Even if you were able to pull off a miracle and find somebody who still has Christmas supplies sitting around in their warehouse and can ship them to us quickly…" He shook his head. "I would still have to have 'em here, hang 'em up, and then take them down in January and find someplace to store 'em for next year. And it's not just Saint Michaels that needs 'em. We shared the warehouse with the towns of Easton, Bozman, and Newcomb. All their stuff went up in smoke too."

"Hmm," said Henrietta. The business opportunity wheels were spinning inside her head. *This could be good news.*

She leaned in close and said, "Chuck, I can solve your problem. Tell you what I'm going to do for you. Mister Mayor, I'll make you a deal. Let's start with Christmas decorations. You get a list of what you need, then I'll get on the phone and track down those Christmas supplies for you. One way or another, I'll find 'em for you. And while I'm doing that, you go back to your fine office at city hall and call those other mayors. You tell 'em you got a deal for 'em that they can't pass up. I'll sign a contract with the towns of Saint Michaels, Easton, Bozman, and Newcomb. We'll get all your Christmas supplies, which you'll pay for cash, up front. I'll have everything delivered here. Then, under a separate multiple-year contract, we'll put them up, then take them down in January and store them until we put them up for next year. Then we can talk about the Fourth of July and your other decoration needs. Deal?"

A smile now returned to his face. "Henny, you got a deal. I have an itemized list back at my office of all the Christmas supplies we needed to give to the insurance company for reimbursement. Let me get going back to my office. I'll call the other mayors, then send you over the list of what we and the other towns need and leave it up to you." He hugged her then turned to walk away, singing a holiday tune, and stopped. "Thanks, Henny. You're the best."

"I know."

Before he reached the front door, she shouted to him, "Mister Mayor? Just remember that there's more to Christmas than hanging decorations."

"You're right, Henny," he said with cheer. "And a Merry Christmas to you and your family."

When he left, Henrietta danced a little jig and shouted to Hilda Mae, "Hilly, get me Steve at Groper's Holiday Supply Company on the line. Then track down some folk to help us unpack and hang all this stuff."

Hilda came from the back of the store and asked, "Who did you have in mind?"

"Well, we can start with Lil' Henry and Sam Carpenter, and anyone else we can think of. We're going to need all the help we can get to unpack, assemble, and hang all this stuff. Quick like. Whew! But one thing I know is we got lots of work to do. But first I got to get on the phone and get some supplies. We're going to bring back the Christmas feelin' to Saint Michaels! Yes indeedy."

Outside, it began to snow. Large flakes flew through the air, sticking to the grass and trees.

# Chapter Fourteen

After Sam and Zack finished tuning the organs scheduled for that day, they made it back to Saint Michaels in time for Zack's date with Clarisse. As Sam watched him drive away from the diner, he noticed that Zack had left his wallet behind on the floorboards of his car. He drove the short distance to the Miles River Inn to return it to him. The streets were becoming crowded at that time of day, and he had to stop at the town's only stoplight before he made the turnoff to the inn.

He made his way to the expansive reception area. "I have something for a co-worker of mine, he's a guest here at the inn," he said to the front desk clerk while holding up Zack's wallet. "It's going to be hard for him to take his date out for dinner tonight without it. If you can just let me know his room number or call him to come down here, then I can just…"

"Sam? Is that you?"

Clarisse, tall and pretty, her long auburn hair falling about her shoulders as she hurried to greet him.

"Oh, hi, Clarisse. I was just bringing Zack his wallet…he left it in the car. Good to see you. Maybe you can give it to him for me."

Ignoring his response, she hugged him, wrapping her arms around him and pulling him close. The strong scent of her perfume was almost overwhelming. Still the same old Clarisse. "I've missed seeing you around, Sam," she said. "A lot." She kissed him on the cheek and took a step back. "I see you're still getting your fashion tips from Motor World Magazine. Jeans, t-shirt, sweater, pea coat, and work boots. Still the same old Sam."

He started to respond but held back. *To what end? Why? She's Zack's fiancée, and she's his concern now, not mine.*

She moved closer to him, now just inches away, holding onto his arm, whispering, "Do you have time for a drink? For old times' sake? Here in the bar or…maybe up in my room? It's very romantic there, overlooking the river. Fireplace. What do you say?" She smiled as she waited for him to accept her invitation.

Sam removed her arm from his and stepped back, away from her. Now he remembered why he had broken up with Clarisse in the first place. They had only dated a few times after he arrived in Baltimore, and he had quickly decided she was not the one for him.

He took another step back. "No thanks, Clarisse. Besides, you're engaged now…to my new boss. I don't think he would care for…"

A lone figure stepped up behind her and walked close to them: Zack. "Hey, Sam," he said. "What are you trying to do? Steal my girl?" He was half joking, but it was Clarisse who responded. "Well, Zack darling, you weren't around anywhere. Sweetheart, what's a girl to do?"

After an awkward pause, Sam looked at Zack and laughed as he handed him his wallet.

"No, no, nothing like that Zack. You left your wallet in my car. Must've fallen out of your pocket."

"Oh, thanks, Sam. I would have missed this later when I went to pay for dinner. I appreciate you bringing it by here."

"No problem. Gotta go."

Clarisse hugged him again, then said, "So good to see you again, Sam. Say, why don't you join Zack and I for dinner?" Then she paused after giving him the once-over, finishing by saying, "After you clean up, of course."

"Thanks for the invite, but I'm going to stop by and see Grace Albright on my way home. See you tomorrow, Zack. I'll order all those parts for the churches we serviced today."

As Sam went to walk away, she stepped in front of him, saying, "Grace Albright? Are you still hung up on her? Sam Carpenter, you'll never change. Pity." She shook her head. "So long, Sammy. Come on, Zack, let's have dinner. I have a lot to tell you."

"So long…" His words hung in the air as they walked away.

It had stopped snowing before any accumulation clothed the grass or the streets, as usual in Saint Michaels. He sat in his car, staring at his phone, studying her name—Gracie. He took a deep breath and could feel his heart begin to beat faster as he dialed her home number and someone picked up the phone.

"Hello?" he said into the silence. "Grace? It's Sam."

"Hi, Sam. This is Bill…Reverend Albright. But I guess you called to speak with Grace, rather than this old man."

"You're not old, Reverend."

"Thanks for that, Sam. But please, after hours, you can call me Bill. Wait a minute, and I'll go get Grace for you. But while I have you on the line, I wanted to ask you if your offer to look at our organ and church bells is still open?"

"Sure,… Bill. It's a busy time for us, but I'll work it in between my other jobs and after hours. I'll stop by Saturday and take a look at it, but I can't promise any miracles."

"That's okay, miracles are in my line. My boss delivers them all the time."

"Your boss? The bishop?"

"No, Sam," he said, laughing. "Think higher, much higher. Think heavenly. Wait, here's Grace. See you soon."

"Yes, Reverend."

"Here's Gracie."

Then he heard her. "Hi, Sam. I'm so glad you called," said the sweetest voice he had ever heard. His heart began to beat faster and pound against his chest. He could not breathe. Again, he tried to say something, but was speechless. *What was going on?* They had always been the best of friends but seeing her the other day in church had awakened something in him. Something he did not understand. He was beginning to have feelings for her, deeper feelings. *Friends? Best friends? Confidants?*

"Sam? Sam are you there?"

Finally, he managed to say, "Hi, Grace. Thought I'd call to say hello."

"Very sweet of you, Sam Carpenter."

He had so much to tell her. "Your dad just said it was okay for me to stop by Saturday and take a look at the church bells and organ."

"Oh, that's wonderful! That is really great. I was just getting ready to call you and see if you would care to stop by for some blueberry pie? Homemade."

He really wanted to see her again, but after looking down at his clothes and his dirty hands, he said, "I would love to, but I'm at the Miles River Inn, and I'm a little bit grimy. Just finished for the day and was on my way home."

"So? You can wash up here if you like. Have you eaten?"

"Zack and I had something to eat on the road, a late lunch."

"Why don't you stop by and at least have some pie?"

"Okay, but I'm all grimy from work and..."

"Sam, that's okay, it's only pie. Besides, I'd love to see you." Then she laughed a nervous laugh. "I say that all the time. I won't be able to see you...but I'd love to see you again. You know what I mean."

"Sure. See ya soon." He began to hum her name as he hung up the phone.

Grace waited for him, standing by the door, but soon it had been longer than she'd expected, and she started getting nervous. *I hope everything's okay,* she thought. *I hope nothing has happened to him. Did he have an accident? I hope he's not in some ditch somewhere? Or slid off the river bridge into the water.* She stopped. *What was going on?* She never worried like this before. But ever since he'd hugged her in church, she felt things change. She could not stop thinking about him. *Whoa! This is Sam. Best friend, Sam. Childhood friend Sam. Get a grip, girl.* But try as she might, her feelings for him were growing stronger. *Warm, tender Sam. Sexy Sam.*

Twenty minutes later, he pulled the car into the rectory parking lot, and she was standing at the door, waiting for him. *He was here.* She wanted to rush to him but waited.

She heard an engine shut off. "Sam?" she shouted from the top of the steps, as she listened to his car door slam shut.

"Hi, Grace," came his voice. "I stopped to get you some flowers at the market, sorry I was delayed. Hope you didn't worry about me?"

"No," she said, trying to appear nonchalant, just happy to hear his voice. "I always stand at my front door for twenty minutes waiting and hoping that nothing..."

"I'm sorry I didn't think. Sorry to worry you."

She heard him walking towards her and said, "It's okay. Come on inside." She felt the bite of a winter wind hit her cheek as she opened the door. "My dad told me about what he said to you, about working on the church bells and the pipe organ. I'm pleased. No, I'm thrilled. Come on inside." She turned and raised her hands into the air and said, "It feels like snow in the air."

"Not in Saint Michaels," he said, reaching the top step as she threw her arms around him, holding him close. But she immediately recoiled.

Puzzled, he said, "Grace? Are you all right? Is everything okay?"

"Hmm. Were you just with Clarisse Matz? I'd know her trademark cheap perfume anywhere."

"Yes, I ran into her by accident, but only to drop off a…"

"Humph," she said, faking a pout.

"Gracie, come on now, she's engaged to Zack Bridges. She's a long time ago in my past."

"You're right. I'm sorry." She smiled a wide grin, as he grabbed her by the arm to guide her—she felt so close—then held out her hand, reaching for his. "But for some reason, that girl always gets under my skin."

His hand felt warm to her touch, different than before. They didn't usually hold hands, but she liked it. Instinctively her fingers touched his. She shivered again at his touch. She loved holding his hand. Warm. *What's happening here?* She thought.

"I know the feeling, "she gets under my skin also." He liked holding her hand and found himself looking for any excuse to touch her.

They walked down the hallway of the small, three-bedroom rectory residence. The red brick building had been rebuilt seventy-five years earlier after a lightning fire destroyed it. Sam looked around and noticed that not much had changed since he was there last. The house was neat, clean, and quiet. A Bible with yellow markers sticking out from the inside sat on the side table in the den, in front of the television.

It always amazed Sam…he had been into hundreds, if not thousands of rectories, and they all had that same clean, almost antiseptic, warm, familiar smell to them. A warm apple pie fragrance smell.

Approaching the kitchen, he leaned in close and said into her right ear, "I've missed you," but he wasn't sure if she heard him. He repeated it, only this time louder so she could hear him. "I've missed you."

"I've missed you too, Sam," said her father with a chuckle, overhearing their conversation, waiting for them in the kitchen. He wore a set of oversized oven mitts as he pulled the pie from the oven. The pastor loved to cook and bake, and their kitchen smelled of hot cakes and freshly baked bread.

"Evening, Bill. Wow, when you said fresh baked pies, you meant it," he said excitedly, taking in a deep whiff. "I had forgotten how good your pies smelled." He led Grace to her chair and helped her slide into place next to him. "And taste."

"This one is apple. It'll have to cool for a bit. But I have a fresh blueberry one I baked earlier. Sam, you can wash up in the sink and then make yourself comfortable."

The reverend set down three pieces of pie and three mugs of freshly brewed coffee. After leading them in saying a prayerful grace, he said, "Enjoy the pie."

Sam cut into the pie, stealing glances at Grace before eating, then said, "Delicious, Reverend. This is really good."

Her father talked about the holidays as the drama unfolded before his eyes, the two making small talk while they ate. Reminiscing about the old times when they were younger. Like little kids. Teenagers. No longer kids but... in love. He could not deny it any longer. There was a strong, soulful connection between the two of them. It had always been there. As they finished their dessert, Bill asked, "Another piece of pie, Sam?"

"Yes, sir. I'm never one to turn down an offer of pie." His hand jutted briefly across the table, brushing against hers before retreating. He looked for reasons to touch her, to be close to her, as he picked up her sweater from the floor. "Grace, you dropped this."

"Thanks, Sam," she said, taking it from him, her hand touching his. She had to catch her breath at the brush of his hand. *What's going on here? This is Sam. Best friend, Sam.*

The reverend handed Sam another slice of pie and asked, "Sam, do you think there's any hope for our old church organ? Or the bells?"

"I don't know, sir, but I'll give it my best."

"I know you will, Sam," he said, as he sipped his cup of coffee.

"What will you have to do?" Grace asked.

"Well, I'll start on the bells first and do a diagnostic."

"How do you do that?"

"First, I'll do a physical inspection of all the bells, checking for any cracks, peeling or corrosion that would cause the off-key sound. Then I'll fire up the program on the bell system and see if it can play a sample chime sequence. And then listen to how they sound."

The reverend smiled, then made an ugly face. "I did that once, many, many years ago. They sounded awful. Some bells sounded good, but others sounded..."

"Sour?"

"Yes. That's a good word to describe it."

"I can imagine. I'll make a note of which ones have gone flat or out of tune. It could be something simple, like the clapper having too much verdigris, mold, or mildew, causing the bell to sound sour. I'll also check for birds or bat nests."

"Bats?"

"Yes, sometimes they have been known to nest inside the bigger unused bells."

"And what's a clapper?" Grace asked, placing her napkin on the table while leaving her hand on the tabletop. Sam glanced at her hand.

"The clapper is the metal piece that hangs down from the top of the bell and strikes the bell to make it ring. I'm going to presume that this problem is something that developed over time, since they used to chime at one point."

"You're right there, Sam. I'm told by some of the old-timers around here that our bells were the best-sounding bells on the entire Eastern Shore of Maryland. People came from miles around to attend church and listen to our bells."

Sam continued, "If that fails to tell me what I need to know, I'll take a sample from the entire carillon and send it off to a friend of mine in New York, Jasef Krasnik at Krasnik & Heidrich Assayers. I'll take a small sample of metal scraping from inside each bell and send it to him."

"What will he do with the sample?"

"As an assayer, it's his company's job to analyze the metal composition of each bell. A proper church bell should have a mix of 80% copper and 20% tin for maximum sound effect and the best harmony. Many times, you'll find a little bit of gold and silver inside."

"Really?" she asked in astonishment.

Her father laughed. "Only traces, my dear. You see, years ago when they were making these bells in bell foundries, rich parishioners and devout churchgoers would throw gold or silver coins into the furnace as the bells were cast. Some people said it was to improve the tone of the bell, while others thought it was for good luck for the parish. Most bellfounders frowned on the practice, thinking that too much alien metal would injure the tone."

He turned his attention to Sam. "But tell me, Sam, how do you know so much about church bells?"

"I spent some time abroad in England as an apprentice, working with a bell founding company," Sam replied. "I worked at Dorchester Bell Founding plant outside of London. Building bells. Testing bells. Installing bells. Repairing bells. Cleaning bells, and yes, retuning bells."

"What's next after that, Sam?" she asked.

"While we're waiting for the report back from the assayer, I'll start to work on the church organ. But it's a two-person job. Someone needs to play certain notes on the organ while I'm inside the loft tuning it. But that's only after I check the generator, the pipes, the felts, and the bellow, which creates the air flow through the pipes to make the sound."

"I can help you with that, Sam," Grace said. "School is out early for the Christmas holidays, so I only have the choir to work with, and of course chores around here."

Her father responded, "Grace, you go ahead and help Sam get our pipe organ working. I'll take care of things inside here."

"Thanks, Dad."

He smiled a smile she never saw.

"When we get the report back from New York, the next step is I'll have to retune the bells on a lathe. But I must warn you, Reverend, it's an irreversible process. It could ruin the original tonal sound of the bells or give them a much more modern sound."

"I have faith in you, Sam," he said, standing and placing his hand on Sam's shoulder. "Total faith. And faith is fundamental in my business." Suddenly he saw Sam in a new light. "You look tired, Sam. Why don't you go home and get some rest?"

"Well, it's been pretty busy."

"When was your last vacation?"

Sam's shoulders slumped. "I've not had a vacation in five years."

"You know the old saying, that on the seventh day he rested. But no preaching tonight, however—it'll make a great topic for my homily on Sunday. Good night, Sam. And if you like, take the rest of this pie home with you. Nothing like fresh blueberry pie for breakfast. See you on Saturday."

"Thank you, Reverend."

"Grace, why don't you pack up what's left of this pie for young Sam here? I'm going to bed. Good night, Sam."

"Good night, sir."

As she covered the pie pan with plastic, he moved closer behind her. She smelled of honeysuckle, sweet honeysuckle. "Did you add honeysuckle to that pie?"

"Samuel Jason Carpenter, you know very well that honeysuckle only blooms in the summertime around here."

He moved closer, then stopped. *It's not fair to sneak up on her like this. Her not being able to see and all. Friends, best friends. Always remember that, Sam. But something is changing. A change for the good. But this is Grace, best friend Grace. Does she feel the same way? I don't want to lose my best friend by coming onto her. But I don't know what's going on here.*

She turned to face him, holding the pie in her hands. "Add some ice cream, and it will taste even better. Everything tastes better with ice cream."

"And bacon."

"Bacon?"

"Yeah. There's an old saying amongst organ tuners, everything goes better with ice cream and bacon."

"Oh." She laughed. "You're so funny, Sammy."

"I love your laugh. Your smile. Your dimples." He moved closer. Then he stopped. He watched her lips move but did not hear what she said.

They walked down the long hallway, she moved past him to open the door, and her chest brushed up against him. He felt her warmth, wanted to reach out and hold her. *Whoa. Cool it, Sam. Don't screw up a lifelong friendship. But I have to know, ask her, somehow. Have her feelings about me changed? Does she feel the same way about me, or does she think of me as just her best friend? Or romantic? Ask her. But how? Somehow, just ask her before it's too late. No don't screw it up.*

He stopped as she opened the door and mumbled, "Grace, thanks for inviting me tonight. I really enjoyed it. And I'm glad your dad is finally okay with me stopping by. I missed not seeing you. But I have to ask you something." His hand reached for hers, and when he found it, she slowly wrapped her fingers around his.

"Yes, Sam. What did you want to ask me?"

*Easy, boy.* "Ah…" *Grace, I think I'm falling in love with you. No, I've been in love with you my entire life, I just never realized it until now when I came back here to Saint Michaels and saw you. But what about…her career? New York? They have church organs that need tuning in New York. Right?* "I was thinking, maybe we could have lunch one day and…talk…"

She moved closer, still holding his hand. "Sure, Sam. Whatever you want to do. Whenever. Just let me know." She kissed his cheek, and he could smell her jasmine perfume. "Whatever you want. Really," she whispered.

Sam caught his breath. "Maybe we could…"

Ring, ring, ring! It was his cell phone: Ollie. Before he answered the phone, he took the pie from her hands and said, "Lunch?"

"Yeah, I would like that. I think we need to talk," she said, slowly releasing his hand from her grip.

"I'm sorry, it's my boss. I have to take this call. Thanks for everything, Grace. Thanks for thinking of me. See you on Saturday?"

She smiled as she reached for the door handle. "Yes, of course. Bye for now," she said, then she raised her hand, in the dark. She guided it to his face and leaned forward to kiss his cheek. "Good night, Sam." As she closed the door behind him, she said aloud with a smile, "See you Saturday."

*Saturday? Seems like years away instead of just two days. I wonder why he stopped coming closer. I never realized how much I'd missed him. It's good to have him back. Best friend, Sam. Old dependable Sam. Sexy Sam. Face facts—I think I'm falling for him all over again. But how does he feel? I hope he feels the same way. I hope.*

# Chapter Fifteen

Once outside in the swirling snow, Sam started his car to warm it up and put the call on speakerphone. "Hi, Ollie. I can talk now. Is everything okay? What can I do for you?"

"Where the heck you been?" said Ollie. "I've been trying to call you all night. I heard back from Zack, but not from you. I want you to check in with me at the end of every day."

"Check in? Seriously?"

"Yeah, you heard me. Check in. Call me. You got parts to order, billing sheets to file, schedules to confirm. Oh, and by the way, I don't like you changing any schedules without me knowing about it. It screws everything up. You hear me?"

"Yes sir, I hear you. It's just that it seems we're doing a lot more service calls here on the Eastern Shore this year. And last year I understand we had two teams of technicians tuning, and they were done in a few days. For years that's the way we've always worked it."

"Well, things change, buddy boy. Oh, and before I forget, when you cleared out your father's office, you must have taken some data sheets on the Reynolds Project your dad was working on. I'll need them back for my Reynolds meeting. E-mail them to me, will ya? Got it?"

"Got it. I'll send them to you first thing tomorrow."

"Tomorrow? No, I need those data sheets tonight. My meeting with them is tomorrow. Get them to me tonight. Understand?"

"But Ollie, it's already nine-thirty."

"Yeah. So, what? I need them tonight. Got it?"

"Yeah, I got it." Sam hung up the phone in annoyance. He loved his job, his customers, but after his conversation with Ollie, the position at Wanamaker's was looking more appealing all the time. But it was in Philadelphia. As he pulled onto the stone gravel driveway leading to the cabin, he saw a herd of young deer rush past him, startled by the car's headlights. In a second they were gone, their tall white tails waving behind them.

Years had passed since he'd stayed at the cabin. When he went inside, he turned on some music and made a pot of coffee, then glanced at the stack of boxes from his father's office; it had been a long day. *Reynolds project? This may take a while. From last year? What kind of project was it? Which file would Dad have put them into?*

There was nothing in the first box, other than some old sketches and repair estimates for some church organs. His father had been meticulous in laying out everything that needed to be done, and the attendant costs associated with each project. *Wish I could be like that. Someday. But I guess that's what comes from running your own business, such attention to detail.*

The second box was a collection of his awards, family pictures, citations, and his apprenticeship graduations. The most substantial framed piece was from Wanamaker's. His father was always proudest of his time as an apprentice there. He'd always said it was the best learning experience he ever had.

Sam continued searching through box after box. The last one contained things his father was working on just before he died. *Dad's life is in this box. Pictures of the three of us. Family. Cherished memories. Oh, how I wish you were here now. I could always talk to you when I had a problem. Like now. Dad, I find my feelings for Gracie are changing. I feel attracted to her and not just as a friend. I think I'm falling for her. But if I'm wrong, I don't want her to think I'm a creep and lose her…as a friend. Never. And I don't know how she feels. I don't know if her feelings have changed about me. I was going to ask her tonight, but chickened out, and then Ollie called. Help me, Dad!* Sam had to sit down. He placed the box on his lap and continued to search.

On his dad's calendar, Sam's birthday was marked with a huge red circle: August 19th. Sam flipped through it. On November 29th, Mom and Dad's anniversary was marked, with a notation to order flowers to take to the cemetery. Other files were neatly stacked on top of one another. He went through each one, stopping only to breathe in deep the aroma from the pine needles on the table and from the fresh Christmas tree in the corner, scents which swirled around the cabin.

He opened the last box. Bingo! The Reynolds Project: a massive church pipe organ restoration project in Washington D.C. *Right. I remember this now.* A piece of paper fell to the floor.

When Sam retrieved it, he saw it had come from the best man at his father's wedding: Don Franks of Franks and Simon, attorneys at law, Chicago, Illinois.

## PRIVATE & CONFIDENTIAL

*Dear Jack—*

 *Good to talk to you again after so many years. Don't be a stranger, and let's get together next time you're in Chicago. I know that Emma would love to see you again. You're welcome to stay at our place anytime.*

 *Per your request, we have reviewed the documents of incorporation of Carpenter and Matz. We can confirm that you own fifty-one percent of the corporation, with the remaining forty-nine percent owned by your partner, Oliver Matz. Your ownership under Maryland law will transfer directly and immediately to your sole heir and beneficiary, your son: Samuel Jason Carpenter.*

 *I hope I have answered all your questions and alleviated any concerns you may have had in this matter. Since this is a sensitive and personal subject, if you require any further action in this matter, just call me at home or on my cell phone. Stay in touch, Jack.*

*All the best,*
*Don*

*Donald Franks, Esquire*
*Franks & Simon Attorneys at Law – Specializing in corporate and contract matters*

Sam reread the document three times. The facts did not change. He owned the majority shares in the company. *As an owner,* he thought, *I can affect a lot of changes. Things that me and Dad wanted to change all along. But now I'm not just an employee anymore. I'm an owner, and a controlling owner at that.* He smiled as he reread the letter. *I own fifty-one percent of the company. Why didn't Ollie tell me any of this? I think I know why, but this is what Dad wanted—for me to take over after he was gone. He must have known something was wrong with his health. That he did not have much time left. Why didn't he say something?*

Sam was confused and suddenly exhausted. He lay back on the sofa. It had been a long day, and now more than ever, all he wanted was some time off. He needed to think everything through. His cell phone rang on the counter, and when he went to get it he saw it was Ollie calling.

"Sam? Did you find it? The Reynolds Project file?"

"Yes, sir, I did. I was just getting ready to e-mail it to you."

"Good. Just in time. Then get some rest, because tomorrow I have you and Zack scheduled for eight tunings, and on Saturday you have nine."

"Whoa, Ollie. Since I didn't have anything on my schedule, I was planning to take this Saturday off. I'm doing some pro bono work on the old Saint Michaels Church pipe organ and bells. Then I've got some Christmas shopping and other stuff to take care of, you know?"

"Yeah, I know," said Ollie, "but I need you to work this Saturday. I just added these churches to the schedule today. I want to pump up our sales figures for this year. Make our numbers look real good. You know what I mean? Good for the profit."

*Hmmm.* Sam eased himself back onto the sofa, still holding the attorney's letter in his hand. *Easy, Sam.* "That's a good thing to hear. I like profit. I like it a lot, but Ollie…I really need some time off, and based on the new company vacation policy as I recall, isn't it use it or lose it? So, I would lose ten weeks of vacation."

"That's right, Sam. Sorry. But if you remember, we published that policy months ago."

"Ollie, if you don't mind me asking, does that policy apply to you, as an owner?"

Silence. Then he heard scrambling and the sound of papers shuffling coming from the other end of the phone. "Well, well, yes and no. As an employee, I'm treated like every other employee when it comes to benefits, but…"

"Yes? And?"

"As an owner, I'm entitled to unlimited time off every year."

"I see. So, an owner doesn't really have to worry about using their vacation time? Or scheduling one? Or not getting paid for it, right?"

"Well, yes."

"The reason I ask is…I came across a letter to my dad from an attorney friend of his, talking about the company's incorporation documents and the ownership status of Carpenter and Matz. He says in his letter that I own—"

Ollie interrupted him before he could finish. "Tell you what, Sam, why don't you take the next few weeks off. You deserve the time off. It's been years since you've had a vacation. We'll talk when you're back in Baltimore. Finish the projects you have on the calendar for tomorrow, and I'll send Zack out to oversee teams to finish up tuning on the Eastern Shore. I'll call him tonight to take care of it."

Ollie sounded frantic. "And I'm going to put off Zack's promotion for a while...at least until you and I can talk."

Sam laughed to himself. He knew he had him boxed into a corner. So, he decided to let him squirm just a little bit longer. "Hmmm," was his only response.

"And...and...and..." stuttered Ollie. "I've had second thoughts about changing your dad's office into a game room. Heck, you're going to need an office when you come back into town. So why not make that one yours?"

Sam stood and walked to the window, looking out across the harbor. With quiet confidence, he said, "Ollie, you're still the CEO of Carpenter & Matz, you can do what you feel is the right thing to do for the company. But I agree, we can talk when I get back. Okay?"

"Yeah, sure. That sounds great," said a relieved Oliver Matz, happy to have time to compose himself and formulate a plan. "Oh, Sam, by the way. Are you going to need anything for your Saint Michaels Church project? The company does have a relief fund to help pay for parts and services to struggling churches. We can tap into that one if you want."

"We have a slush fund?"

"No, no, no...not a slush fund, it's an appreciation fund. That's what I call it. I use it to help out struggling churches."

In all his years with the company, he'd never heard of such a fund, and was surprised to listen to the offer coming from Ollie. "Well, I know I'm going to definitely need to replace the leather on the bellows, and the felts, the belts, the stops. Everything short of a complete overhaul. It hasn't been tuned in years."

"Got it. I'll overnight you whatever I think might be of help. Anything else?"

"I'll let you know," said Sam.

"Merry Christmas, Sam."

"Merry Christmas Ollie." *Very interesting,* he thought as he hung up the phone. *This could change things quite a bit at work. Very interesting indeed.*

# Chapter Sixteen

Grace finished fixing her hair, then searched the closet with her hands for something to wear. She always arranged the clothes in her closet by color to make it easier to coordinate and stitched knotted threads into the labels to signify color. That always made it easier to match her outfits: one knot was for blue, two for brown, three for black.

Her room was small, but her bedroom window overlooked the harbor. While she could no longer see the view, early in the morning, as the sun rose in the sky, she sometimes opened the window and breathed in deep the misty salt air off the water. She learned so much from smells and sounds. She could hear the traffic on the street below, the seagulls squawking and flying high in the sky, the smell of fresh bacon from the diner, the engine sounds from the fishing fleet making its way out of the harbor.

The floorboards creaked as she walked down the steps and into the kitchen to join her father. "Dad? Dad?" Silence. "Father?"

"Yes, Grace?" came his voice. "Down in the basement. I'll be right up. I found those old Christmas ornaments I was looking for everywhere. The old ones we had when you were a kid."

She heard him enter the kitchen. "I know," she said, "I can smell the ornaments and the old cardboard they were packed in. Old ornaments have that special smell that comes from the thin piece of tin used to hang them from Christmas trees. Brings back so many memories." *Memories of Mom. Memories of the family together for the holidays. Baking cakes. Cookies. Pies. Oh, how she loved to bake. Maybe that's why Dad bakes so often?* She brushed a tear from her eye.

Her father rooted around in the box. "I even have some of the old ones that you and Sam made in school. Talk about memories."

Grace's hand felt around the old shoebox and found the old popsicle sticks magically transformed into Christmas trees. And ornaments. Old soup can lids now repopulated as a shiny, hanging ornament.

"Memories. So many memories." Christmas had been everybody's favorite time of the year. Her mother loved to save the lids from the soup cans, and they would clean them, polish them, and hang them from their Christmas tree. Oftentimes, Grace and Sam would scavenge the woods for oversized pinecones, and then dye them in Christmas colors and hang them from the mantel. She started to cry. The brave young woman who had been through so much, now reduced to tears by wayward pieces of metal and old wood.

"Gracie, you okay? Is there something wrong?"

"No. I'm okay, Dad. Sometimes it's just too much."

"I know, dear, I understand." The house seemed quiet as her father held her tight, kissed her head, then tousled her hair before he poured them each a cup of coffee. Setting the box on the table, he said, "Why don't we share these with Sam, for his Saint Michaels Christmas tree? He has so little here. No family. No…"

"Good idea." She was quiet, as her fingers molded and felt the old ornaments from years gone by. "You're right, let's share these things with him. Later, I'll call him, but for now, I gotta go."

"Where are you off to?"

"I'm heading into town to hand out these circulars, urging people to join our choir. Remember, the bishop is coming into town for Christmas. In a couple of weeks. Not much time left."

"Wait, let me put some shoes on and I'll drive you."

"Daddy, I can walk. It's not far. I'll be just fine. Really."

"Okay. Are you sure?"

"I'm sure. Besides, it's only a couple of blocks. I love you. Don't worry about me, I won't be gone long."

Her father watched her as she struggled to put on her oversized topcoat, then her gloves. Grace's dress was down beyond her knees, her clogs were faded, and he wished he had time to cut her hair again before the holiday season. *Where does the time go?* he wondered.

He watched her make her way down the church sidewalk and walk towards town. "Independent cuss," he muttered under his breath. But she would have it no other way.

As he watched her leave, he thought about how well Grace had endured the loss of both her mother and her sight. He had tried to help her as much as he could, but maybe that help—buying her clothes, doing all the cooking, driving her everywhere she needed to go—had become just another crutch for her to hold onto.

He smiled a knowing smile, which grew larger as he thought about a plan of action to help her. Then he opened the local Saint Michaels phone directory and picked up the receiver. It was time to make some changes.

Grace, meanwhile, walked towards downtown and could feel the winter sun on her face, warming her against the midwinter chill. She could still feel a frosty wisp in the air which told her of snow. Her black and white walking stick moved methodically from side to side in front of her. Her feet touched the nubs in the sidewalk at the street corner, alerting her to a stoplight. The beeping began, and she walked faster to the other side. It was then she heard recorded Christmas carols. *Must be Ye Olde Christmas Shoppe*, she thought. *Henrietta and Hilda Mae.*

Her stick tapped two steps. She walked up and opened the door. "Merry Christmas," she said aloud, as the bell over the door rang, announcing her entrance.

"Well, lookie, lookie. It's our favorite princess," said the unmistakable voice of Hilda Mae Copper. "And a Merry Christmas to you too. What are you doing down this way?"

She held up her circulars. "I'm trying to get more people to sing in our choir. The bishop is coming in for Christmas Eve services, and if we don't fill the church, they may close us down."

"What? Oh my! Can't be. How can we help?" came Henrietta's voice as she appeared from the back room.

"If you could put up one or two of these circulars in your window, I'd really appreciate it."

"Well, of course, girl. We'll do even better than that. I'll spread the word at our church and tell everybody to also come to your church for Christmas Eve services. Lordy, we don't want any church to close, especially not yours. Everybody loves you and the reverend."

*I am so lucky to have such good neighbors and good friends like Hilda Mae and Henrietta*, she thought. "Oh, thank you so much."

"Anything for you, Gracie. By the way, young Sam Carpenter stopped by here to say hello. He was askin' 'bout ya. Just thought you would wanna know."

"Thank you. I saw him last night, and he's coming by the church on Saturday to work on the bell tower and the church's pipe organ."

The two older women smiled at each other, giving each other a wink and a silent high five. "Really," they responded in unison.

"Yes, really," she said, then turned serious. "Any word from Frankie, Hilda Mae?"

"No, ma'am. But there's always hope. I just sent out a bunch more letters. Every day I hope I'll get a call or a letter or an e-mail or a postcard from her. But who knows. Lordy, I miss her."

Grace opened her cane and said, "We'll all keep hoping with you. And praying. But in the meantime, you both have a nice day, and you two behave yourselves." After she opened the door, she said, "It's going to snow. I can feel it in the air. A good snow." She waved her hand over her head, saying as she left, "Merry Christmas!"

"Merry Christmas!" they shouted in response.

Her next stop was the bakery. Ashley and her mom also agreed to post the choral posters in the window. The cookies smelled so good, so fresh, she resisted the temptation. But she walked back inside two minutes later to order a dozen warm chocolate chip cookies, her dad's favorites. So good.

Grace walked along Talbot Street and stopped at many of the other stores along the main street. Wilson's antique store. Mason's general store. Saint Michaels Hardware store. Charley's Restaurant and Grill. Every place she stopped and asked for help, they all agreed. Now she could only hope and keep her fingers crossed. Her last stop was the diner. As she approached the front door the smell of the diner's crab soup, french fries and cheeseburgers were so enticing.

"Hi, Gracie," said Molly when she walked in. "I've been hoping you'd stop by." She leaned in close, touched her right arm, and whispered, "The second booth on your right is open. Homemade crab soup today. Cobb salad? Light raspberry vinaigrette salad dressing. Green tea?"

"Perfect," she said, tapping her cane until she reached her seat. Then she removed her coat and pushed it to the side of the bench seat.

"Be right back," said Molly.

Molly returned ten minutes later and set her meal in front of her, saying, "Soup. Very hot. Twelve o'clock. Close. Soup spoon at three o'clock. Crackers at two. Tea at one o'clock. Okay?"

"Yep, thanks."

She sat down across from her and leaned in close to whisper, "All right. All right. Tell me all about it. Sam came by? And? And?" Molly was forever the matchmaker in town.

Grace held up her hand to stop her then made a face, saying, "Good golly, Miss Molly!" She laughed. "And how are you doing today, Grace? I'm fine, thank you. And how are you, Molly? Good? Oh, so glad to hear it. Oh, I'm fine too. Give me a little time to get my bearings, will you, please?" She paused with a grin and slowly ate spoonfuls of their delicious homemade lump crab soup, flavored with the slightest hint of sherry. Impatient fingertips tapped the table across from her. Tap, tap, tap. Molly coughed impatiently.

The younger woman held up the last of the posters her father had made for her. "Oh, and Molly," she said, "before I forget, can you put these posters up on the store window for me? It's for the choir and…"

"Yes, yes, of course, I'll put them up." Molly was waiting for more information, but none was forthcoming. "Grace, this is not Christian-like, to torture someone like this. And you being a minister's daughter and all. It's just not right. Now tell me, did you see Sam?"

Grace hesitated before responding, "Did I see Sam? No. I have not seen him or anyone else for over three years."

Molly stared at her, and then it was her turn to laugh. She started to get up from her seat and leave. "Okay, okay, have it your way," she said, as she wiped down the table with her towel. "I have work to do around here, and I can't be sitting around…"

"But I did talk with him," she said, lowering her voice.

Molly eased back into her seat. "Yes? Tell me more."

"He came by the church, and we talked. When my father saw him, he was furious and said he never wanted me to talk with him again. Sam even offered to tune the church's organ and the bells."

"Really? He still blames Sam for the accident that caused your blindness?"

"Yes. Then Sam called me when he finished work for the day, and for some reason, my father had a change of heart. He told Sam he wanted him to come by and work on the church bells and the organ. See if he could fix them."

"He did? Wow, that's a change."

"Yes. And Sam asked if I could help with him as he worked on the organ, and then he stopped by to have some pie a little later."

"What's with your father's change of heart?"

"I don't know. He came by after his church visit and was a changed man. I don't know, other than he didn't want to discuss it all, but what I do know is that I'm happy about it. That's the first of the good news."

"What? There's more?" she said, absentmindedly wiping the tabletop with her ever-present dish towel.

"Yep. A man has been at the church for the last couple of days when I was in the church alone, singing."

"Yes? And?" she said, leaning in closer, afraid she would miss something. "This sounds exciting. Tell me more."

"Well, he really liked my singing and thinks I have enough talent to make it on my own. He wants to sign me to a contract to manage me and sing professionally."

"Wow, Grace, that's great news."

"But the only thing about it is, I would have to move to New York, to live. Then go through vocal training and then be on the road for a few years, with some other singers he manages."

"You mean leave Saint Michaels?" she said, unable to hide her shock at the thought of Grace moving.

"Yep. I love what I'm doing here, but this is a once in a lifetime opportunity, and I must be practical. If the church and school close, I'll have to find something to do. But to leave Saint Michaels…I don't know about that."

"That's a big step Grace. But I am so happy for you. You deserve every bit of happiness that comes your way. What does Sam think about your singing career? And your move to New York?"

"I think he would be happy for me. That's the way Sam is. Always was very supportive of anything I ever wanted to do."

"So you haven't told him, have you?"

"No. I haven't. Not yet. I'll tell him when the time is right. He'll be supportive of this too. As always."

Molly watched her eat her lunch, and for the next half hour, the conversation drifted to Christmas and other local news. Finally, she spoke. "So, you're going to spend the next week or so with Sam. Working with him. Talking with him and…"

"Yes, Mol. But remember, we're just friends. Best friends. But I must say, I've missed him. And…please don't tell anyone, but…"

"My lips are sealed."

"I find myself looking for ways to spend more time with him. To be with him. This is terrible…but I think I'm falling for him. He's my best friend. I wouldn't want to jeopardize our friendship. And I don't know how he feels. Everybody jokes about us being a couple since kids…the dreaded buddy word. I don't know what to do. I've missed being able to talk with him, to call him, to joke with him, to…"

Molly interrupted. "You know, Clarisse is in town. She's stayin' at the Miles River Inn."

"I know, but she's also engaged."

"That's never stopped her before."

"I know. But not much I can do about it, is there? I am what I am."

"You're right," said Molly. "Nothing you can do about it. It's just…"

"What?"

"Nothin'."

"What do you mean? It's just…come on, spit it out. You're dying to say something, I've known you for too long."

"All I was going to say was that…well, Sam Carpenter's going to be in town for a couple weeks, and you're going to be working with him every day, while he tunes the bells and organs. And maybe we force his hand, that's all. Find out once and for all what he feels about you. In the meantime, we do a little fixing up."

"What do you mean?"

"Well girl, you may want to put a little bait on that trap, that's all I'm tryin' to say."

She laughed. "What do you mean?"

"Well, you look like your father dresses you. Buys your shoes. And cuts your hair. And does your makeup."

"He does. I mean, he helps me with clothes I buy, but I go shopping with him…sometimes. It's easier that way. But so what?"

"Well, Grace, now don't get me wrong, I love your dad to death, God bless him, but he doesn't have a woman's eye for fashion. And I must say it's time for an update. Past time, that's all. Need to get you some clothes that show off your girlish curves and youthful figure, paint your face, add a little style to your haircut. And *voila!* The trap is set, just waiting for young Sam Carpenter to come sniffing around. Then you spring it. What do you think?"

"I think you've been watching too many of those outdoor reality shows, that's what I think."

Molly held her ground. "Well, is he worth fightin' for or not, my young friend?"

Grace blustered at first, standing in defiance, before sitting back down, her shoulders slumped in defeat. "Yes, of course he is, but Mol, I can't do it. Not by myself. I need help." Then she smiled a mischievous smile. "Your help."

"Whoa, girl," she said as she raised her hands in front of her. "No, no, not me. You're too headstrong. I'm not goin' to be fighting with you about clothes, haircut, shoes, boots, and the like. No siree, bob. Not me."

"Mol, please. You're a good friend. Can't you help me? I promise I won't buck you."

"Promise?"

"Yes, I promise."

"Okay then, let's go."

"Now?"

"No time like the present. I'll get a hair appointment for you with Phillippe. Then I'm going to have Marci show you the proper way for a blind person to do makeup. She's helped her sister for years. First, we do clothes shopping: some nice form-fitting jeans, then some snazzy tops, stylish sweaters, boots, shoes. Then jackets, scarves, gloves. The works. That'll bring him around. And a black dinner dress and shoes. Gotta have shoes."

"Whoa, wait a minute. I don't want to scare him away. We're just friends, old friends," she said, then added with a smile, "Close friends, but still just friends. Besides, he hasn't asked me out to dinner…and dinner out, at a fine dining restaurant, with a blind person, can get a little tricky, if you know what I mean. So I don't think that …"

"Grace. Remember what we just talked about? That you would not buck me as we enter this new phase in your life? And what about your singing career considerations, girlfriend?"

"I'm still thinking about it. I'm not sure what I'm going to do yet. But please don't tell anyone while I figure it out."

"Your secret is safe with me. Besides, you'll still need a new wardrobe if you go to New York. Right?"

"You're right. But wait a minute, I'm not sure how much money I have in my checking account, so I may have to talk to my dad about an advance."

"Already taken care of. Your dad called me earlier and said to tell you this spending spree is on him—an early Christmas present. Charge it on your credit card, and he'll pay for it. So come on, let's get started."

Her face tightened as she said, "Wait a minute. You had this whole thing all planned out even before I walked in the door?"

"Yep. Still, want to do it?"

"Of course. Whoop whoop!" she shouted.

Three hours later, Molly drove her home, with Grace sporting a chic new hairstyle, wearing new clothes, and feeling like a new person. After Molly parked the car, both of their arms were loaded with bags of clothes, boxes of shoes and boots as they walked up the steps.

"I feel like a million bucks," said Grace.

"That's about what it cost," she joked.

Her father greeted them at the door, nearly in tears at the way Grace looked. "Gracie," he said, "you look wonderful. Just like your mother. Thank you, Molly," he whispered. "Thank you so much."

"My pleasure, Reverend Albright," she said, then paused before adding, "She looks great, doesn't she?"

"Yes...yes, she does. Thanks again. Merry Christmas."

Molly hugged her and said, "Well, the bait has been set. Now it's all up to you. Good fishing."

"Thanks, Mol."

As Molly strode to her car, it began to snow. "Merry Christmas, Reverend. Merry Christmas, Grace."

# Chapter Seventeen

It was a cold winter that year in Los Angeles. *No snow here,* thought Frankie Cooper, as she stood in line at the soup kitchen on Polk Street. She pulled her coat tight around her and saw another new hole appear near her pocket as she poked her finger through it. She wiggled her thumb and laughed.

The line for food snaked around the building, and Rick Mason, the manager, smiled when he saw her. "Evening, Frankie," he said. "Haven't seen you around lately. How ya been doin'?"

"Good."

He leaned over to whisper to her, "Listen, I need a volunteer to help serve meals tonight. Includes a bed and breakfast too." She nodded with a smile at his generosity, then grabbed her torn canvas tote bag and moved past the others in the serving line. No one else ever volunteered because it meant being the last to eat and losing their place in line. But Frankie had lived on the streets long enough to know you took whatever you could get when offered.

The meal at the soup kitchen was not like back home at her mother's. The meat they served was usually some sort of mystery meat and served lukewarm. The cornbread and biscuits were mushy, and the gravy was runny, but it was a meal, and she was always grateful for being able to sleep inside. She knew the room and bed he offered would be clean but sparse, and she didn't have to worry about anyone stealing her "stuff." This was one of the better ones.

When Frankie finished serving the remaining stragglers, she sat down by herself off in the corner to eat, shoving extra rolls and bread into her coat pockets for later. *You never know when you may need something to eat,* she always told anyone who cared to listen.

"Frankie, I have something for you. I been savin'

'em for you, hopin' I'd see ya around." Rick reached inside his back pocket and handed her two envelopes.

She recognized the handwriting immediately—it was her mother's—and a glance at the return address confirmed it: Hilda Mae Cooper, Saint Michaels, Maryland. The front of the envelope was covered with different yellow forwarding labels.

"Thanks, Ricky," she murmured, and quickly shoved them in her pocket, as her eyes darted around her to make sure no one had seen her. Had to be careful. Others there could think the envelopes contained money, which always invited trouble.

As he walked away, he told her, "Oh, Frankie, Merry Christmas."

"Yeah, Merry Christmas, Rick." *Yeah, Merry Christmas. Some Christmas this is going to be.*

Her bed for the night was in a small room at the back of the stairs, which she shared with mops, brooms, buckets, and a little brown field mouse. The steady drip of water from the leaky faucet into the rusted sink was drowned out by the whirring of the heating system emanating from the room beside her. But it was warm, safe, and dry. *What more could a girl want?* She thought to herself. *How about a hot bath and a mani-pedi?* said a laughing voice deep inside her. *And maybe some of Mom's fried chicken, a big pile of mashed potatoes and gravy, and some of Henrietta's homemade pie.*

A lightbulb dangled above her cot, twisted in the air as it illuminated the room. Rick had set out a pillow, blanket, and sheet for her; this was much better than the cold bench she had slept on the night before. Her back was still sore from the raw steel slats. *Letters?* She pulled them from her back jeans pocket and looked at the yellow forwarding labels, slowly opening the oldest one first, hesitating. Taking a deep breath, she opened the first one and began to read.

> *Hi baby,*
>
> *Hope all is well with you, and that you're enjoying yourself in California. Lordy, girl, you do get around—back and forth from one city to another. It's so hard to keep track of you except for your postcards, which I love readin' by the way.*
>
> *Everybody here asks about you. Saint Michaels is pretty much the same, it never changes much, as you well know. The farms look barren without their crops of corn, wheat, and soybean. Old man Courtney planted a hundred acres of sunflowers this past summer at the Miller farm. Prettiest thing you ever saw. Always made me*

*smile when I drove by on my way to work. Bright yellow and brown faces followin' the sun to keep you company. Real friendly-like.*

*The Christmas store is doin' fine, and Henrietta sends her love. We had Thanksgiving at her place, and I had Henny set a place for you, just in case you showed up and surprised us all. Bet you had a lot of turkey and stuffin' to eat that day. You always loved Thanksgiving and my homemade pumpkin pie, topped with thick spoonfuls of fresh whipped cream. Pastor Williams from the First Baptist Ministry joined us this year since Pastor Theo got sick. He said grace for the Reverend Theo and a special prayer for you. We all missed you.*

*The town is getting ready for Christmas, and I always tell everybody it ain't the gifts or the presents or the parties, but instead it's what's inside you that is the Christmas spirit. That's what my momma always told me.*

*Henrietta told me that young Henry will be graduating from Morgan State University this year with his MBA and probably movin' back to Saint Michaels. Can you imagine that, Lil' Hank, a college graduate? He's a fine boy. He always asks about you when he calls and tells me to say hi to you. Every time I see him, I swear he's lookin' more like his daddy, rest his soul. Handsome boy that young Henry is.*

*Well, it's early, and the sun is comin' up. Time for me to get movin'. Takes a little longer every day to get the old motor runnin', if ya know what I mean. You be good now, sweetheart, and take care of yourself, ya hear me? I miss you, girl. You're my best friend. I miss not havin' you around to talk to. Got so much to say. Write if you have a mind to, ya hear.*

*Love Ya,*
*Momma*

She missed home but she could never go back. Not now. Frankie's stomach let out a deep rumble, the sound filling the silent room. She was hungry again. Holding the second letter in her hand, she stared at it for the longest time, and only looked away when she heard a noise at the door. It lasted for a few moments, then stopped, as she opened the second letter.

*Hi baby,*

*Hope you are doin' good. Saint Michaels is puttin' on all its holiday fineries. Lights, Christmas trees in the front windows of people's homes, and carolers walkin' up and down Talbot Street. It all looks so pretty, and people are so friendly. Lordy, brings you to tears sometimes, this town does. I love it here.*

*I'm afraid I got some bad news, the Reverend Theo passed away over the weekend. He was getting up in age, even though he was younger than Henny and me. He was a good man. The church was full of well-wishers, and even the Reverend Albright came to pay his respects and say a few words. His daughter Gracie was there too and was askin' about you.*

*I know you must be a busy girl, so I'll get right to the point. I want you to come home, to Saint Michaels. I miss you. And I forgive you. I don't care about the missing money, never did, but I do care about you. You're family. Reverend Theo's passin' made me think about how we spend our time on this planet, and I would dearly love to spend more time with you, darlin'. Just call me. Call me collect at the store if you want. Call me, and I'll send you a bus ticket home. I never asked you for anything, darlin', but I am askin' you now, come home. Everybody misses you. Love ya baby.*

*Merry Christmas,*
*Momma*

Frankie folded the letters and put them back into the envelopes as tears dripped from her eyes. Two years earlier, she had left town in a huff after a fight with her mother. A nasty battle. She would show her, she thought at the time, she was going to make it on her own. Now she wished she was home. Warm. Clean. Home. Family.

The noise at the door began again. She froze. A mouse? A rat? The doorknob started to turn, and an urgent voice came from the other side of the door, "Frankie? You still awake? Are ya hungry for some dessert?" It was Rick. The doorknob turned again, and the door began to bulge open but was stopped by the mop handles she had wedged between the door and the wall.

"Not tonight, Rick. See you in the morning," she called out. She fell asleep hours later, still shivering. Tomorrow was another day, she thought, but it would probably be the same as today. She would panhandle downtown until the cops come by. Have a meal of samples at the grocery store, washed down with a bottle of cola from the shelf, as she walked around the store. Make some money putting carts back at the airport or grocery store at a quarter apiece. Then try another soup kitchen. This one was getting too friendly.

Just as her eyelids began to close, she felt something on her leg in the dark, way too big for a mouse. She kicked it off and heard a loud hiss, coupled with a squeal. Frankie Cooper did not sleep that night. Instead, she thought of home. Of Saint Michaels. Of her mother and her friends. She thought of the warm bed, the plentiful table, and the warmth of her hometown. She missed home. Maybe...

# Chapter Eighteen

A light dusting of snow greeted Sam as he awoke the next morning and saw the fog lift from the water behind the cabin. His first service call was Saint Luke's Episcopal Church in Berlin, Maryland, almost two hours away from Saint Michaels. The drive was through the smallest of towns which dotted the eastern shore. He smiled as he parked in front of the old white clapboard church on the outskirts of Berlin. The church was surrounded by acres of fallow cornfields awaiting the spring plantings.

"Welcome, Sam. Good to see you," said the Reverend Manchester, the longtime pastor of Saint Luke's. He looked the same as he did twenty years earlier

"Morning, Reverend."

"I was getting a little worried."

"How so?"

"I got a call a few days ago from a fella named Zack, and he said he'd be coming here to tune the church organ. Then somebody else called and said you'd be here and then…well, I just didn't know what to think. You're not leaving the company, are you, Sam?"

"No, sir, not today."

He laughed. "Good. It wouldn't be the same without you. Don't ever leave."

"Well, you never know, Reverend. Things happen."

"It wouldn't be the same without you, Sam."

"Thank you, Reverend. But since my helper seems to have deserted me…"

"Your office called this morning and said he wouldn't be coming today and was going to be overseeing another team. But I'll be happy to play the organ and operate the manuals and stops for you if you like?"

"That'd be great. I'm a little shorthanded today."

"Well, at least you got the weekend coming up, and you can rest and take it easy for a few days."

"Well, I'm taking the next few weeks off and spending it working on Saint Michaels church bells and organ."

"Really? Good luck with it. I recall old-timers around here telling me about the sound coming out of Saint Michaels Church. There was a big rivalry among the downtown churches until after the war. And then when the Saint Michaels church bells went silent…well…so did everybody else, I'm afraid."

"Yes indeed. Should be interesting," Sam said, as he disappeared inside the dark church organ loft anteroom to begin his tuning.

"You know," called out the reverend, "I always used to tell your father that your company could have a full-time crew here year-round and keep them busy."

"I believe you're right Reverend," came the echo from inside. "Or have someone live over here on the Eastern Shore full-time."

Two hours later, Sam emerged for the last time from the dusty loft and said, "Okay, Reverend. Let's see how it sounds. Want me to play you a holiday favorite?"

"Great."

Sam's fingers struck the keys, opened two stops, and the organ seemed to come alive with his touch as he played "Hark the Herald Angels Sing." He loved to play as much as he loved to tune. When he finished, the pastor told him, "If you ever tire of tuning, you could always make a living playing the organ at the local churches."

"No thank you, Reverend. But Saint Michaels Church may be looking for a part-time organist after I tune it. If you know anyone, pass it on to the Reverend Albright."

"Will keep it in mind, Sam, and I'll pass the word around with other pastors. Merry Christmas."

When Sam finished for the day and arrived back home, he found a pile of boxes sitting by his front door marked with express labels. He made a cup of maple-flavored cocoa and brought the boxes inside to begin sorting through them.

The largest box contained a huge leather hide. Perfect size to replace the bellows on the old church organ at Saint Michaels Church. Other boxes included felts, tuning forks, stops, chambers, everything he needed. A note was attached to one of the bags:

*Sam,*

*Hope this covers what you need. Let me know if I can help.*
*Enjoy your time off. You've earned it.*

*Merry Christmas,*
*Ollie*

He sat back and began to relax, sorting out his options, when his phone rang. "Hello?"

"Hello, Mr. Carpenter," said the voice on the other end, "this is Carson Wright at Wanamaker Organ Company. Sorry to be calling you so late in the evening. Is this a good time to talk?"

*Wanamakers!*

"Yes. Of course," he stuttered.

"Well, I'm calling to let you know that you have made it into the final round of consideration for employment here at Wanamaker's. Your credentials are impressive, your education is right in line with what we look for in new associates at Wanamaker's, and you scored very high on your telephone interview. And it doesn't hurt that your father apprenticed here early on during his career. His apprenticeship allows us to consider your application for employment first since you're a legacy. We would like to have you come and visit here for four to five days to see what life is like here at Wanamaker's and show you around the city of Philadelphia. See how you would like your new workplace, new colleagues and the like."

*Philadelphia?* He loved the idea of working for Wanamaker's, but now he had to deal with the thought of moving to a new city, new people, new job, new coworkers, just when he was starting to enjoy the holidays at Saint Michaels...and Grace. "Oh. And when would that be?"

"I'll call you back in the next few days to arrange it. We want to have the position filled and have whoever we hire as our new associate on board by the first of the year. I just wanted to call to make sure you're still available and interested in the position. You are still available and interested, right, Mr. Carpenter?"

Sam didn't say anything for the longest time until he responded, "Yes, yes, of course. I'm still interested."

"Good. I'll talk to you again once all the arrangements have been made. Merry Christmas, Mr. Carpenter…Sam. Looking forward to having you come aboard. Good night."

"Merry Christmas." Sam looked at the pile of supplies; organ parts were strewn about the floor. He plopped down on the sofa and stretched out his arms. *Sleep. Wonderful sleep.*

The foghorn from an incoming ship blared into the night as he warmed some cocoa and went outside on the back porch to try to sort through his feelings. The slow-moving Miles River usually provided comfort to him in its journey past his cabin, but that night, it only added to his confusion. *What to do? Wannamakers? Gracie? New York? Saint Michaels? Baltimore? Too many decisions and no answers.*

Looking towards the town of Saint Michaels and the houses surrounding the harbor, he could see Saint Michaels Church, Grace's home with the lights still on, and the church steeple standing proudly beside it. He missed her and whispered her name, "Grace? Gracie, can you hear me?" No response, other than the hooting of the night owls somewhere deep in the woods surrounding his home.

On the other side of the harbor, Grace Albright turned out the light in her bedroom and walked to the window, slowly opening it. She breathed in deep, taking in the chilled night air—the Christmas breeze she called it. Grace heard voices and laughter from people passing by down below on Talbot Street. She smelled the strong smell of chestnuts roasting with the corner vendor on Willow Street.

Suddenly, she wished she could see the moon on the water over the harbor, the way she did when she was younger. Or see the twinkling Christmas lights of the town. Or the light from Sam's cabin. To see Sam again. To touch his face. To see his smile. A tear drifted down her cheek. Then another. *Yes … to see him again.* She took in a deep breath, then whispered, "Sam? Sam? Can you hear me? Sam…I think I love you."

# Chapter Nineteen

There was frost on the grass the next morning, and the fog lifted from the water as Sam drove into town. It was early, and the streets were nearly deserted. He slowed to pass an eighteen-wheeler blocking his lane in front of the Christmas shop and waved to Henrietta, who was acting as a volunteer traffic guard, directing cars as the truck was unloaded.

"Morning, Sam," she called out with a huge smile.

"Morning, Henrietta. Big delivery?" he asked as he lowered his window.

"You bet. Our biggest ever. We filled up the garage out back, the storage room upstairs, and are now just unloading the last of it temporarily into the store and the basement storage area. After you talked with Charlie, he came to visit me and placed an order with us to replace the Christmas items destroyed in the fire earlier in the year. He also talked the mayors of some of the other towns around here into doing the same. Which they did. And now here it is. Can you believe it? And all paid for up front! God bless 'em." She stepped back and directed a van around the big delivery truck before returning to his car.

"Yep, now all I gotta do is unpack all this stuff, put it together, and hang it about town. Whew."

He put the car into park. "Henrietta," he said, "I'm pretty busy down at Saint Michaels Church refurbishing their church bells and organ today, but I have the next two weeks off. I'd be happy to come by in my free time and help you out if you need me?"

"Oh, baby boy, that would be wonderful. I got young Henry coming to help, and you were on my list to call. Thank you so much. I really appreciate it."

A large snowflake landed on his windshield, then another.

"Grace Albright said there was snow in the air, and she was right." The woman lifted her head to the sky as snowflakes drifted down. "Maybe even a white Christmas this year in Saint Michaels."

"Grace? Almost forgot. I better get going. I want to get an early start. Lots to do. I'll see you later, Henrietta. Merry Christmas."

"Merry Christmas to you too, Sam," she said. "Give my best to Grace and her dad. And tell her I have already had several people ask about the flyer we put up for her. About the choir."

"Will do. Gotta go."

It began to snow harder as he soon parked the SUV on the church parking lot and rang Grace's doorbell, his heart pounding in his chest.

"Morning, Sam," Grace said, taking him in the shadows towards the kitchen and leading him to the table. She liked holding his hand. Firm. Strong.

"Morning, Gracie," he said. Once in the light of the kitchen, his eyes followed her about the room, looking at her as if it was the first time he'd ever seen her. He could not take his eyes off her: her clothes, and how her snug, form-fitting jeans and sweater outlined her curves in all the right places. It was as if he'd never seen her before. So beautiful. So sexy-looking.

"You look amazing, Grace," he said. "I must tell you, you look...different. Way different."

"You like it?"

"Yes, of course, I like it! You look fantastic, not that you didn't look great before, but now...wow! New hairdo. New clothes, jeans. New shoes. I love it. You look great."

"Thanks, Sam," she replied, with a slight unexpected blush. She was getting embarrassed with all this new attention. Changing the subject, she asked, "Snowing?"

"Yes. How did you know?"

"Your jacket sleeve is cold and wet. It's too cold for rain, so it must be snow. Care for some coffee? Donuts? Bagels? I can whip up an omelet for you if you like."

"I'll just have a coffee, if you don't mind. Then I'd really like to take a close look at your bell system and get started. I got a lot to do."

"Sure."

Her father entered the room, and after landing a good morning peck on her cheek, said, "Morning, everyone."

"Morning, Dad," she said.

"Mornin', reverend," said Sam.

"Well, Sam, are you ready to start your examination and see if we can bring our patient back to life?"

"Yes, sir. I thought I'd start with the bell system first, the electronics, the tuning, and a physical inspection of the bells themselves. How long exactly has it been since the bells were last used?"

"As best as I can tell, it's been over seventy years since the bells last rang. Just before the war."

"Okay," Sam replied. "Once I have them working, and when I'm sure everyone in town is awake, I'll try to ring them and make a note of those bells that may be out of tune. You have thirty-three bells in your *carillon,* and each one is numbered by pitch and tone."

"Carillon?" Grace asked.

"It's French for a set of church bells that are played together, either mechanically or manually. They can weigh up to a ton."

"That's a big bell."

"Yes, it is. After I ring them, then I'll take a sample of each bell and identify which bell it came from and ship it off to an assayer company in New York for him to test it. It's his job to analyze the sample and come back with a report that tells me the metal composition of each bell. Jasef is an old friend of mine in New York. He owns Krasnik & Heidrich Assayers. From his report, I'll be able to see if it's on the mark as to what it should be."

He finished his coffee, and Bill asked, "Are you ready, Sam?"

"Yes, sir."

The three of them walked through the rectory, into the church, towards the organ. The reverend glanced at the organ pipes and said to no one in particular, "I can't wait to hear the bells and organ again. What a wonderful Christmas present." Turning to Sam, he asked, "Do you think you can pull it off, Sam? I mean, make them sound good again? I mean really good?"

"I'm going to try, Reverend."

They walked past the organ door and the door to the bell tower room. The door creaked when the reverend unlocked and opened it. But the room was clean, almost spotless. Sam turned to the minister with a questioning look on his face.

Sheepishly, the reverend said, "One of my few extravagances. I have the cleaning service clean this room once every other month, just hoping and praying that one day we could use it again."

"That's good. It will help in the maintenance of the system."

A trapdoor was on the floor in front of them, with a long steel coiled cable hanging from the top of the tower, tightly secured to the wall. "Sam, I've always wondered what they use this for?" he asked.

"To raise or lower the bells. If they ever need to replace or repair a bell, you can raise or lower it by using this cable to lift it up inside the tower. Sometimes, but not often, they'll have a couple replacement bells underneath the trap door, and then all they have to do is attach it to one end of the bell, hoist it up, and make the swap. That's easy compared to getting them to sound right together. You see, a bell must not only sound right alone, but they all also must harmonize together. Just like a pipe organ. That's the tough part."

Sam looked at the bell control panel. "Let me see what we have here," he said, taking off his jacket and examining the keyboard and the system. "You have an early version, but it uses a play chart, much like a player piano. But first I have to turn it on. Let's see if it works." He flipped the switch; nothing happened.

Pressing the button on the panel, he said, "Our first goal is to get this little green light to turn on. That tells us that the electric is working." Nothing happened. He tried again. Then he checked all the connections. No luck. He went around the back of the control mechanism and began the process of rewiring the connections with the new wire that Ollie had sent him from Baltimore.

Her father watched him, then stood and said, "Well, I must get ready for the bishop's visit, so if it's okay with you, Sam, I'll leave the two of you here alone and be on my way. Call me on my cell phone if you need anything. Anything at all. See you later this afternoon. Good luck with the bells."

"Thank you, Reverend."

"Bye, Dad."

As Sam began rewiring the system's connections, he lost himself in his work. "One of these has to be bad. I just have to find out which one. Grace, after I rewire each one, flip the switch when I ask you."

"Sure, Sam."

It was just the two of them in the small control room, sitting on the bench. He could feel her closeness. She felt warm as she leaned over him, her chest gently pressing into him. Soft. Warm. "Did you find out what was wrong?" she asked innocently.

"No, everything is fine," he said, then swallowed, still feeling her chest pressing softly against him. He turned to look at her, her face, her smile…he needed to stand, and went around to the back of the panel. "Try it now," he told her.

She flipped the switch. Nothing happened. "I'm glad you're home, Sam," she said with her hands on her lap, looking like an angel. She had the prettiest smile, a smile that lit up a room when she came inside.

"Me too," he said, as he lay out of sight on the floor, rewiring the harness. "I never realized how much I missed Saint Michaels. Try it again."

She flipped the switch. Nothing. "Nope." Then she said, "You know, my father was so angry at you for years. He blamed you for me losing my sight."

"Did you?"

Her voice rose in pitch. "No, I never blamed you, Sam, never. Doctors said it was a freak accident. As a matter of fact, I missed you when you left, but I never blamed you."

"I missed you too," he said, as he sat down next to her on the bench. "I felt guilty for the longest time after I left. Like I caused your blindness and then abandoned you. I wished it had happened to me instead of you. I felt like a real jerk."

She threw her arms around him. "Sam, it wasn't your fault. You didn't abandon me. And the doctors and all the specialists we went to still don't know what caused it, but it certainly wasn't your fault."

Sitting there, next to her, so close, he had an overwhelming urge to kiss her. He moved a wild strand of hair from her face and placed it back around her ear. His hand lingered on her face. *Oh, this is not going to be easy, at all,* he thought. "Back to work."

Two hours later, they were still trying to get the bell electrical system to function properly. He tested and replaced all the fuses. No luck. Replaced all the wiring. No luck. Checked the contacts. No luck. Frustrated, he finally asked, "Try the switch again."

She flipped the panel switch. "Nope. Still nothing."

He attached the final wires and sockets and again sat down next to her on the bench to rest and dust himself off.

She moved closer to him. "We never did get to talk," she said, and after an awkward moment of silence, asked, "So how have you been? Work? Love life? All the juicy details. Don't leave anything out." Her hand rested casually on his leg.

Sam laughed at her directness, the kind that only old friends can share while glancing at her hand. He held it for a few seconds, it felt warm, soft. "Nothing on the love life front for quite a while. Not since…" He stopped, then was quiet for a minute. "Living in Baltimore for the last couple of years, I guess I never found the right girl. But work has been good. One of the old-timers of the tuning crew at Wanamaker's is retiring, so I applied for the job."

"Wanamaker's? In Philadelphia? Really? Wow! That's fantastic. Hasn't that always been your dream job?"

"Yes."

" So what happened?"

"Well, I completed a phone interview with them—twice."

"And?"

"They called me late last night and want me to come to Philadelphia for a working interview and visit. Sounds really good. But to be truthful, I'm still not sure, that's all."

She was quiet for a moment. "And you would have to move to Philadelphia?"

"Yes, unfortunately. That's the only bad part. I would also miss the interaction with all my customers. I love traveling to the different churches and working with the pastors. My customers are like my friends, my family. But I have to explore it as an option. I've also given some thought to chucking it all and just opening a pipe organ tuning shop down here on the Eastern Shore."

She was genuinely excited upon hearing this. "Your own business? Wow, I'm impressed. That would be great. But whatever you decide, I hope it works out for you, if that's what you want."

"Yeah, I guess. What about you?"

"Well, we have the bishop coming in, and Dad is really stressed out about it, although he tries not to show it for my sake. The church needs more parishioners. I've formed a church choir, hoping that will draw more people in. We need more people and their support. It's critical."

She was quiet for a moment, then her face brightened when she said, "I told you about the man who stopped by the church the other day when I was singing. I was alone in the church at the time, it was very early. It was cold in church, very cold. I like to sing like that in the morning, especially at Christmastime. I love to sing. It calms my nerves for the day and…"

He had to laugh; she rambled on when she was excited. He interrupted, "Yes, so, you had a man stop by the church, and…"

"Oh yes, I get a little carried away sometimes, and I can't believe it. This is exciting news."

"Gracie…you met a man and?"

"Oh yes, well, he loved my singing. He has a talent management agency in New York City and offered to help me find a job to sing professionally. I would have to go through some vocal training initially, but he thinks I have what it takes."

"Gracie, that sounds wonderful! You've always loved to sing," he said, sounding genuinely excited for her. "However, I hear a but coming on."

"But I would have to move to New York, but then I get to travel…and see the world. New York. London. Tokyo. Paris. Rio. The world!"

"Is that what you want? To see the world?"

His choice of words stopped her from saying anything further. A tear rolled slowly down her cheek. Then another. She could hear the excitement in his voice, but she wanted to see his smile, his face.

Her words came tumbling out. "I want to see again," she blurted out barely above a harsh whisper. "In the morning I want to feel the sunrise on my face at my window. But now I want to see the sunrise and the sunset. I want to see the fireworks on the Fourth of July. I want to see lightning bugs in my backyard. I want to see the winter geese flying low in formation over the water. I want to see the snowflakes falling from the sky before they hit my face. I want to see…"

Tears streamed down her face. She reached out her hand to touch him. *I want to see your smile again.* Grace brushed away the tears. "I'm sorry, Sam. I don't mean to bother you with all my troubles, but I can't tell anyone else.

My father takes it personally like he has failed me and hasn't been able to help me."

Sam reached for her hand and said, "I understand. Grace, I know a doctor in Baltimore, an eye doctor. A good one. One of the best in his field. Maybe he can help. I can make a phone call and…"

"No, Sam, I don't want any more false hopes. Besides, my father has taken me to the best eye specialists from Richmond to Boston. No luck. No hope. We are even on the list at the Winston Eye Clinic for the experimental stem surgery. Saturna. The one they call 'the last hope.' But even if they did call, don't ask me how we would ever pay the hundreds of thousands of dollars for the procedure."

She could feel his warmth. She wanted to reach out and touch him. To hold him, to kiss him.

"I'm sorry, Sam," she said as she dried her eyes, holding his hand, trying to appear brave. It all came rushing out. "But enough about me and my whining," she said attempting to change the subject. "I've been holding it in for so long. It is what it is, and I must accept that in my life. But what I can't accept is why we can't get these old church bells ringing. Come on, Sam. Have you double-checked everything?"

He reached for her, putting his arms around her, holding her close. "Oh, Grace, I wish I could just wave a magic wand and make that hurt disappear. Make you see again, but I can't." He brushed the tears away from her eyes. "All I can do is be here, now, with you, and try to help in any way I can."

She felt his arms around her and felt something more, something else inside her, warm feelings stirring. She breathed deep, then had to swallow, her hand still on his leg. *What am I going to do? My feelings for him are getting stronger every day. I want to be with him. I want to…*

She moved away and swallowed deep saying, "Have you double checked everything?"

"Yes, of course. I rewired all forty-three connections. Changed all the fuses. Cleaned all the circuits. Checked all the backstops. Everything."

"Hmm. Then it should work. And you turned on the main switch, right?"

*Main switch?* He blinked, and his eyes searched until he found the blue button on the side in all capital letters: MAIN. He discreetly pushed it in, coughing to cover the sound of the button being turned on. "Yes. Of course, it's on." Then turning to Grace, he said, "Try your flip switch again."

He watched as her hand searched for the switch. "You know, Grace," he said, "I really do have some close connections in Baltimore, within the medical community. I could call in a favor and see if I could..."

"No, Sam. I've been down that path too many times. I've tried everything. I've even prayed for help."

"Try again."

"Praying?"

"Yes, that of course, always—but try the flip switch again."

Her hand continued to search for the switch until he leaned closer and gently took her hand in his to guide it there. He leaned closer as she flipped it, and then they both heard a whirring noise growing louder and louder. The green light was on!

He grabbed her by the arms and yelled, "The light's on! The light's on!" He hugged her. "It's working! It's working!" In all the excitement, he pulled her close and kissed her. A first kiss. The sweetest kiss he had ever experienced. At once, he recoiled away from her. "Sorry, Gracie, I guess I got a little carried away."

She smiled. "That's okay, Sam, no apologies necessary." It was a warm and tender kiss, just the way she thought it would be, even if it were by accident. *Or was it?*

The panel beeped.

"Holy smokes!" she shouted. "Now what?"

"Now let's ring the test bells. Grace, press the square button next to the flip switch. To the right. It's just to the right of the flip switch." Again, he took her hand to help her find it, then pressed it. Soon a long, sweet, beautiful bell rang out from the steeple overhead. "Again," he whispered. The sound of the bell ringing out made people hurrying on the street outside the church stop, look up to the bell tower, and listen. "Again," he said. Glorious.

"So, the main switch was turned off? Right?"

"Well, well...I would have had to rewire those wires eventually anyway. I just did them early."

Her hand reached up to touch and trace the lines of his face. "Samuel Jason Carpenter, you'll never change. You goofball, you need to check the main switch. That's why you need a woman in your life."

"To ring my bell?" he said impishly.

She chuckled, then laughed, something she had not done in a very long time. "Yes, to ring your bell."

They were interrupted at the door by the sound of her father as he burst into the room, completely out of breath. "Wow! It's working?" he shouted. The reverend had a huge smile on his face as he listened to the long silent bells ring out. "They sound glorious, Sam. Good job."

"Yes, but that's only the test bell. This carillon has thirty-three bells with a four-octave range. Next, I need to test all the bells, then I'll take a metal sample from each bell and send it off to the assayer. The real test is when I do a full sequence through the entire carillon."

The Reverend asked, "When will you do that?"

"Right now. Are you ready?" he asked, as he pulled his notebook from his briefcase.

"Yes. Ready and excited," said the reverend.

"Me too," said Grace.

Sam reached over the top of the console and pressed the TEST SEQUENCE button. The church bells of Saint Michaels began to ring, one at a time. Ding, ding, ding, ding…ding, ding, dang, DANG, ding, dang, ding, ding, DANG. Of the thirty-three bells in the tower, seven had rung sour.

"Very strange," said Sam. "There's no rhyme or reason why these particular bells don't ring true. Some of the sour bells are in the lower octave range, while others are in the higher. Odd. Very odd."

"Now what?" asked Grace.

"I'm going to climb the bell tower and do a physical examination of the bells. Make sure none of them are cracked or bent. Then I'll take a metal sample and number each one from inside each bell for the assayer. When I'm done, I think I'll start working on the organ while I wait for the report to come back. I have the materials for a new organ bellows. But I'll take some measurements to be precise before I cut the pattern."

The reverend looked at his watch and said, "Grace, don't forget you have your choral group in the church for rehearsal."

"Oh, no, I forgot all about it. We have twelve new additions to our choral group."

"They're all a result from the flyers you posted around town," smiled her father. "It brought more people into the church last week as well."

Grace stood and reached for her cane. "I gotta go, Sam. Are you coming to the parade and Christmas Festival in town tomorrow?"

"Wouldn't miss it for the world." He watched her unfold her cane and couldn't take his eyes off her. Her new clothes, haircut, and whole air of confidence were inspiring. He breathed in deep; he wanted to hold her, to kiss her, but he would have to tell her, so she wouldn't be startled. *Don't do it, Sam. You can only call one kiss an accident. Kissing her again will only make matters worse and tougher all around. She has New York, and you have Wanamaker's. So cool it.* He held himself back, content with merely watching her, her mouth, her gentle hands, her... *leave her be, Sam.*

She turned to him and said, "Hey, after the parade, how about dinner tomorrow? You can help me finish the Christmas decorations."

He was quiet for a minute, lost in thought, but responded, "Sure, sounds great. I'm going to program five of the good bells to ring tomorrow morning before church services. It'll sound awesome."

"Why only five?"

"I must program around the dead-sounding bells. But trust me, it'll sound great."

"Wonderful. I can't wait."

As Grace made her way through the church, she heard the sounds of voices singing from her choir at the front. They stopped when she approached. "Good morning," she said. "I'm Grace Albright, your choral director, for those of you that are new here."

"Love the new hairdo, Miss Grace," she heard Billy Collins say.

"And love your new clothes, Miss A. Really steppin' out there," echoed Alison Parker.

"Thank you, thank you, thank you. I appreciate the compliments. But now on to business. Since we may have a new organ for Christmas, I thought we would practice 'O Come All Ye Faithful,' on page 43 of your hymn book. But first, I understand we have some new members to our choral group. Welcome, everyone. I heard some wonderful voices coming up the aisle. If you don't mind, shout out your name so I can hear your voice, take a head count, and see where you would sound the best." She pointed to the right. "Let's start there."

"The n-name is Jared, ma'am, Jared Butler," sounded out a deep baritone—with a stutter.

"Welcome, Jared. You can stay right where you are. You have a wonderful voice—have you been singing long?"

"T-two years, ma'am."

"Jared, you're welcome here. And I can't wait to hear more of your voice."

"Thank you, ma'am. I appreciate that. I love to sing. It helps me out a lot."

Next came the sweet alto voice from the back row, "Cindy Rohm, Miss Albright."

"Welcome, Cindy. I think I'd like to have you join the other alto voices over to my left if you please. But come closer to the front. Your wonderful voice gets lost in the rear with all the others."

"I've always kind of stayed in the background. Sort of a habit, I guess."

"You're welcome to stay there if you like, but I don't think there's a need to put your angelic voice in the rear or under a basket."

The young voice laughed. "Sure, Ms. Albright."

"Next."

"Michael Simmons, Miss Albright," said a strong, confident voice. "I'm kinda new in town. And don't really know anyone here. I work for the Maritime Authority here in Saint Michaels."

"You can stay right where you are for the time being. Welcome. On second thought, why don't you stand over by Ms. Rohm? Perhaps you can both share insights and learn from one another."

"Great, I'd be happy to, Miss Albright."

"Next." But Grace was interrupted by the ringing of her cell phone in her purse. She searched and searched. Three rings. Finally, on the fifth ring, she answered, "Hello, this is Grace."

"Grace? Hi, this is Justin, Justin Reynolds. We spoke the other day in church about my company representing you professionally. Remember me?"

She held up her hand and slowly walked away from the group.

"Oh yes, of course, I remember you, Justin. How could I forget you?"

"Well, I'm sorry to bother you, but if you remember, I told you sometimes we have small group sessions organized to train our new clients. You train with each other, then sing and travel together to help accelerate your career. Well, I have some good news for you. We have a new group starting next year and thought you would be perfect. You would travel, take vocal lessons, sing with groups, go through our imaging program, help shape your brand, the whole works. It would move your career along at a much more rapid pace."

"Wow, that sounds great. When does it start?"

"In two weeks. So I would need your answer soon."

"How soon?"

"I hate to do this, but I'll need to know within the week. Please think about it and let me know. I'm sorry for the short notice, but we have a lot of things we would need to prepare for you to give you the best professional experience. Booking vocal coaches, hotels, transportation, and things like that."

*Leave Saint Michaels? In a week? I'm not sure. There's so much going on in my life now. So much unsettled. Dad? The church. And now Sam. And Wanamaker's?*

"I see. Let me think about it and check my calendar. Can I get back to you?"

"Sure. Call me. Talk to you soon, Grace. Merry Christmas."

"Merry Christmas, Mr. Reynolds." She was lost in a fog; a once in a lifetime opportunity before her was now taking center stage in her life. *Why does all of this have to happen at the same time? A new career. The bishop coming to give his decision about closing the school and the church. Dad. Sam coming to rebuild the bells and the organ. And of course, Sam.*


Sam Carpenter slowly made his way up the narrow steps leading to the belfry at the top of the tower. It was a road less traveled, as evidenced by the dust and many abandoned birds' nests he passed along the way. At the top of the tower, he saw the magnificent bells arrayed around the trapdoor in the center floor, leading to the ground floor three stories below. Upon examination, he found that none of the bells were cracked or damaged, but he did notice that the seven bells which had sounded out of tune didn't match the others. They were of a different style, from a different bellfounder, but bore no name or identifying marks as to their origin other than a raised, stylized cross just below the crown. None of the bells were chipped or cracked. None contained rust. None were covered in verdigris. *Very strange*, he thought to himself.

Sam took a metal scraping from inside each bell, marked it, and numbered each individual one for Josaf, the assayer. He put all the samples into an envelope and addressed it to his old friend in New York. Some of the bells sounded dull, and Sam knew Josaf would be able to tell him their composition. Typical bell metal should be 80% copper and 20% tin, but these didn't sound like that at all. There was no verdigris, no cracks, no outward signs of stress, but something was causing them to sound sour.

When he finished with the bells, he made his way downstairs to examine the church's beautiful old organ. It was as he expected, the bellow providing the air for the system was dry rotted and incapable of holding the air needed to power the organ pipes. The felts were long gone, the mechanics needed attention, and the generator did not start.

Next, he measured the bellows, and it was then he heard the choir practicing the Christmas hymns downstairs. For the first time in years, he heard Grace sing. Her voice rose high inside the church, its sweet echoes surrounding him. It was a glorious sound. He had never realized what an incredible voice she had until then.

With a voice and talent like that, she would go far in the music business. Nothing could stop her if she decided to pursue a professional career. She had to share her voice with the world. Yes. His smile drooped as he listened. His soul ached, for he knew what he had to do.

Once back home working in his father's workshop was usually calming for him. He laid out the leather hide, measured it, and cut it for the new bellows. Then, using a special fish-based glue made specifically for securing leather bellows together, he carefully applied the adhesive and set it aside to dry as he began to work on other pieces for the organ. It was going to take some time for him to finish all of it. While working to piece together the odd assortment of parts, his gaze continued to return to his cell phone on the workbench. He remembered what Grace had said. She was adamant in her refusal for help, but this was different. One last thing he could do to help. Finally, he picked up the phone, took in a deep breath, and dialed the number.

A woman answered, "Hello?"

"Coleen? Hi, this is Sam. I need a favor, a big favor."

"Sure, Sam, anything. You know that."

"Can I speak to Malek?"

Her voice filled with concern, she asked him, "Is everything okay?"

"Yes, I think so. I hope so. I need to speak with Malek…please."

"Of course. Hold on while I get him."

She must have told her husband of the urgency in his voice because Malek answered the phone and came right to the point. "Sam? What's wrong? What can I do to help?"

# *Chapter Twenty*

The next day, Sam went to Ye Olde Christmas Shoppe on Talbot Street to help Henrietta and spent hours unpacking and putting together the Christmas displays. Next, he loaded them onto a rented truck to help deliver and install them.

"Hiya, Sam," came the sound of a deep, thundering voice. "It's been a long time."

It was Lil' Henry, though his childhood nickname no longer seemed appropriate. Sam reached out to shake his hand. The young, skinny boy Sam remembered as a kid helping his father in the delivery business was now some eight inches taller than Sam. He was broad at the shoulders, with coal black hair and matching dark eyes. But he still had that flashing, warm smile.

"Hey, Hank. Good to see you," he said, as they each picked up boxes to carry outside and load into the waiting truck. "You sure grew up, Lil' Henry. What have they been feeding you in college?"

He laughed. "Well, whatever it was, it sure wasn't as good as my momma's home-cookin'. She's still the best cook on the Eastern Shore."

They walked back inside, each grabbing another box, when Sam asked him, "Have you finished your schooling yet?"

"Yep. Momma and Hilda Mae came up for the ceremony. She cried the whole time, kept saying she wished my daddy was there to see it. She was so proud. I got my bachelor's in computer science and my MBA in Finance." He set down the box to tell him, "You know, Sam, I got job offers from all over the country. Got offers to go to work from big banks, big insurance companies, venture funds, high-tech companies in California, you name it."

"So what are you goin' to do?"

He stopped for a minute, obviously reflecting on his decision. "I gave it a lot of thought, and I think I'm comin' back here to Saint Michaels. It's a good place to live, friendly people, everybody knows your name, and it's home. A good place to raise a family. I just love it here. Always have." He smiled that wonderful smile of his, then said, "Come on, we got work to do, and Momma will start yellin' if she sees us just standing around doing nothin'." Sam smiled. Lil' Henry was right, Saint Michaels was a great place to live and raise a family. Yes, yes indeed.

When people heard of Henrietta and Hilda's dilemma, it seemed that the whole town turned out to help. Unloading, unboxing, connecting the wires, and assembling the decorations to hang from the streetlights in town. Sam moved from box to box and table to table, wherever he could help out.

"Hi, I'm Sam," he said to the man next to him, an unshaven man, wearing a worn army fatigue field jacket—the homeless man from the diner before. "We've never officially met."

"Good to meet you, Sam. I'm Gabriel, but you can call me Gabe," the man said with a warm smile and a deep traveling voice. "And thanks for the help at the diner. Merry Christmas." He smiled, and that was all he said, but his eyes—sharp, piercing, warm eyes—said the rest.

Sam persisted, "That waitress must be new at the diner, because Molly is much more tolerant. She would have never embarrassed you like that."

"No bother, no bother at all. Thanks again." He merely smiled but said not another word.

Sam added, "Happy to help out." Gabe moved more boxes than anyone else that day and kept busy until they were finished.

They moved boxes for hours, stopping only to eat the hot ham sandwiches and coffee that Henrietta and Hilda had prepared for them. Sam grabbed a plate and rested on a box next to Gabe.

Silence.

"Army?" he asked him, while pointing to his ragged army fatigue jacket.

"Yes. Army medic."

"Where were you stationed?"

"Wherever I was needed."

"Oh." *Not a talkative cuss at all. Very strange bird, likable, but strange,* thought Sam.

Over the next four hours, the group unpacked, set up, assembled, and loaded the decorations into the waiting truck with volunteers, who rushed to hang them around the small village. They hung them from streetlights, lampposts, and shrubs all through town, according to the plan that the mayor had laid out for them. Henrietta wanted to have everything hung before the upcoming traditional Christmas parade. She smiled when the last truck left, and she knew they were going to make her deadline.

At the end of the day, Sam was so tired he could hardly keep his eyes open. When the group finished for the day, Henrietta thanked all of them. "I can't thank you enough. All of you. Merry Christmas and thank you," she said nearly in tears. "It's times like these that you can tell who your friends are, and that the Christmas spirit comes alive. Thank you all again and see you at the parade tomorrow. It'll be the best in years."

As Sam and the stranger walked past the veteran's tree, now filled with hanging dog tags, the stranger stopped and looked at the tree.

Henrietta walked up beside them and whispered, "It started out by accident, but now look at it. Now we have over fifty sets of dog tags and our own commemorative tags hanging from this tree. We started with the bare tree, the flag and the sign at the bottom of the tree—*We Thank You for Your Service*—and now look at all the dog tags to honor all the vets, POWs, and MIAs."

Gabe raised his hand to salute those who had served. "Yes. Amazing, but it's missing something," he said, standing there motionless. He slowly removed the chain from around his neck and placed the star-shaped object at the top of the tree.

Sam moved in closer behind him to see what Gabe had hung from the tree. It was the Silver Star, one of the highest honors that America can bestow on its veterans. Sam was speechless. This man was a decorated war hero.

The ragged veteran stepped back and remarked, "Now it's complete. Let's finish up." Without another word, he walked away towards the garage warehouse at the back of the building.

At the end of the day on his way home, Sam saw the reflection of the moon off the water behind his cabin on the Miles River. It reminded him of past Christmases with his parents. Singing Christmas carols. Baking cookies with Mom and handcrafting Christmas tree ornaments with Dad in the shop. Hanging decorations and garlands about the house. Drinking cocoa on the back deck, looking out over the water. He recalled all the

Christmases his family had spent here together, and on the lake in the boat. Good times. He smiled a weak, torn smile.

Sam missed his mom and dad. The times they spent decorating the cabin, cutting down their own Christmas tree, decorating it with homemade ornaments, hanging stockings from the fireplace. The presents. The baking. He could smell the pies his mom would make by merely closing his eyes. He missed those Christmases from years gone by.

He had missed Saint Michaels more than he ever thought he would, but now he had the most significant move in his career right before him: to be on the exclusive staff at Wanamaker's. A once in a lifetime opportunity. Wow! But what about Grace? Then again, she might be going to New York. To start her career. With her incredible, beautiful voice, she should go to New York. With everything going on in his life, he was confused, but he was not going to stand in her way. He wanted her to be happy. That's all he ever wanted for her.

Sam looked across the water at the church steeple and the lights. He could see the church and Grace's house in the distance. He listened to the night birds as they cooed and flew overhead. The lights near her home twinkled in the moonlight. "Good night, Grace Albright. I love you, I have always loved you," he whispered. It felt good to say it now, without any repercussions. Nobody's feelings being hurt. "I love you, Gracie."

# Chapter Twenty-One

On Sunday morning, the village of Saint Michaels, Maryland awoke to a holiday surprise. At precisely 8:50 A.M., the long-silent church bells of Saint Michaels Church rang out across the town, calling the faithful to church services. Even though only five bells sounded that morning, it made for a cheery addition to the holidays.

Pastor Bill Albright smiled as he greeted his growing flock before they made their way inside the church. Grace took her place in the choir loft and whispered to herself a soft, "Thank you, Sam."

It took Sam a little longer than usual to find a parking spot at Saint Michaels. People rushed to find a seat inside as Sam greeted the pastor.

"Morning, Sam," said Bill. "God bless and Merry Christmas to you."

"Mornin', Reverend Albright," he said with a smile. "Bells sound glorious, don't they?"

"You bet. Sam, you did a great job. I can't wait to hear them when all the bells are ringing." He glanced at his watch. "Gotta go. Got a flock to tend to inside."

"And a growing flock at that," Sam said, as he looked around.

"Yes indeed, thanks to you and Grace. I just hope it's enough to impress the bishop when he visits." He turned to walk inside and said, "Wait until you hear Grace sing her solo today. Spectacular. Oh, and you're going to join us for dinner tonight, right?"

"Yes sir, Reverend."

"See you then."

The church was crowded that day, so Sam sat at the rear of the church and saw Gabe close by, kneeling in prayer. He looked different that morning for some reason. Maybe because Sam had thought of him as an aimless, destitute person, much like the dozen or so who made their home under the bridge every night. But that day in church, he saw him as a vet, a hapless hero who put his life on the line to save his fellow vets and defend his country. Gabe raised his head and glanced around. When he saw Sam watching him, he smiled a sweet smile, then motioned a quick hello.

At the end of the service, Grace stood. All dressed in her new dress fringed in lace and her new white shoes, she began to sing. She looked like an angel as she breathed in deep and the words flowed forth: *Hallelujah, Hallelujah…*

Her sweet, strong voice rose in pitch with the hymn filling the church, echoing through the hallways. The congregation stood to listen to her incredible voice, and when she finished, they applauded wildly. Her voice was magnificent, and Sam knew she was destined for greater things beyond Saint Michaels. He watched her approach him and heard the tapping from her cane, holding out her hand and tucking it inside his arm for support.

"Ready to go to the parade and the festivities in town?" he asked.

"I'm ready."

"Let's go, then." As they walked outside, she buttoned her coat and wrapped her scarf around her neck. She pointed her face to the sky and took in a determined breath of air. "It's going to snow, I can tell. I predict a white Christmas for us this year. I know it. I can feel it."

"Grace, we haven't had a white Christmas in Saint Michaels for as long as I can remember. Years and years. Flurries yes but…"

"Then we're due for one. It's the law of averages. Right?"

He had to laugh at her logic. "Right." Then, still laughing, he added, "If you say so."

"I *know* so. Come on, let's go."

Everyone smiled at them as they passed by, greeting them with a warm and sincere hello. Sam leaned in close and whispered, "You sounded magnificent today in church, Gracie. Like a real professional."

"Thank you," she said, then leaning in close, confided to him, "Mr. Reynolds, the talent agent, called me and said they have a program starting soon and wanted to know if I was interested in joining them early."

"When do you have to decide?"

" I only have a week."

Sam looked at her and stopped walking. "What did you tell them, Grace?" He felt his heartbeat quicken as he waited for her to respond.

"I told them I had to think about it. Too many decisions. Leave my job as a teacher and choir director. Leave my father. Leave home. Go on the road. But on the other hand, it is a wonderful opportunity. Fulfill my dream of singing professionally. My dad checked him out on the Internet, and everybody had nothing but glowing things to say about him."

Sam wanted to reach out and touch her, hug her, comfort her. But that would only make matters worse. *I'm back in Baltimore in two weeks, or Philadelphia if I get the Wanamaker job. Don't make it any more complicated for her, Sam. But maybe I could just stay here, in Saint Michaels? Or go to New York with Grace...if she'll have me. But that won't work either, she'll be traveling a lot with her new career.* He glanced at her and breathed deep. *I don't think this is going to work, Grace and I.* He pulled her closer and said, "You're right, Gracie, that's a lot of decisions you have to make."

They walked arm and arm down Talbot Street, making their way through the crowd assembled along the way, looking for the best vantage point to watch the parade. And then it was upon them. The Saint Michaels High School marching band came strutting down the center of the main street, followed by an original Saint Michaels antique fire engine, complete with a brightly decorated spotted Dalmatian proudly sitting on the front seat next to the driver. The Dalmatian mascot barked every time the siren was activated.

A team of horses pulled a wheeled sleigh directly behind the fire engine. A parade of old antique cars followed the procession, with young college girls dressed as elves tossing candy to the waving crowds of children who lined the main street. Another high school band from Easton, Maryland marched in unison, followed by the girl's glee club from Cambridge. They were followed by a brightly dressed Santa and Mrs. Claus, riding in a vintage white Cadillac convertible.

In town, every store now sported strands of clear, bright Christmas lights around their windows, with green garlands draped above their doors. Sam could not help but notice that every city streetlight had a new Christmas wreath, candy cane, or reindeer hanging from it, the same way they had when he was younger, all courtesy of Henrietta and the mayor. The town was always decorated for the holidays. That's one of the things he'd missed when he moved to Baltimore. That hometown feel, with hometown people, friends, neighbors. Nothing better.

Sam and Grace continued walking and passed a stand run by the local Knights of Columbus selling freshly made cocoa.

"Want some cocoa?" Sam asked.

"I'd love some," she said with a grin. "My favorite Christmas drink. I could smell it two blocks away."

Beside their table was a stand selling homemade gingerbread cookies. Some plain, some with nuts, some with jalapeno peppers. "Cookie? Gingerbread?"

"Sure, but not the ones with hot peppers in them."

"Okay. But how did you know some had..."

"I can't see, but my sense of smell just keeps getting better all the time. Since I can't see, I have no distractions and I..." A tear rolled down her cheek. Then another. "Take me home, Sam, please? I'd like to go home."

He put his protective arm around her shoulders and said, "Whatever you say, Gracie." It was just like when they were kids; she always looked up to him, and he was always there to protect her. Always.

"Is everything okay?" he whispered to her.

"Yes. I'm fine. Just please take me home."

"Hold on tight to my arm."

Once home at her front door, she opened it, and without turning she said, "See you later Sam. Dinner at six?"

He touched her shoulder and eased up next to her, turning her around slowly to face him. "Gracie, are you okay? I can't stand to see you cry, ever. Please talk to me."

She struggled to stop her sniffles but did not say anything.

"I mean it, Grace," he said as his arms encircling her, holding her.

She buried her head in his chest. "I know you do, Sam. That's one of the things I love about you. You're always there. Always caring. I love the way you stand up for people. I love the way you help me. I love..." She stopped and pulled away. Then, wiping away the tears from her eyes, she said, "I'm fine now. Really. Sometimes I get a little emotional, you know? Sometimes I just want to be able to see again. Sometimes I want to be able to see people's faces. It normally doesn't bother me, but now because...I guess it's Christmastime, that's all."

"Are you okay?"

"Yeah. I'll see you later. Six?"

"See you then."

A snowflake brushed against her cheek, then another. Her face brightened. "See, I told you we would have snow for Christmas."

He touched her nose with his finger and said, "One snowflake does not a white Christmas make, my dear," kissing her on the forehead.

She laughed, then said, "Six o'clock, and don't be late."

As she closed the door behind her, she took a deep breath. *What am I going to do? I so want to sing on my own, but leave Saint Michaels? What about Dad? Sam?* As she made her way up the steps, the phone rang. Her father was in the kitchen making dinner and hollered out to her, "Can you get that, Grace? My hands are covered in pasta sauce."

"Sure, Dad." Her hands searched for the phone on the small table in the living room. She smelled a whiff of brown sugar in the air. Then again. *Strange,* she thought. *Mom loved baking with brown sugar.* "Good afternoon. Saint Michaels Rectory. Grace speaking. How can I help you?"

"Ms. Albright?"

"Yes, this is Grace Albright. Can I help you?"

"Miss Albright, this is Doctor Malek Winston from the—"

She interrupted him, "Oh, Doctor, hold on for just a minute, please. You probably want to speak with my father, the Reverend Albright. Hold on, I'll get him." She put the phone to her chest and shouted, "Dad, it's for you, a Doctor Winston. There must have been an accident in town somewhere with one of our parishioners. He needs to speak with you."

"Coming," he shouted from the kitchen.

She returned her attention to the telephone caller. "Doctor Winston, please hold on for just a minute. My father will be right with you and…"

"Miss Albright? I was calling for you."

Grace was surprised. She didn't know a Doctor Winston. She knew very few doctors who would call her personally at home, other than the specialists she and her father had visited years before. Any time one of their parishioners was in an accident, the doctors from the local hospitals would always call her father to come to the hospital and sit and pray with the family.

"You said you need to speak with me?"

"Yes, Miss Albright."

"I'm sorry, sir, but have we met?"

"You spoke with my staff a few years ago during an evaluation for a procedure we perform here at the clinic."

She was puzzled. Her memory was excellent, but she didn't remember this doctor. "What staff? What clinic?"

"The Winston Clinic, in Baltimore."

All at once, she connected the dots. Doctor Winston. The Winston Clinic. Baltimore. Renowned eye surgeon. Now it all made sense. Her knees weakened, her voice cracked, she could not swallow, she felt faint, and could not breathe or talk. Her hand searched for the sofa to support herself as her heart began to beat faster and faster. Plopping down hard onto the old couch, she finally said, "Oh yes, Doctor Winston. How nice to talk to you."

She felt the reassuring hand of her father on her shoulder as he sat down next to her. He patted her hand to calm her as he touched the speakerphone button on the phone.

"I hope I'm not calling too late. And I apologize for calling on a Sunday."

"That's quite all right, Doctor Winston."

Her father gripped her hand in his.

"Well, let me come right to the point. You tested here two years ago as a possible candidate for our gene therapy procedure called Saturna, enhanced with a new technique called CRISPR. At that time, all of your receptors tested positive—which is a good thing. And then you were placed on a waiting list of potential recipients, once all the other hurdles were cleared, such as insurance, availability, costs, etc."

Her heart sank. "Yes, Doctor, I understand. Your staff explained it all to my father and me a few years ago. They also told us that most insurance companies do not pay for the procedure, and there was a ten-year waiting period for those who did."

She heard him murmur in acknowledgment. "That's all true. Well, the good news is we had a cancellation on our schedule."

She swallowed hard, squeezing her father's hand. *Now the bad news: the cost.*

"I presume that you're still interested and available to go forward with the procedure."

"Yes, of course, more than ever, Doctor Winston, but..."

"Good. Which leaves us with the question of cost. After checking with your insurance company, we discovered that they do not cover the cost for this procedure. Which is not unusual, as I said earlier." He paused to let them process the information. "We do two injections, one day apart. Then you go home and wait for it to work its magic. Over the next few days after the procedure, you will need to see one of our approved local doctors to examine you regularly and change the bandages. It's very routine, something that can be done in the doctor's office. You will know the results within a few days to a week, whether or not it was a success. The cost of each injection is $425,000 for each eye or $850,000 for a total cost."

Grace gasped, then began to cry as she gripped her father's hand, squeezing it tight. The tears rolled down her cheeks. She could not breathe. She gasped again, waiting for a miracle.

"However, the manufacturer has allowed us to provide the operation at no cost to certain individuals chosen at random. It's called a beta test. And I'm pleased to inform you that you have been chosen to participate in that program, at no cost to you or your family."

In her excitement, she dropped the phone to the floor as she hugged her father, saying, "I can't believe it. I can't believe it. Oh, thank you, Doctor Winston. Thank you so much! Doctor Winston? Doctor Winston?"

"Wait, Grace, let me pick up the phone," said her father, retrieving the phone from the floor and turning the speakerphone back on. "Hello? Doctor Winston? This is Grace's father, Bill Albright."

"Pleased to meet you, Mister Albright. Just a few housekeeping chores we need to attend to first. I'll need your daughter to visit one of our approved local ophthalmologists in your area. I believe that Doctor Richard Cassel, in Easton, Maryland, is the closest one to you. He will perform some tests and do the follow-up visits."

"Oh yes, I remember him. He was the doctor we saw a few years back when we first applied for the procedure. A very nice man."

"Good, then he'll also have those test results to compare the new ones to. I'll have him send me a copy of both. Just routine to make sure there have not been any drastic changes in your daughter's ocular condition. He will also be the one to change the bandages after Grace's procedure. Miss Albright, Grace, can you hear me?"

"Yes sir, I'm right here. I'm just trying to recover from this wonderful news you've given me."

"I understand perfectly. After I receive Doctor Cassel's report, we would like you and your father to come to Baltimore for the procedure. You'll need to be here for a few days before you can safely return home. Just as a precaution."

"Okay, okay, we can do that."

His voice turned serious. "Lastly, Grace, I must warn you this is a one-time procedure and can never be performed again. The receptors in your eyes can only be injected once without risking serious harm to your health. It either works, or it doesn't."

"What is your success rate?"

"Our current success rate is 58%, but if you're one of those success stories, you will be able to see again, drive again, and watch the snow fall within a week. Pretty amazing stuff, wouldn't you say?"

"Yes, I would. But let me ask you, Doctor Winston, what's the downside of this procedure?"

There was silence on the other end of the line. "If it is not a successful operation, well…you will never see again."

His bluntness shocked her as she brushed the tears from her eyes. "Which is exactly where I am now, right, Doctor?"

"Exactly. So, unless you have any other questions, I'll let the two of you enjoy the rest of your evening. Good night, Grace, Reverend Albright. Call me if you have any questions at all. Merry Christmas."

"Good night and Merry Christmas, Doctor Winston." As she hung up the phone, she began to cry. Tears of happiness burst from her eyes, streaming down uncontrollably. Between the tears, she cried out, "I can't believe it! I'm going to see again. You don't think it's a prank call, do you, Dad? Who would do something like that? It can't be."

"I don't think so," he replied. "Nobody would be that cruel."

She brushed the tears from her eyes. *To see again?* She thought. The words sounded like the miracle she secretly prayed for every night.

"It'll all work out, sweetheart. Trust me," her father said.

"I know, I know. It's so wonderful. It's just too much for me to take in all at one time. But I have so much going on in my life. I love teaching. I love my work with the choir. I want to help to make sure the school and the church remain open. I love Saint Michaels and being here with you. But most of all, I love singing. And the opportunity in New York…or do I stay here and move in with Karen? The operation, a new career…it's all overwhelming. And then there's Sam. And his career prospects with Wanamaker. It sounds like he may have a shot at the job he has wanted his entire life. And now I will see again."

She stopped crying and whisked away her tears, whispering, "I care deeply for him, daddy, and I think he's holding back taking the job because of me. He's always told me that Wanamaker was his dream job. I want him to be happy, but I don't want to lose him now…not now." In exasperation, she threw her hands in the air and said, "It's all so confusing."

He patted her hand, hugged her to comfort her, the way he had always done since her mother passed away. "You don't need to make any decisions at all, Grace. Don't feel like you're being forced to make a decision. Whether it's about the operation, the singing, the apartment, the school or the church, it's all in God's hands. And Sam? Well, Sam cares so much for you he would support you no matter what you decided to do. And speaking of which, he's going to be joining us for dinner tonight, so you better fix your makeup, get dressed, and be ready to greet our guest of honor."

"Right. In all the excitement I nearly forgot about him coming here." She kissed him on the cheek and, with a smile, said, "Thank you, daddy. You always know just what to say."

"It's my job, pumpkin. Now go on, get ready."


Driving home, Sam was lost in thought until he pulled the car into the driveway and saw a green sedan parked beside the cabin. Opening the cabin door, he was greeted by the smiling face of Clarisse Matz.

"Hiya Sam," she said sweetly and hugged him tight and close. She kissed his cheek while still holding onto him.

Sam stepped back, feeling awkward and uncomfortable with her being inside his house alone. It was then he saw Zack getting up from the sofa.

"Hey Sam, how ya doin'?" said Zack.

"I'm good."

Before Sam could ask any questions, Zack said, "I hope you don't mind us walkin' in on your place, but there was no answer when we knocked."

"…and the door was unlocked," interjected Clarisse.

"It's fine. Really. Sit down, make yourselves comfortable. What's going on?"

"Well, lots," said Zack.

"And we didn't want you to hear it secondhand, and…" added Clarisse. Zack shot her an imploring look which temporarily silenced her.

Zack looked serious. "I gave my two weeks' notice today. This VP job is not for me…it's really yours. You've earned it. You deserve it, and you're more qualified than I could ever be. Ollie told me about the ownership agreement and…"

"And we broke off our engagement. So, I'm now a free and single woman," said Clarisse, with an alluring smile.

"Clarisse, please let me finish," said Zack, giving her a look to silence her.

"Well, okay, but you always leave out so much when you…"

"Clarisse, please."

"Okay, okay."

Zack continued, "It's your company, for you to do as you see fit. Besides, I was never cut out to do this job, and you were made for it. Even after Ollie put me into the job, you helped me learn so much in such a short time. I realized then how much I didn't know, so I'll probably move back to Boston and…"

Sam raised his hand to stop him. "Zack don't sell yourself short. I wish you would wait before leaving. A few weeks is all I ask. I think you can bring great value to the company. You're great with marketing ideas, with social media, and you're up on the latest in technology. The rest you can learn. You just need to remember that at our company we work together as a team. Don't be afraid to reach out to people. So please reconsider, stay for a few more weeks and then make up your mind."

"Sam, I don't know."

"What do you have to lose?"

"Are you sure?"

"Positive."

"Okay. I'll stay, and we'll see what happens. Thanks, Sam. But you know the funny thing is, Ollie said the same thing, but I told him I wanted to talk with you first." He paused as if searching for the right words, before saying, "Have you heard back from Wanamaker's?"

"Yes," Sam said with a smile. "They want me to come up to Philadelphia for a few days and spend some time there. I'm just waiting to hear back from them about a date. But I'm torn. Do I stay here and see where it takes me? Or go back to Baltimore? Or do I move to Philadelphia for my dream job? It's an opportunity that only comes around once in a lifetime."

"That's a tough one. Good luck with the decision."

Clarisse chimed in, "Yeah, Sam, good luck." She paused. "I hear Philadelphia is a great town. Lots to do, with great restaurants, wonderful ballet, and theater." Then, in her sweetest voice, she said, "Funny how things work out, I'm visiting Philadelphia after the holidays to see some old college friends. Maybe we could have coffee and…"

He turned to her. "Clarisse, you're a sweet girl, but let me tell you, it was never going to work out between you and me. And now I may have somebody in my life I care a great deal about, who's also struggling with her own career decisions. I want to give her space, for her to make her own decision. I know it'll take some time for her to sort things out, but in the meantime, she needs her space. And time."

"You're a good man, Sam Carpenter. And she's a lucky lady."

"I know, I'm very fortunate. And tonight, I'm going to have dinner with her and her dad very shortly, so if you'll excuse me, I have a lot of work here I have to finish."

"Need some help?" asked Zack.

Sam was surprised by the offer. "Sure. I have to refit the organ pipes, the felts, and the bellows. And I need to finish it for tomorrow."

"Can we help?" asked Clarisse.

Three hours later, they'd finished their work, and Sam said, "I can't thank you enough… both of you," he said. Their faces were dirty, their hands smudged with piano grease.

"No, I should thank you, Sam," said Zack, "for being so understanding. We'll be around town for a few more days working with the crew, as we finish tuning the last of the local church pipe organs. So maybe we can get together and talk…if you have some time available."

"Sure, Zack," responded Sam. "Any time."

Clarisse walked to him, touching his face with her hand. "You take care, Sam, and if you ever need someone to talk to, I mean really talk to…as a friend…call me day or night." She looked like she had when they were kids: funny, young, and vulnerable.

"I will, Clarisse."

"Promise?"

"I promise."

# Chapter Twenty-Two

As Sam drove through the town to join Grace and her dad for dinner, he could not help but notice that the tiny hamlet seemed to have suddenly come alive with the Christmas spirit. Every mailbox was covered in green garlands, bright red ribbons, or pine branches. From the store windows hung multicolored blinking lights. At the corner Sam noticed carolers walking along the city sidewalks, singing Christmas carols. He stopped at the traffic light, rolled down the window and could hear them singing:

> *Jingle bells, Jingle Bells*
> *Jingle all the way!*
> *Oh, what fun it is to ride*
> *In a one-horse open sleigh!*

He sang along with them, so loud it sounded more like shouting:

> *Jingle bells, Jingle Bells*
> *Jingle all the way!*

A young family of three walked by in front of his car and waved to him: the Mueller family, on their way to the traditional bonfire at the town square in the center of town. The log fire blaze was an annual tradition in Saint Michaels, held in front of the town's Christmas tree, which was adorned with blinking colored lights, gold and silver ornaments, and tinsel waving in the wind. As kids, he remembered roasting marshmallows at the bonfire with Grace and her dad and then chasing her around the tree. He had forgotten how much he missed this town at Christmas, how much he had missed Saint Michaels…home. And Mom. Dad. Molly. Henrietta and Hilda. The Reverend Albright. And of course, Grace. Small town living at its best. He had missed it so much. He watched the flames from the fire dance in the wind until someone behind him honked their horn to speed him on his way.

The parking lot at the church was nearly empty, except for the reverend's old blue and white Chevy station wagon.

Just as he was about to turn off the engine, his phone rang. The caller ID said: Unknown Caller.

"Hello?" said Sam.

"Sam? Mr. Sam Carpenter?" said an unfamiliar man's voice.

"Yes, this is Sam," he responded reluctantly, expecting a sales pitch to follow. Credit card pitch, timeshare, computer problems, and the old standby, a free cruise.

"Hi, Sam. This is Carson. Carson Wright."

"Carson?" *Do I know a Carson?*

"Yes, Carson Wright, with the Wanamaker Organ Company."

"Oh yes, that Carson. Of course." He fumbled at not recognizing the name. "You see, I know so many people named Carson."

"Oh, I see."

"How are you? What can I do for you?" he responded, feeling slightly apprehensive for some unknown reason.

"Well, I wanted to get back in touch with you to arrange for your final interview and thought the best time to come is during our busiest time: Christmas. We do maintenance and at least three performances per day during Christmas. I should tell you that after speaking with all the managers involved, who had interviewed you over the phone, we've decided that we are very interested in you for the job. So we were thinking about having you come up here and spend four or five days. You can see how we operate, meet your team of coworkers, and see how you would like it at Wanamaker's."

"Ah, yes. I guess that would be for the best."

"Say Tuesday?"

"Well, I'm finishing an organ and bell tuning project here in Saint Michaels. It will take me a few more days. Then I have to test the bells and see if I can find out what's wrong with them, and see if I can find a replacement, so that could take me a few more days or another week…"

"You're still interested in the position, aren't you, Sam?"

"Ah, yes. Of course. Who wouldn't be interested in working at Wanamaker's?"

"It's just you sounded a bit hesitant. We've passed over quite a few other outstanding applicants because we thought you would be the best fit for our team, especially since your father interned with us years ago. But if you're not interested, please let us know now so we can move on to other candidates."

"No, no, I'm still very interested. Can I call you back in a little while after I've looked at my calendar and can commit to some firm dates to come to Philadelphia for a visit?"

"Sure, sure, of course, Sam. Call me back later. Take care, talk to you soon."

*Everything happens at once. Visiting Saint Michaels. Owning the majority share of the company. The promotion. Wanamaker's. Zack. Clarisse. And of course,...Grace. Nothing is ever simple.*

Sam sensed something was different from the time Grace opened the door and hugged him, holding him just a little longer than she had before. "Long time no see, my friend," she said, laughing.

He could tell she was nervous but seemed excited about something.

"But I still can't see you. Of course not, I'm blind and..."

He squeezed her hand and murmured to her, "Grace, is everything okay? Are you all right?"

"I couldn't be better. Come on into the dining room. We have some news."

Her father was waiting for them, mixing the last of the simmering spaghetti sauce. "Evening, Sam."

"Evening, Reverend...ah, Bill."

"You're in for a treat, Sam. Homemade pasta. Homemade sauce. Freshly baked bread. All delicious." He smiled a devilish smile. He was holding something back.

Sam gave them his arched eyebrow look, always sure to bring on a confession, before saying, "Okay, okay, you two. Give it up. What's the secret that the whole world seems to know except Sam Carpenter."

Her father poured a glass of champagne for each of them, and they stood in a circle, facing each other. "Here's to good news." Then, looking at Grace, he said, "Go ahead, Grace, you tell him."

"Sam, I just got a call from the Winston Clinic in Baltimore, and they've selected me for this new surgical procedure called Saturna. It takes two injections, and then a few days later...I find out if I can see!" She was bubbling with enthusiasm like a young schoolgirl. She paused, swallowed, then said, "Fifty-eight percent success rate, according to Doctor Winston. Fifty-eight percent! That's pretty good, right, Sam? Right?"

He brushed the hair away from her face, his hand lingering on her cheek. "Yes, that's very good. Excellent indeed, Gracie. When does all this happen?"

"Next Wednesday, but first I visit a doctor here on the Eastern Shore for a pre-op exam, and then next week I leave for Baltimore to have the procedure. I stay there for a few days, then come back home, and then a few days later they take the bandages off, and I'll know. It's exciting, isn't it, Sam?"

He was so happy for her. "That is fantastic! What great news. Cheers to a successful operation." Her father poured the champagne, and they all raised their glasses to toast the future.

Grace smiled and said, "Doctor Winston was so nice and thoughtful. I feel like I'm walking on air since he called to tell me the news. I can hardly believe it."

Sam looked at her and said, "Grace, that's wonderful. You'll do just fine. You're the greatest."

"Thanks, Sam." She sipped her champagne and thought, *Just like Sam, always there for me. Always rooting for me. He would do anything for me, but maybe now it's time to let him go. Let him get on with his life.*

She swallowed hard. "Oh, and there's more—regardless of what happens with the operation, I've decided to sign up with Mr. Reynolds, the talent agent, and move to New York."

Her father nearly spilled his glass of champagne. "Grace are you sure that's what you want to do?"

"I'm sure, Dad. It's what I want to do. It'll all work out. Trust me."

"Okay, it's your decision," he replied, trying to muster enthusiasm for her decision. Finally, he resigned himself to the fact she had made up her mind. "Good for you, cheers!"

They again raised their glasses into the air and toasted, "To Grace!"

Sam smiled and added, "Well, as long as we're toasting, I also have some news."

"Really?" said Grace.

"Yes, just as I pulled into the parking lot here, I got a call from the human resources guy at Wanamaker's. He told me that they want me for the job. They need me to come to Philadelphia for a few days to make sure

I like it, and to fill out the paperwork before they go through all the expense of moving me." He laughed. "I only have enough stuff to fill my car, some tools, and all my books. I need to let them know I want the job, then that's it," he said, taking another sip from his glass.

"Oh," said Grace, surprised at the news, but both happy and sad for Sam.

"Cheers," he said in a hollow toast, as they all slowly clinked their glasses together.

The dinner table was unusually quiet that night; the usual chitchat and joke telling were more subdued.

Grace thought to herself, *You said you had to let him go, now he's leaving. I got what I want. I should be happy. Why am I so sad? I'm so confused.*

As dessert was being served, Grace asked him, "When do you leave?"

"Next week sometime, just as soon as I finish my work here on the organ and the bells. But it'll take longer than usual because it's usually a two-person job. One person to tune the pipes, and another to play the organ."

"I can help you with that, Sam. I play the piano and can learn how to play the organ. At least enough to play the keyboard to help you. It's not too different from playing the piano, is it?"

"Totally different. Organ playing is different in that the bellows makes the air blow through the pipes, much like a trumpet or saxophone. I could use the help, but aren't you going to be busy yourself, with the doctor appointments, your trip to Baltimore, and the choir?"

"Yes, but that won't take long. I'd still like to help you."

Happy to have a conversation around the table, her father joined in the discussion, saying, "Sam, I kept meaning to tell you, I had someone stop by after church services and volunteer to be an organist for the church. She's moving from Chicago to Saint Michaels to retire. She wants to be closer to her grandkids who live in Cambridge."

"That's great! I can use an extra set of hands tomorrow when I start tuning the organ."

The reverend made a face. "Well, she said she was going to the DMV to get her driver's license on Monday but would be available to help out starting on Wednesday. Her name is Maria Gomez. Very nice lady. A widow."

"And I'm available on Monday and Tuesday, so that works out perfect," responded Grace.

"Yes…yes, it does."

There was an awkward silence as Sam glanced at his watch. "I better get going. I still have some work to do in preparation for tomorrow."

"You need a hand?" she asked, reaching out her hand to couple with his.

"I'm just about done,… but you can walk me to the door. I guess I'll see you tomorrow."

"Yes," she said, walking him to the door. "Looking forward to it. You can teach me everything there is to know about how church organs operate. Okay?"

"Sure," he responded, giving her a slight kiss on the cheek. "See ya tomorrow."

She stood at the door and listened to his footsteps fade away in the cold night air before she slowly closed the door. It was getting colder in Saint Michaels.

The cool mist of winter was in the air as Grace sat by her open window that night, listening to the owls outside, thinking of Sam. *It's the right thing for him to do—go to Philadelphia. Wanamaker's is the job he has wanted his whole life. I had to let him know it was okay. He would not go there if I didn't push him. Everybody is getting what they wanted, things to make them happy. Why are we all so sad?* Then she stopped for a minute, her hands covering her face. *Oh no, what was I thinking? Stupid. I don't want him to leave, not now, not ever.*

# Chapter Twenty-Three

Grace was up early the next morning and met her father for breakfast. "Morning, Dad."

"Morning, sweetheart," he replied. "Sleep well?"

"Yeah, kinda. Not really. I was up most of the night. I have a lot on my mind and never really fell asleep."

He touched his daughter's head, stroking her hair as he always did when she was upset. "It'll all work out okay," he whispered. "Trust me. It's out of your hands. Say some prayers. But for now, come on, sit down and have your breakfast." He then gave her directions as to the location of things on the table. "Tea is at one o'clock, next to your knife. Toasted muffin is next to your knife, butter is at noon, and eggs are—"

"Dad, I appreciate everything you do, but I must get back to standing on my own two feet. I must find things on my own. In New York, I won't have you around to help and protect me. I must try. Okay?"

"Okay, if you insist. Are you sure you want to do this New York thing? All the travel? Moving away from Saint Michaels? Away from friends and family."

"Yeah, well, I guess I have no other choice," she said, as she began her breakfast.

"Like I said, it'll all work out okay. It's in God's hands."

"I know." She finished her breakfast, then said, "I have the next two days alone with Sam, and I'm going to make the best of it. Speaking of which, I gotta go. I told him I'd meet him in church. He's always early, but this is one time that I'm going to be earlier than him."

Her father had to laugh at the two of them: always competitive, even as kids. "Here," he told her, "take this plate and mug of coffee with you for Sam. It's a hot egg sandwich. Tell him I said hi."

"Will do. Love you, daddy."

"You too, sweetheart. Now off with you. I got stuff to do. Got the bishop coming into town."

*The bishop!* The sound of the words brought her back to reality. Would he really close the school that she loved so dearly? And the church, which had been in operation for hundreds of years? Never. He was a kind and wise man, but she could not bear it if that were to happen.

The church was quiet as she entered and made her way to the rear, where the organ was located. She heard humming and a noise coming from behind the organ as she sat down on the organist's bench in the rear.

"Sam?"

No response.

"Sam? Is that you? Are you here already?"

"Yeah, back here. Got here an hour ago," came a muffled response. "I just installed the new bellows that I made. Now just keep your fingers crossed and hope it works. I just got a little more work to do before…"

"I got a hot breakfast sandwich out here for you." She heard movement from the area behind the organ.

"Really? Be right out," he shouted.

"And coffee!"

"Wow, you sure know how to spoil a guy, now don't ya?"

"Well, to be truthful, my father did it all, but I carried it over here for you."

Grace felt the warmth of his body as he sat down next to her. His leg touched hers. She sat still, not moving, swallowing.

"Thanks, Grace," he said, as he took the plate and coffee from her.

"So, tell me," she said, "what do we have to do today to get this old organ humming again?"

She could hear him eating his breakfast, but he stopped to say, "First, I need to make sure the new bellows I installed works, that it will hold air. You see, it blows air through the pipes to make the sounds which are controlled by the manual."

"Manual?"

"Sorry. On a piano, it's called a keyboard but, on a pipe organ, they call it a manual. Then we'll test the manual to make sure that all the pipes are clear. No bird or bat's nests inside to clog them up and prevent them from making music. Then I'll have you play each pipe to make sure it's in tune and…"

"And if it isn't?"

"Then I'll use my tuner and my ears to make sure they sound the way they're supposed to. Each pipe must sound good by itself, and then in tune with the others, just like the bells are supposed to sound." He finished his breakfast and said, "Ready?"

"Yep," she said, and was on her feet. "Just make sure the main switch is on. Okay?"

"Ha, ha, funny," he said, as he quietly flipped on the main switch. Then the ON button. The lights on the manual flashed on. A massive swooshing noise filled the air as the new bellows began to fill with air for the first time. The fish glue held.

"Hee-haw! Merry Christmas!" he shouted in his exuberance. "Sit down on the bench Grace, and let's test these pipes." He guided her and sat down next to her, taking her hand in his.

His hand felt warm. *I don't know if I can do this*, she thought to herself. *And we've only just begun this process.*

"While we wait for the bellows to fill up," he said, "let me kind of explain how an organ works. We're going to be using this manual today and the other one tomorrow. You see, the organ is a hybrid, kind of a mixture of a piano and a wind instrument, like a saxophone. It produces sounds by using air coming from the bellows and then vibrating in the pipes. Some are as thin and short as a pencil, while others are over sixty feet long. And the size and diameter of each pipe determine the sound, not the amount of pressure that the organist uses to press down on the key, like on a piano."

"Got it."

"I'm not boring you, am I?"

"Oh no, of course not."

The red light above the keyboard went on, then the amber light. "It won't be long now," he told her. "The pipes are organized in sets of similar size, called ranks. Much like you organize your choir into bass, tenor, baritone, soprano, and the like. This one has over two thousand organ pipes."

"That's a lot of pipes."

"You bet. And they all must sound good, alone and together. That's the key to a well-tuned organ. And the shiny tin pipes that everyone sees here in church, or in any church, are for decoration only. That's not where the sound comes from at all. It's from the pipes behind the facade."

"Really?"

"Yeah. You know, this is the most fun I've ever had tuning an organ."

"Me too," she laughed.

The green READY light went on, indicating the organ warm-up was completed. "I guess we're ready. Pull out the first stop."

"What?"

"The first stop." He guided her hand in his to the knob above the manual. "Here. Pull. Then press this key on the manual." She liked the feel of his hand on hers. The sound bellowed like a lark in winter. High, pure, and sweet, almost angelic.

"Fantastic. Now tell me what a stop is."

He chuckled. "An organ has its own language, its own vocabulary. A stop, or a register, is a set of pipes grouped together. It may consist of one rank of pipes, or it may include multiple ranks. When an organist selects a stop that combines ten ranks of pipes, for example, then depressing any key on the keyboard will open all ten pipes concurrently. You've heard the saying, 'Pull out all the stops'? That's where it comes from."

"I never knew that." *This is entirely different than playing the piano.*

"And because the ranks all have different sounds, the stops that an organist selects will determine the organ's music at any given moment. Stops have names that reflect either what kinds of pipes they're composed of or how they sound. Some of these names are simple, like Flute, or Trumpet, like what we just heard, while others are more complex. Got it?"

"Got it. That was a beautiful sound," as he played one.

"Yes, it was. Are you ready?"

"Yep."

"Now I need you to press on the pedal and pull one stop, then press the first key here," he said, holding her hand. "Press each key slowly and let me tune it before we move onto the next one." He moved her hand to the first stop and held it there. "We'll start here and work our way down the keyboard."

They spent the entire morning playing one key at a time as Sam disappeared into the back room, which held all the pipes. Then, as they moved from one stop to the next, he would join her, take her hand from one stop to the next. His hand would linger on hers at times, and each time he sat closer and closer to her. She waited for him to join her on the bench after he tuned each pipe. Occasionally, he would direct her to which key to press by touching her and hugging her. She was in heaven.

For the next few hours, Grace diligently pressed one key after another while patiently waiting for Sam to tune the pipe and listen for the organ to respond, before moving on to the next key.

When she played three keys, she shouted, "Wow! It sounds wonderful. I had forgotten how good they sound. It's been years."

He stuck his head out from behind the organ to say, "Eighteen years, to be precise, according to the register. And according to the logbook back here, my father was the last one to tune it."

"Then it was meant to be," she said softly. "Like many things."

"How many more pipes do you have to tune?"

"Fifteen hundred."

"Oh."

He could see she was fading. "What do you say we take a break? Let me buy you lunch at the diner."

"Sounds like a delicious idea. Let me grab my coat and cane."

As they walked down Talbot Street to the diner, he leaned in close to say to her, "I hope it goes well with the doctor. Your surgery." Fresh baked cookie smells from the bakery made her happy and hungry. A winter wind had begun to blow, as flakes of snow swirled down the street. *A white Christmas?* She thought to herself.

"I'm a little nervous. No, I'm very nervous," she said, managing a short laugh.

"It'll all work out fine. You'll be in good hands. I understand Doctor Winston is the best there is in his field." He looked at her; she was always so determined, so resolute, so sure of herself. That was one of the things he loved about her. "After your surgery, what's the first thing you want to see?"

"Oh, that's an easy one," she said, rushing to reply, "I want to see a sunrise. Then my dad and...you. But maybe not in that order."

"Ah," he said with a chuckle. As they walked, he reached out his hand for hers and squeezed it gently. "I only hope that you get what you want and that you'll be happy in New York. That's all, Grace. I just want you to be happy."

"Thanks, Sam. I knew I could count on you for support," she said, grabbing hold of his arm and squeezing it tight. *I won't be able to do this in New York*, she thought to herself.

It began to snow, and the sidewalks became slippery as he pulled her in closer to him to help support her. "I guess it'll be nice to see a snowflake before it hits your face, right? No surprises."

"Yeah." Grace had heard someone else say that same exact phrase recently but couldn't remember who. She had to know some answers and was quiet for a few minutes as they walked. Finally, she asked, "Sam, are you really going to move to Philadelphia? For the Wanamaker job?"

He held her closer and asked, "Are you really going to move to New York?"

"That's not fair. You're answering a question with a question. Are you going to…"

"I don't know, Gracie. There's a lot to consider."

"Like Clarisse?"

He stopped and turned to her. "Grace, there was never going to be anything with Clarisse and me. Believe me when I tell you that. I have never lied to you before, and I'm not about to start now."

She smiled and searched for his hand. "Good." She smiled and laughed, taking his arm, just as a huge flake collided against her face. "Will you be finished in time before you leave for your trip to Philadelphia?"

"Yes. I hope to be finished by tomorrow, or the next day at the latest. Then, of course, there are the bells to consider. That may take a while as well."

She was quiet because she knew that when he finished his work at the church, he would be gone. And he had never answered her question.

As Sam walked down the street, arm in arm with Grace, he thought aloud, "I just wonder why it's taking so long to hear back from the assayer? I told Jasef that I needed the information quickly to finish my work on the bells. He's usually been pretty quick with a response in the past. Very strange."

"Maybe he's busy this time of year? It's the holidays. You'll just have to wait around until you hear back, I guess. Could take years," she said with a smile.

New York City was just waking as Jasef Krasnik sat in his office, rereading the assay reports that his staff had given him that morning. "These can't be right," he muttered to himself, taking another sip from his old coffee mug. His desk was peppered with many circular reminders of where he had carelessly had set his cup in the past. It had been his father's desk, and while the rest of the company was outfitted with the latest technological tools, equipment, and furniture, he preferred the feel of his father's well-oiled leather chair and antique cherry desk.

He compared the results one last time: identical. He didn't care for what they'd told him, even though he had the best staff in the country working on the tests.

There was a knock on the door. "Sorry to bother you, Jasef," called out his assistant, Demetri.

"No, it's good. Come in. I have waited for you. What did you find out?" Jasef said, in a heavy Hungarian accent.

Demetri, with his dark, coal black hair, and piercing eyes was Jasef's first hire when he started the business. His longtime employee was dressed in the usual blue coveralls and steel-toed work boots as he made his way into his office. He handed the test results to his boss and said, "I reran the tests, and they came back with the same result. When I use the electrolysis, most of the pieces check out okay, right on the money, eighty percent copper and twenty percent tin, but with seven of them…it's crazy. On them, the composition is all wrong. Way off. I can't figure it out."

"Run the tests again—one more time."

"But Jasef, I did it three times already, and each time…"

His boss looked up from the report and removed his glasses. "I know, I know, I hear you. But this is critical, and if we're wrong, it could be embarrassing for many people. This is important. So run the tests one last time. Please?"

"Okay. But I don't think that will change the results at all. But I'll rerun the tests."

"You let me know, you find out."

Two hours later, the phone rang on his desk. "Hallo?" he said as he answered it, already knowing who was calling him.

"Jasef, it's me, Demetri. I wanted to let you know I reran the test, two more times and I got the same result each time. Sorry."

"No problem. Thank you for letting me know."

"Hey, can I ask what's so important about these tests?"

Jasef laughed. "You'll read about it in the newspapers. That's all I can say. Thanks again." He rubbed his eyes with the palms of his hands, then reached for the phone and dialed the overseas number.

A professional, efficient voice answered the phone in a foreign language. "*Bonġu.*"

Jasef responded, "*Bonġu.*" While the Hungarian spoke seven languages, Maltese was not one of them. "I need to speak with Antonio Bennetti, please. This is Jasef Krasnik in New York. Urgent, please. Tell him it's about the 'sisters.'" He paused, then added, "He will know what I mean."

"Yes, sir. Please hold while I ring his office."

He waited, glancing through the report one last time until a deep voice came on the phone. "This is Antonio. You have information about the sisters?"

"Yes, sir. I have found them, here, in America."

"Santa Maria! Our search is finally over," Antonio said.

Jasef heard a noticeable sigh of relief on the other end of the phone and knew that he'd made the right decision.

"Where are they?"

"Near here, not far, from Washington D.C., in a fishing village. Saint Michaels, Maryland."

Antonio laughed. "How appropriate." Then his tone turned serious. "I'll begin my preparations to bring them home. Thank you, *signore*. Thank you."

# Chapter Twenty-Four

The next day greeted the town with a light dusting of snow, covering the grass and trees, but only lasting until the glint of sunrise melted its memory.

Grace had not slept well the night before, tossing and turning: again, thinking about singing, New York, Sam, Philadelphia, Wanamaker's, and of course, Clarisse. She cleared her throat to practice what she was going to say to him. "Sam, we need to talk. I have something to tell you," Grace said. "No, that won't work. Let me start again. Sam, I don't want you to go... anywhere. Stay right here in Saint Michaels." She shook her head. Too desperate. "Be more direct," she said aloud. "Tell him exactly how you feel.... Sam, I love you, Sam. Don't go. I want the two of us to be..."

"Is that you, pumpkin?" said her father. "Everything okay? Are you alone in there? I heard voices."

"Just practicing my speech, Dad, that's all."

"Okay, but you better get a move on. Sam's car is already in the parking lot, and this afternoon you have your choir rehearsals."

"Right. I nearly forgot."

After a quick bite, she carried a coffee mug and a breakfast plate for Sam to church. "Morning Sam," she said, in a cheerful voice and heard a shuffling noise behind the keyboard as he slid out from underneath the organ.

"Morning, if you can call it that."

She could tell by the tone of his voice that he was troubled and distracted, so unlike Sam. "Breakfast?"

"No thank you, maybe later."

Now she knew there was something wrong. Turning down food was so unlike Sam. "What's wrong, Sam?"

He came out from behind the organ, with a detached, faraway sound in his voice. "The main switch keeps blowing fuses, and I don't know why. And now I'm running out of fuses. I have to find out what's wrong." Soon the smell of a fresh, hot breakfast sandwich sitting on the nearby plate was overwhelming. "Is that for me?"

"No," she said jokingly. "It's for the Sam Carpenter that I know and love, not some grumpy guy with a chip on his shoulder who keeps blowing fuses."

"Sorry," he said and leaned in closer to kiss her good morning on the cheek.

"Forgiven. Merry Christmas. Now here, eat your breakfast," she said, handing him the plate and the mug of coffee.

"Thanks." Halfway through, he looked around the church and remarked, "You know, this is such a beautiful church. I read once in the local library that the red bricks it's made from were made right here in Saint Michaels. And I love the beautiful stained-glass windows with curved arches, and the dark oak benches stained to a weathered finish by constant use. I miss coming to this church every day."

She nodded in agreement. "I miss being able to see the beauty of it all." She stopped, cleared her throat, and started to say, "You know, there was something I wanted to tell you, Sam. When we were alone. Together."

"Oh, this sounds serious."

"Well, it is…in a way. We've known each other for a very long time, and I wanted to tell you that when you're gone, I miss having you around and…"

POP! A fuse blew again, and the stench of acrid smoke filled the air. The light went out on the console.

"I've been thinking the same thing." He reached for her hand. "But that's no surprise, we've been doing that since we were kids. Thinking the same. I miss you when you're not around, and I don't see you."

"But what are we going to do? You have Wanamaker's to consider. I have New York to think about." She continued to hold his hand in hers. "And Dad has the bishop. And it's all happening at the same time. So confusing."

"We'll have to wait and see, that's all. Nothing we can do now but wait." He kissed her forehead and hugged her. He watched her and felt so helpless.

"But in the meantime, I have to figure out what's wrong with these fuses, or your father won't ever speak to me again. That's my last fuse. What am I going to do now?"

Sam sat for a minute looking at her, wishing there was something more he could say or do to help her. He took in a deep breath. "Let me think, let me think. I called the office earlier to see if they had any spares and no luck. Maybe one of the other techs in the area may have some extras, but that won't help. It's liable to blow again unless I can find out what's causing it."

He knelt on the ground and retrieved some tools from his toolbox, then removed the side panel of the console and shined his flashlight inside. Looking. Searching for the culprit. "Aha! I found it."

"What is it?" Grace asked in a distracted voice.

"Two lead wires are crossed, causing them to overload and short-circuit the panel and blow a fuse." He moved deeper inside the anteroom cavity. "Done. Now all I need is a fuse. Any idea if you have any extras? Or where they might be?"

"If we have one, it would be in the storage room, over there, down one level, in the basement under the bell tower." She pointed to her far left.

"Underneath the bell chamber?"

"Yes. You want me to show you?"

"No, thank you. I'll find it myself." He grabbed his flashlight from his toolkit and proceeded to the door at the back of the chamber, making his way down the shadowy, cobwebbed stone walkway. It was dark and musty.

The feeble light from his flashlight gave just enough light to see a few feet in front of him and opened the door. He was now directly beneath the bell tower, where they stored extra clangers and clappers, replacement bells, and ropes.

Sam walked into the mechanical room. Flickering flashlight shadows bounced off the walls. His hand felt for a light switch near the door. Flipping it on, he was bathed in light from an old bulb but was amazed at what he saw. Boxes of fuses lined the shelf: 5w, 20w, 30w, 60w, 75w, and large ones at 150w. Perfect. But there was more: rows and rows of church bells.

*Wow!* Thought Sam. *I need more light. What are they doing here? I must investigate this. No time now. I'll have to examine this later when I finish the organ tuning.*

He closed the door behind him and made his way to Grace. "Sorry to keep you waiting," he said to her, as he dusted himself off and sat down. He was excited and puzzled at his discovery. "I found more bells downstairs. Lots of bells. And it looks like they were moved there for a cleaning and never hung back upstairs. But where did the other bells come from? The ones hanging in the bell tower now. And why do we have so many extra bells? The ones in storage look clean, no cracks in them. They also match the other bells up there in the tower. And..."

She took in a deep breath and told him, "Well, if you're going to have a one-sided conversation with yourself, you certainly don't need me. I have work to do. I have choir practice. I must pack for my trip to Baltimore. Then prepare for New York. But first, I have a doctor's appointment early tomorrow morning and surgery next week. Oh, and the bishop is coming into to town next week for an important visit, and with all that to do, I certainly don't have the time to listen to..."

He kissed her. The church was quiet, and so was Grace. Sam looked at her and said, "I'm sorry, I don't know what came over me, but..."

She swallowed hard. "Did you kiss me to shut me up? Or because you wanted to kiss me?"

"A little of both," he said sheepishly.

Twice was no accident. She had been waiting for years for that to happen, and then it was over, too soon. She took his hand. "Sam, listen to me. There's so much I've wanted to say to you, and so little time, and..."

A door slammed behind them, and a woman's voice from the back of the church cried out, "Hello? Hello? Is there anyone here? I'm looking for Sam Carpenter."

He was quiet at first, his eyes trained on Grace, then he turned and shouted, "Over here, at the organ."

An older, well-dressed woman approached them. She wore a smiling face and a bright red coat with a green beret, covered in a light coating of snow. "My name is Maria Gomez," she said. "I'm the organist. I finished my errands earlier than I thought, and had some spare time, so I thought I would...come by if that's okay?" She looked at them. "Unless I'm interrupting something. I can come back later if you like."

Sam looked at Grace, then reached for her hand, his face turning back to Maria. "Ah, no, Maria. We were searching for a new fuse for the organ.

And we found one. Just now." He held up the blue and white circular glass fuse. "See?"

"Oh yes, I see."

Grace stood up and said, "Well, I better get ready for my choir practice. Talk to you later, Sam?" She didn't want to leave. She wanted to talk more with him, but what more could be said? She agreed with Sam, they'd just have to wait a little while longer. But she was getting tired of waiting.

"Yes, count on it. Bye, Gracie." Noticing the snow on Maria's clothes, Sam leaned closer to her and said, "It's snowing outside."

"Of course," said Grace. "Bye for now, Sam," she said, as her hand drifted away from his.

He watched her go, then turned to Maria to say, "Ready?"

"Yes. But first, I think you should marry that girl and have lots and lots of children."

"It's complicated."

"It always is. Good luck. Now how far have you progressed with tuning this magnificent pipe organ?"

# Chapter Twenty-Five

Early the next morning, Bill Albright drove his daughter to Cambridge, Maryland, to meet with Doctor Cassel, the ophthalmologist recommended by Doctor Winston. He watched Grace as they drove through town, and he wasn't sure which one of them was more nervous. It was only a forty-five-minute drive from Saint Michaels to Cambridge, but it seemed to take forever. He reached over and patted her hand. "It's all going to work out okay, Grace. Trust me."

She took his hand and managed a weak grin. "I hope so daddy. I tried so hard to adjust, and I was just beginning to accept my blindness as a way of life. Now this. I don't know what to expect or hope for. I don't want to get my hopes up."

They pulled into the parking lot of the Cambridge Medical Specialty Center, just off Church Creek Road. It was a tan brick, three-story building just off the main street in downtown Cambridge.

The office was decorated with a wreath on the entrance door, a Christmas tree in the corner, and soft Christmas music playing over the intercom of the busy office.

"Good morning," said the receptionist. "You must be the Albrights. Please have a seat and complete this paperwork for me, and the doctor will be right with you." Ten minutes later, they were escorted to an office at the very rear of the building. The office was filled with family photos on his desk, his credenza, and file cabinets. His multiple medical diplomas from Harvard, Duke, and Johns Hopkins lined the wall. Patient files were stacked everywhere on the floor, awaiting review.

"Good morning," said the doctor as he walked inside the office, carrying a manila folder and an electronic tablet. "Still trying to get used to these new procedures. I've done things my own way for the last thirty-five years, and now we have to change everything. A nuisance, but I'm finally getting the hang of it." Looking at them, he said, "I'm sorry, I'm Doctor Cassel... and you must be Grace and Mr. Albright. I think I remember you from our last visit years ago." He had kind eyes.

Grace smiled. "Yes. I remember you as well, Doctor Cassel. I must say, you haven't changed at all. You still look the same."

He smiled and started to say something before he broke out laughing. "Very funny. Very funny indeed. I see you still haven't lost your sense of humor. I can tell we're going to be fast friends. What do you say we get started? Doctor Winston has asked me to do a few routine tests, and then some other exams specific to the gene therapy needed for his procedure. Shall we begin?"

"Sure," said Grace.

"I have just a few questions for the two of you first." He began to write as he asked her father, "Growing up, did Grace ever have rheumatic fever, scarlet fever, mumps, or measles?"

"No."

"Ever have scarlatina?"

"No."

"Rubella or shingles?"

"No."

"Meningitis?"

"No."

*Is this all good or bad?* Grace wondered to herself.

He turned to Grace. "Have you ever been diagnosed with Multiple Sclerosis?"

"Heavens no," responded Grace.

"What about tuberculosis? Or viral encephalitis?" he asked.

"No, no, no, Doctor Cassel. I think we both would remember if she had any of these conditions," responded her father. "Can I ask you, what's the connection between Grace's loss of sight and the conditions you mentioned?"

"Sometimes the loss of sight experienced the way Grace did can be the first symptom of these ailments. But in Grace's case, I don't think so. But I must be thorough and pursue all avenues. You understand, don't you?"

"Oh yes, but of course, Doctor," said Grace, beginning to shake.

When he was finished, he said, "I am going to dilate Grace's eyes and perform an OCT test. This is a vision test, which allows me to look at the nerves at the back of her eyes. It's similar to an eye exam but more comprehensive." Turning to her father, he said, "The exam should take approximately an hour, Reverend Albright. If you like, you can wait in the waiting room, and I'll have one of my staff come and get you when we're done."

After the eye drops took effect, one of the nurses led Grace to a chair in the examining room. "Have a seat," she said, "and the doctor will be right with you."

The doctor performed all of his tests and was very thorough. But while he tried to make it sound like a routine visit, she could tell from his voice that something was wrong.

"Is everything okay, Doctor Cassel?"

His voice remained calm, yet detached. "Everything is fine, Grace. Fine. Now, don't you worry, but I'm just going to run some of these tests a second time. For confirmation. Please be patient. Not too much longer."

Two hours later, Grace returned to the waiting room, and her father rushed to greet her. "Grace, is everything all right?" he said. "I've been going crazy here! The people are nice, but they just kept telling me to wait and somebody would be right with me. I've never been so happy to see you. Is everything okay? What's going on?"

"I don't know," she said. "The doctor redid some tests and exams a couple of times and wasn't as chatty as he was earlier. They told me to wait here, and I guess we should know something soon."

They waited patiently for the next forty-five minutes until another nurse appeared at the door. "Ms. Albright? Mr. Albright? Would you please follow me?"

*I don't think I like the sound of this,* thought Grace. Her hands began to sweat and shake as her father led her down the hallway, back to the doctor's office.

"Please have a seat," said the nurse. "The doctor will be right with you."

Within minutes, the door reopened, and Doctor Cassel walked inside. "I am so sorry to have kept you here for so long," he told them.

*Now for the bad news,* thought Grace, as she listened to his tone. Even before her blindness, she'd had a sixth sense for moments such as these.

"I'm afraid I have some bad news for you," said Doctor Cassel. "I re-ran these tests just to make sure, and while the retinal scans all seemed normal, your Choroid Receptors at the back of your eye, which are necessary for

Doctor Winston's procedure, may not be strong enough to accept the stem implant. I'm sorry. Usually, this exam is a routine pre-op visit, but I'm afraid after comparing your test results to those of your last visit a few years ago, there has been some gross deterioration. I'm afraid I can't recommend you for this procedure. I'm so sorry."

A tear rolled down her cheek, but she said nothing, accepting her fate.

Her father watched her, then turning to the doctor, said, "Has Doctor Winston seen these test results? Or seen the comparison of the two different ones from a few years ago?"

"No, I normally wouldn't bother him with such pre-op details."

Her father was nervous but determined. "Could you make an exception, please?"

The doctor sat back in his chair and retrieved his glasses from his desk. "That would be highly unusual."

The Reverend Albright picked up a picture of the doctor and his family. "A lovely family you have here, Doctor Cassel. Very lovely." Their eyes met, father to father. "Please?" he whispered.

"Perhaps you're right, Reverend Albright. That would be the next course of action. Excuse me for just a few minutes while I have my assistant forward these results to his office. Would you care for some water? Tea? Coffee?"

"No, thank you," interjected Grace. "We'll be just fine, thank you." Her hand reached for her father's as he returned to his seat next to her. "Pray," she whispered, as Doctor Cassel left.

After what seemed like an eternity—but by the clock on the wall, it measured only thirty minutes—the doctor returned. "I have Doctor Winston on the phone," he said. "If it's okay with you, I think we'll use the speakerphone so we can all participate in the conversation."

"Yes, that'll be fine."

"Ready?" he asked them.

"Yes," they said in unison.

The doctor pressed the blinking button on his desk phone, then the speaker button. "Hello? Doctor Winston?"

"Hello, yes, I'm here."

Doctor Cassel leaned in close to the phone. "Doctor Winston, I have Grace and Bill Albright in my office with me. Thanks for taking the time to speak with us."

"No problem. Hello, Grace. Afternoon, Reverend."

"Hello, Doctor Winston. Yes, we're here," they both replied.

"Well, I've reviewed the results that Doctor Cassel sent me," he said, "and compared them to the accompanying results from your examination a few years ago. The degradation is definitely there, and I concur with Doctor Cassel that it could be a far riskier procedure given this new information. I'm so sorry."

"I understand," said her father. The disappointment was evident in his voice.

Grace sat up in her chair and asked, "How much riskier?"

"Well, the usual rate of success with this procedure, as I mentioned to you earlier, is about 58%."

"And with this new prognosis, what are my chances?"

There was silence on the other end of the phone. Finally, the doctor spoke. "Miss Albright, I wish I could be more optimistic…your chances are now thirty percent at best."

Grace swallowed deeply, then without hesitation, spoke firmly. "I'm still interested in having the procedure done, Doctor Winston."

"Are you sure?"

"Yes, more than ever."

"Then I'll need you to come in sooner for your procedure. In your case, time is of the essence."

"We're scheduled for next week."

"I would like you in earlier. As soon as possible. Like tomorrow or the next day."

"That sounds ominous."

He laughed, then to ease her fears, said, "Nothing ominous, Ms. Albright, but can you be here tomorrow or the next day? I think it's better for you if we do it sooner rather than later. It'll give you some time to rest over the holidays."

"Oh yes, sir. Of course. We'll be there. Thank you, Doctor Winston. Thank you for caring."

"I'll alert my staff to the schedule changes, and they'll begin the preparation."

"We'll leave soon and check in with your staff when we get there."

"My assistant will make the arrangements and give you all the info you will need for the procedure. See you soon."

"Goodbye, Doctor," said her father.

Driving back to Saint Michaels, Grace was quiet in the car. She rolled down the window and then whispered, "Dad, please don't tell Sam about the changes. He'll worry that something is wrong and will want to come with us to Baltimore. He has his interview at Wanamaker's, and...he needs to make his own choices. Without any pressure."

"But Grace, he's going to want to know! And I'm sure he'll suspect something is wrong."

"I know. Let him suspect all he wants, but I don't want to tell him...at least not yet. Let me wait until the time is right. I want to see his face... again."

"But Grace..."

"Please, Daddy?"

"As you wish. I won't say a word." He was quiet for a moment, then whispered to her, "Have you told him yet?"

"Told him?"

"Told him how you feel about him?"

"No. I started to, but...it's all very confusing, with so much going on in both of our lives. I have a lot of things to sort through."

As they pulled into the church parking lot, her father said, "Sam's car is still here."

She sighed. "Why don't you go inside and get ready? Let me talk with him for a minute, and then I'll be right in."

"All right, baby. Don't be long. We leave soon."

"Okay," she responded, kissing him on the cheek. She wiped the tears from her eyes, fixed her makeup as best she could and made her way to the church.

Sam was packing up his tuning bag, getting ready to leave, when she arrived. "Hey, Grace," he said. "How did your appointment go today?" He knew immediately something was wrong, very wrong.

"Good," she stuttered, trying hard to be normal. "And Doctor Winston called and said that he could take me earlier, so we're going to Baltimore tonight. Isn't that great news?"

She heard his packing movement stop and could feel him move closer to her. "Yes, that's wonderful, I guess," he said, a tear forming in his eye. "You know, I'm just about done here. Today, or tomorrow perhaps, I could come to Baltimore and keep you company? Moral support, so to speak?"

"I'll be fine, Sam, really I will. You're waiting for your Wanamaker call. You don't want to screw that up, now do you?"

"No, I guess not, but I can always go there later," he said, not taking his eyes off her. "Is everything okay, Gracie?"

She tensed, he knew her too well. "Yeah, everything's fine." Then thinking quickly she said, "You see, if I go in for the procedure now, I can be home for Christmas. Then I go into Doc Cassel to have the bandages changed and then...hope for the best." She stopped when she heard no reaction from him.

"Sam, I just wanted to tell you what was going on with the procedure. I'll be fine. See you next week," she said without thinking. *I hope.* "I better go," she said, and turned to leave, stopping long enough to say, "I'll call you once the procedure is done and let you know everything is all right. How's that? Okay?" She wanted to continue their conversation from earlier in the day, but now things in her life had changed. *Only a thirty percent chance of seeing again?* A tear ran down her cheek. *What else could possibly happen?*

"Yeah, sure. That'd be great. Take care, Gracie." He watched her walk away to the steady tap-tap-tap of her walking stick. He stood and went to say, "Grace?" Too late, she was gone.

# Chapter Twenty-Six

Sam was at the church early the next day, and he and Maria completed tuning the last of the organ pipes in record time. She waited for him to finish packing up his tuning forks and sit down next to her at the organ.

"I think you should be the first to play...you know...the inaugural hymn, so to speak. Be my guest, Sam," she said with an ever-growing grin.

"Okay," he said, as he sat at the console and rested his hands on the manual, pulling out stops number three, six, and seven. The organ awoke from its long, deep slumber at the hands of a master, as he heard the wind rushing through the pipes, both large and small. Then he began to play, one hymn then another, bringing tears to Maria's eyes. The sound was heavenly. It had been a long while since she had heard an organ played so well.

"Bravo," she exclaimed, clapping her hands.

They heard the continued clapping at the back of the church. It was Gabe, the homeless man. "Well done, young man," he said, still clapping. "You missed your calling, Sam. You should have been an organist. Well done." He walked closer and, for some reason, seemed taller that day than he had before.

"Thank you, Gabe. It'll need to be refurbished this summer...that is, if the church stays open."

"Why do you say that? This past Sunday, there were a lot more parishioners here."

"Yes, but I don't know if that's going to be enough. The church needs more people attending. More families for the school."

"Pray. It'll all work out for the best, trust me. Merry Christmas and...good luck," said Gabe, buttoning his coat and putting on his hat and gloves.

"Thanks," said Sam.

The church was quiet again as he and Maria looked up at the massive pipes.

She said to him, "I must say, the organ sounded wonderful, and you play it so well. Now if we only had the bells working. I understand years ago when they were working they sounded wonderful." She glanced at her watch. "Gotta go meet my daughter for lunch. Bye for now. Good luck with the bells."

*The bells?* Thought Sam. "Yes, the bells. I'm going to go down to the storage room and take a closer look at them. Thanks again, Maria. Merry Christmas."

Downstairs, the room was narrow, the musty smell of age all about him. He turned on the hoist and moved it over the smallest of the seven bells, attached the harness, and pressed the button to lift it. Once it was at shoulder height, he grabbed the clapper strap and pulled it. The bell resonated with the sweetest sound he had heard in many years. He returned it to the ground and repeated the process with the next one. The bell sounded heavenly. Perfectly tuned. He climbed the many steps up the bell tower to examine the entire carillon in the belfry. Looking down from the tower after his examination, he knew at once. *The ones in the storage room are the rightful replacement bells. But where did these other ones come from? The ones here in the tower, the ones with the cross emblem embedded on the side of the bell. The sour ones.* He scrutinized them. *Where are they from?*

He turned to look skyward, then examined the hoist. *I can switch all of them with the crane, but this is crazy,* he thought and shook his head. *This is a two-person job. I'm going to need some help.* He pulled out his cell phone and searched for a number. "Hey, Zack, this is Sam."

"Hey, Sam," said Zack. "How ya doin'?"

"I'm doing good, but I need a favor…and some help. Can you come to Saint Michaels Church and give me a hand with something?"

"Sure. I'm finishing here at Christ Church in Easton with my crew, but I can be there after lunch sometime. Say, around three?"

"Great. See ya then."

Shortly after three, Zack appeared at the door of the old church. "Whatcha need?" he asked with a smile.

"Let me show you something," said Sam, leading him past the organ, then down the steps to the storage room.

"Did you get this old church organ working?" Zack asked as they made their way down the steps.

"Yeah, and it sounds great." He pushed open the door to the storage room and turned on the light.

"Um, delightful place you got here, Sam. What's with all the extra bells?"

"I'm surmising that these bells were taken down for cleaning while the others were temporarily hung in their place. I have duplicates of some bells, seven to be precise, and the ones hanging upstairs are sour. But the ones stored here in storage sounded perfectly tuned."

"So what's the plan?"

"Well, I thought we would move these bells from the storage room up to the bell tower, hang them as we replace the ones up there with these. Bring those down here. Do a simple swap. Later, we have to figure out where they came from, but all of this is a two-person job."

"Got it. Let's go."

They opened the trapdoors in the bell room, above the storage area. One by one, Zack attached the lifting harness to the bell collar of each bell and using the electric hoist, began raising them up the bell tower to Sam. In the light of day, Sam could see that the condition of the stored bells was even better than he'd first thought. Positioning them one by one, he began the arduous task of attaching the harness to the tower bells. Slowly, he directed Zack to lower the sour ones to the storage rack below. Most of the bells they were moving were the larger ones, but all contained the same unusual cross emblem at the top. Very interesting, thought Sam.

The process of replacing all the bells took almost three hours. It was dark by the time they finished.

"I'm finished up here," shouted Sam from the belfry.

"Sam, come on down and let's see how they sound," replied Zack, now filled with excitement and anticipation about the completion of the project.

Sam glanced at the bell tower and smiled, rubbing his hands to keep warm. The bells upstairs were all back together, like a family. He rubbed the largest bell and whispered, "Merry Christmas." Then turning to Zack below, he shouted, "Down in a minute, Zack."

As he entered the storage room, Zack asked him, "Do you know what to make of the funny emblem, the strange crosses on these old bells?"

"No, not at all. Never seen it before. But it looks European. And the sheen is something I have never seen, like a golden hue."

"I don't know. Let's try to ring these bells."

Sam glanced at his watch and said, "Let's wait a few minutes until six o'clock, just so we don't scare anyone with ringing bells."

"Good idea." The minutes clicked by, and precisely at six P.M., they rang the bells in sequence. The bells rang out over the water to the other villages nearby, a glorious sound, echoing through Saint Michaels. Sweet, strong, and beautiful. It was something to hear. So pure, so sweet and all in perfect harmony.

"You did good, Sam," said Zack. "How did you figure out we needed to put those bells up there?"

"Lucky guess. But the sizes match, so I figured it was worth a try."

They stood outside as the snow began to fall and the bells continued to ring out loud and clear, tolling for the first time in over seventy years. What a glorious sound they made. Sam closed his eyes and listened, then smiled, as he heard people cheering in the streets. He and Zack listened to them until he was interrupted by his ringing phone. "Hello?" he said.

"Hi, Sam. This is Carson, Carson Wright with Wanamaker?"

"Oh yes."

"I wanted to let you know I booked a room for you at a hotel nearby, and we were hoping we could count on you joining us here?"

"Ah yes. Well I…" He paused. "Yes, I'm available anytime." He walked away from Zack, just far enough to have a private conversation.

"How about tomorrow? Or Saturday? It's our busy time, we play at least four times a day. We could really use the extra help to keep old Ben working in top shape."

"Big Ben?"

"Yeah, that's our nickname for the organ. Big Ben."

"Oh, I see. I thought I was the only one who did that sort of thing."

"No, we do it here too."

"I'll see you tomorrow."

Ten minutes later Zack approached him, all smiles. "Wow, I'm in the wrong business. I've never heard such a sound. I love those bells."

"It's a wonderful melodic sound, isn't it?"

"You bet. Well, Sam, if we're all done, I have to run to dinner with Clarisse."

"Yeah, we're done. I just have to close up shop and do the shutdown of the organ, the bell tower, and the console. You go ahead. And Zack, I really appreciate all your help."

"Anytime, Sam, anytime."

He had a lot on his mind as he went through the closedown. *Wanamaker. Grace. Philadelphia. Saint Michaels.* As he started his car, he stopped. *Did I complete my shutdown list for the organ? Yes, of course I did. Tomorrow— Wanamaker's.*

The organ at the back of the church continued its quiet hum for a few minutes longer, becoming louder and louder until a loud, distinctive noise filled the empty church: POP! The lights on the console flashed, then went dark as a wisp of black smoke curled above the keyboard.

# Chapter Twenty-Seven

The ultra-modern medical building which housed the Winston Clinic was located adjacent to the world-famous Johns Hopkins Medical Headquarters in downtown Baltimore. Early that morning, Grace and her father walked from the nearby hotel to check in at the front desk of the clinic.

"Good morning," said the middle-aged receptionist at the front desk. "How can I help you, hon?" she asked with a smile.

"We're here for an appointment with Doctor Winston."

"Your names?"

"Grace and Bill Albright."

She typed in some information on her keyboard while her eyes scanned the screen. "Oh yes, I see it here. I'll inform the doctor's office you're here. Please have a seat and make yourself comfortable."

Ten minutes later, a well-dressed young assistant approached them. "Hello, I'm Avril. I've been assigned to be your guide while you're under our care here at the clinic. Please follow me to Doctor Winston's office." As they walked along the plush, blue-grey carpeted hallway, she said, "If you have any questions, issues, or requests, please do not hesitate to bring them to my attention. At the Winston Clinic, we want your stay here with us to be as pleasant and productive as possible." She stopped them in the hallway and said in a sincere voice, "I understand you may be a little nervous. Not knowing what to expect. But trust me, you're in good hands. I have worked for Doctor Winston for over twelve years. He's the absolute best. He's not only kind and caring, but he's also one of the best in his field."

Grace felt relieved. "Thanks for that. And yes, I am very nervous."

The nurse responded, "No problem. Did you bring the paperwork with you from Doctor Cassel?"

"Yes, we have it right here," said her father, handing her a folder.

"Excellent. Right this way." She led them down other wide corridors, past many different offices all staffed with white-coated assistants and took them into the doctor's office. "Please have a seat. The doctor will be with you shortly."

Grace sat while her father looked around the office. It was a corner office, containing a large teak desk, two leather side chairs, and off to the side, an expensive-looking Italian leather sofa. Bookcases lined the wall, filled with medical reference books and files and folders. The high gloss cherry conference table was cluttered with files stacked on top of one another, spilling over to stacks on the floor surrounding his office.

On his credenza was a picture of an attractive woman playing the piano. Next to it was a picture of the doctor and his wife, in formal attire with the mayor. The photo was flanked by photos of the doctor shaking hands with two former American presidents, a British prime minister, a Hollywood star, and a Saudi sheik.

The door opened, and in walked the man from the picture. "Oh, good morning. I'm Doctor Winston. I hope I haven't kept you waiting long."

"No, not long at all. I was just admiring the photos on your credenza."

He smiled as he retrieved the picture of his wife sitting at the piano. "She's my one true joy in life. The light of my life so to speak. And hers is playing the piano, which I have tuned regularly by an excellent tuner." He laughed as he returned the picture to its place of honor.

"Now, just give me a minute to review these documents again from Doctor Cassel. I received them electronically, but I'm from the old school and like to see the hard copy," he said, without taking his eyes off the paperwork he was so intently reading. "I'd like to spend some time to perform my own OCT and eye exam, if you don't mind."

"No, not at all, Doctor," said Grace.

"Follow me, will you, please?" He led them both to a small examining room adjacent to his office. He placed some clear drops in each of her eyes and then repeated the process a few minutes later with yellow eye drops. After a few minutes, he turned off the lights and began his examination. When he was finished, he handed Grace a tissue to dry the drops from her eyes. Then he had her sit in front of the OCT machine and rest her chin on the support cup. When they had finished, he said, "Please join me in my office. I have a few questions."

He sat down at his desk, and once they were comfortable, he asked her, "Grace, have you ever had Lyme disease?"

"No. Not that I'm aware of, at least."

"Have you ever been diagnosed with MS?"

"No," she replied, her voice quivering with worry. Doctor Cassel had asked her that very same question in his office.

"Have you ever been assessed as having any of the following ailments: demy eliminating disease, autoimmune neuropathies, sarcoidosis, or anterior ischemic optic neuropathy?"

She shook her head rapidly after each one. "No. No. None. I think I would remember those. Is that good or bad?"

"It's very good, I assure you," he said in a soothing voice. "Have you ever had chronic sinusitis?"

She sat up in her chair and said, "Yes, yes I did. Right before the accident. The people at the doctor's office called it an allergy or possibly summer sinusitis. The doctor said I would get over in time, but I couldn't shake it, regardless of what I did or what medicine I took, including multiple antibiotics."

"At that time, did you experience headaches, runny nose, nasal congestion, fatigue, sore throat for a period of a few weeks?"

"Yes," responded Grace, and nodded.

"I see. For now, that's all the questions I have. I suggest you go back to your hotel and rest. Tomorrow is a big day for you."

"And after the procedure?" Grace asked him in a nervous voice.

"You go home and wait. And wait. Have patience. After a week, you can return to your everyday life."

"Just no swimming, right Grace?" her father interjected to lighten the mood while squeezing her hand.

"Swimming?" asked Doctor Winston.

"Yes. That's what started all this mess, the water at a local swim club."

Doctor Winston looked at him strangely. "Swimming wasn't the cause of your daughter's loss of sight, Reverend Albright. This could have happened to her anywhere, at any time. It was a virus that caused this."

"Virus?"

"Yes, a virus. The same virus that caused Grace's sinusitis caused her blindness. It's a condition called Optic Neuritis. It can happen when your optic nerve becomes inflamed, and stops receiving optic signals causing blindness. That's why I wanted her to come in early—her recent deterioration was very rapid."

His face lost its color. "And all this time I've been blaming Sam Carpenter for this tragedy, since he was the one who took you swimming to that watering hole."

Grace reached for his hand. "He never blamed you, Dad."

"I have to make it up to him. Somehow. How did all this happen?" he asked the doctor.

"Grace's chronic sinus infection somehow caused her optic nerve to become inflamed. The inflammation usually only causes temporary loss of sight in one eye, but in Grace's case, it only got worse. Most people recover in a month or two, usually no longer than a year, but in Grace's case, her severe infection compounded the injury. Young females between the age of 18 and 45 are at the highest risk to develop optic neuritis, but they also recover the fastest. For future reference, for your own health, I suggest not swimming until you're over any sinus infection. But swimming didn't cause your blindness."

He closed the folder and addressed them quietly. "Any other questions at this point? I'm still very concerned about the deterioration in your optic receptors, but these test results tell me we are definitely in the workable range."

"What happens tomorrow?" her father asked.

"The procedure tomorrow is pretty routine. Tomorrow morning, you'll be met by Avril, who will escort you to the waiting room, where you'll dress in a surgical gown and then be sedated. I will inject one eye with a stem cell injection. And then do the next eye the following day. Any questions so far?"

"No, Doctor," Grace responded.

"Once you're back home, I want you to rest and wait. You'll visit Doctor Cassel's office every other day for an examination and to have the bandages changed. This will be done in the dark, and your eyes will not be tested for several days. At the end of the waiting period, he will remove the bandages permanently. There are usually no half measures with this procedure, Ms. Albright, Grace—it either works or it doesn't. Once the receptors have been breached, the procedure cannot be done again. For now, only time will tell."

"What restrictions will I have after the procedure?"

"The first day, just take it easy. Doctor Cassel will change the bandages a few times, and once the bandages are removed for the last time, you can resume your normal activities, hopefully with one major difference. You'll be able to see."

He stopped to read the relief on Grace's face. She was strong as she held back the tears.

"Go back to your hotel room and get some rest, and I'll see you first thing in the morning."

The next morning, Grace was wheeled into the procedure room, and one hour later, she was awake.

"See, I told you it was a snap. You did real good, Grace," said Doctor Winston, as he entered her room. "Tomorrow we'll do the other eye."

She reached for his arm. "Doctor Winston, when will I know if it's a success?"

He patted her hand. "Not until the bandages come off for good will we know if the procedure has taken, but some patients have said they experienced an itching sensation in one or both eyes after the procedure. But that's not a foolproof indication. Get some rest, and I'll see you tomorrow."

In her room that night, she tried to send Sam a text, but the signal was not strong enough: only one bar, then two, then none. She dictated a text to Sam, hoping at some point it would go through.

*Sam—Procedure went well. Have to wait until tomorrow for the next one.*
*Nervous.*
*But the doctor is sympathetic, and very kind.*
*Wish me luck.*
*Miss you.*
*Grace*

When she woke up the next morning, she heard a beep. A waiting text on her phone from the night before. She hit the voice button for voice conversion.

*Grace—*
*Happy to hear it went so well.*
*Working late. Sorry it took so long to get back to you.*
*I miss you too. A lot.*
*Hope to see you soon.*
*Sam*

That day was a repeat of the prior day. When the doctor came to visit her and her father in her room, he asked, "How do you feel, Grace?"

"Tired and hungry."

"That's to be expected. I want to keep you overnight, then I'll sign your release papers, and you'll be free to go. Remember, just don't overdo it. No strenuous activity and no swimming."

They all laughed.

"Check in with Doctor Cassel when you return home tomorrow and have your bandages changed every other day. Any questions?"

"No, Doctor. No matter how this turns out, I can't thank you enough for finding room in your schedule for me."

"Don't thank me. Thank your guardian angel."

"Guardian angel?" asked her father.

"Yes, Sam Carpenter. He's an old friend of the family. He made a personal plea in your case to have me see you and perform the procedure. But for now, let's just hope that it works. You must excuse me now. I have a few other patients to look in on before I head home. Merry Christmas."

After dinner that night in her room, her father asked, "How ya feeling, Gracie?"

"Better, I think. Just tired."

"Get some rest. You've had a long couple of days. I'm going back to the hotel room and making some phone calls. I have the bishop coming into town in a few days. And Christmas services. And I must get some things ready for your return home. Say some prayers."

"Dad? Can you hand me my cell phone?"

"Sure, pumpkin. But don't be on the phone for too long now. You need your rest. Besides, it's a very weak signal in the hospital they may even have a blocker.. But you can try." He laid her phone in her hand and kissed her forehead. "Say goodnight, Gracie."

Grace laughed. "Funny. Good night, Dad."

After he left, she lay in bed and listened to the steady rhythm of activity outside her room slow as the day wore on. She listened to the sounds of quiet footsteps, made by white soled nurses' shoes, as they pattered by her door. She heard a voice on the intercom page a Doctor Green to call extension 101. She dozed off, and on when she woke her cell phone fidgeted in her hand. She needed to hear his voice—she had to hear his voice. She put the phone close to her mouth, pressed the voice prompt, and said, "Call Sam Carpenter."

The phone responded, "Midtown Carpet?"

"No, dial Sam Carpenter."

"Quick Carpet Cleaning?"

"No. No. No. Sam Carpenter."

The phone rang.

"Hello, it's Sam."

She sat up in bed and said, "Oh, hi. I told you I would call and let you know what was going on...I mean, after my procedure." She brushed her hair back with her hand, happy to once again hear his voice.

"How ya doing, Gracie?" he asked quietly.

"Better now that I can talk to you. Did you ever hear from Wanamaker's?"

"Yes, they offered me the job, and I've been in Philadelphia for the last couple of days working, trying it out. I tried calling you a couple of times yesterday, but kept getting a busy signal on your phone."

"They said the hospital has blocked calls or something like that. You accepted the job and moved? How is it?" she gulped. *Gone? To Philadelphia?*

"It's good," said Sam. "The pipe organ is in a department store, and the building is close to a hundred years old. It takes up seven stories. And this pipe organ is the biggest thing I've ever worked on. It has over 28,000 pipes. Can you believe it, 28,000 pipes? And Gracie, get this, they have a staff of four full-time people tuning and maintaining it. It's the largest pipe organ in the world."

She could hear the excitement in his voice. She was happy for him; he'd found what he really wanted to do with his life. He had made a commitment. In Philadelphia. *Good for you, Sam, you deserve some happiness. How can I crush his dream now that he finally has the job he's always wanted? But what about...us?* "This is such a clear connection. It sounds like you're right here in my room."

"I am," he said, and she realized he was standing at her door.

She stuttered, "What?" She could feel his weight as he sat on the bed.

"I couldn't get through to you, and you didn't call me...so I thought I would drop by and visit."

"You drove two hours from Philadelphia just to be here. You're crazy," she said with a chuckle.

"Yeah, I am." He leaned closer, holding her hand, then pulled away. "When do you go to New York?"

"After the first of the year."

*So it's a done deal after all,* he thought. "I wish you luck with that, Grace. You have a wonderful voice." He paused. "How did the surgery go? What did Doc Winston say?"

"Well, he said that you didn't cause my blindness, and I have a guardian angel by the name of Sam Carpenter looking out for me who made a phone call to him to ask if he would consider performing the procedure on me." She felt something brush against her lips, something warm. A kiss?

"Sam Carpenter, did you just try to kiss me? Are you trying to shut me up again?"

"Hmmm. Is this a multiple-choice question?" Changing the subject, he asked, "When do the bandages come off?"

She pressed her lips together and waited for a few moments before she replied. "They need to be changed by Doctor Cassel every other day. When he takes them off for the final time,… then we'll know. Won't we?"

"Yes indeed. Good night, Grace. I must get back to work. We do most of the maintenance work on the pipes and the organ at night when the store closes. After hours. Tonight, we're refinishing the largest metal pipe in the organ. But it's a labor of love."

"Sam, when will I see you again? I mean, when will…"

"Soon."

"I know this is silly, but can you stay here with me until I fall asleep? I don't want to be alone. Not just yet. Just hold my hand?"

"Sure."

She felt the whoosh of the bed's mattress as he again sat down next to her. Fifteen minutes later, her eyes closed. She was dozing when she whispered, "Sam? Sam, are you still here?"

"Yes," came a voice in the dark. "I'm still here."

She reached for his hand and kissed it. "Good night, Sam. Merry Christmas."

"Sweet dreams, Gracie. Merry Christmas."

As Sam made his way on the beltway to I-95, his phone rang. "Hello," he said, using the car's speaker connection.

"Sam," said a thickly accented voice, "this is Jasef. Jasef from New York."

"Hi, Jasef. What news do you have for me?"

"I mail the report to you from today, on your bells."

"Today?"

"Yes. It took longer than I expected. If you have a question, you call, yes?" he said in his sing-song Hungarian English voice.

"Okay, will do. But tell me, what caused the bells to sound sour? Salt water from the ocean? Hurricanes? Bad casting?"

"Difficult to say on the telephone. You'll see. You have full report soon. Read and call me. No? Okay?"

Frustrated, Sam replied, "Okay, Jasef. I'll look at the report."

Before he hung up, the old Hungarian asked him, "Sam, I have a question for you. If you have something that no belong to you, you want to return to the right people, no?"

*Strange question,* thought Sam. "I don't want anything that's not mine, if that's what you mean, Jasef?"

"Yeah, yeah. Thank you, Sam. You call me. Yes? Good night."

"Good night, Jasef." *That is the strangest conversation I have ever had with him,* he thought, *the very strangest.*


It was late in the evening in Saint Michaels as Hilda Mae closed the store for the day. Business was picking up, and sales for the week were brisk. *It'll be a good Christmas,* she thought. *Almost a great Christmas, if only...*

Hilda closed the back door, locked it, and was beginning to walk away when she heard the phone inside the store ringing. It was late, she was tired, and her feet and back ached terribly, but it could be a customer or Henrietta needing something.

She trudged back up the steps, unlocked the door, turned on the light, and picked up the phone. "Hello, Ye Olde Christmas Store. How can I help you?"

The voice on the other end of the phone was so weak, she could barely hear it. "Hello? Hello? Anyone there?" she said.

No response. As she went to hang up the phone, she heard a small voice say, "Momma? Momma? It's me."

"Baby? Is that you, Frances?" It took all her strength to hold back the tears.

"Yes, Momma." There was the longest pause before she said the words Hilda had been waiting to hear for all these years. "Momma…I wanna come home."

# Chapter Twenty-Eight

Grace had recovered well over the week she was home on the days leading up to Christmas Eve. She went into town to deliver Christmas presents to her old friends. The overhead bell rang on the door as she entered Ye Olde Christmas Shoppe.

Henrietta Brown hugged her close. "Oh, dahlin', it is so good to see you. How was the operation? Are you able to see yet?"

"I won't know until they take off the bandages for the last time. But tomorrow I go to see Doctor Cassel again, and when he replaces the bandages, I'm going to peek. The suspense is killing me."

Hilda Mae, as usual, jumped into the conversation. "The doctor's workin' on Christmas Eve? Well, I never…"

Grace smiled. "He's only coming in to do paperwork. He's seeing me as a special favor to Doctor Winston, who did the procedure. Doctor Cassel is one of the nicest doctors I have ever had to deal with. "

Hilda smiled broadly. "Well, that would be one heck of a Christmas present, you betcha, girl. I just got my best Christmas present," she said, beaming a smile as broad as her face. "My Frances is coming home for Christmas. Will be here soon. I can hardly wait."

Grace smiled. "That's wonderful, Hilda. Absolutely wonderful." She handed them each a box covered with brightly colored Christmas paper. "Merry Christmas to both of you."

Hilda Mae shook it. "What's in it?"

Grace whispered, "A box of chocolates."

"Um, I better check this out in private, away from pryin' eyes. Merry Christmas, girlie girl. Your present was dropped off at the rectory this morning. See you at the Christmas Eve services tomorrow. The bells sounded wonderful, thanks to that young Sam Carpenter. Good luck with the bishop."

"The bishop comes in tomorrow. Christmas Eve, so say a prayer."

"Will do…again. Bye bye, Grace." Hild Mae shuffled her feet as fast as she could to the back of the store, all the while muttering the words, "Chocolate, chocolate, chocolate."

Henrietta walked closer to her, saying, "Thank you for the present, Gracie. You didn't have to do that, but I'll enjoy them nonetheless." Then whispered, away from the prying ears of Hilda Mae, "Have you heard anything from Sam?"

"No. He's still in Philadelphia, working at Wanamaker's. He calls me every night and we talk. He's settling into his new job and new place. He says he's happy, but he sounds homesick. I tried not to sway him one way or another or put a guilt trip on him about his decision. He has to do what he wants to do, what makes him happy. That's his choice, and I only want him to be happy. It's only been a couple of days, but I miss him. It's killing me not being able to have him here."

"And what about you? You goin' to be leavin' us too, I hear? Headin' for the bright lights of New York City?"

"Yep. I leave Jan 5th," she said, not too convincingly. "Already got my ticket. But as much as I want to follow my dream, I'm going to miss singing in the choir on Sundays and the annual Christmas choir. I will really miss summertime here in Saint Michaels. I won't have any saltwater clams. My mouth already is watering for fresh oysters, and Maryland blue crabs with freshly shucked corn. I'm going to miss walking along the Miles River down by the harbor, and the old plays at the Saint Michaels Theater. I'm going to miss my dad. And you. And Hilda Mae. And Molly and everybody else here in Saint Michaels."

"Home is where the heart is, darlin'. Sounds like you still got some decidin' to do."

"I guess you're right, Henrietta. But enough about me, what about you?"

"Well, I'm happy. I have my health. My friends. My family. I didn't tell you, Lil' Henry graduated from college with his MBA and will be working for the bank right here in Saint Michaels. He'll be helping me out part-time on the computer stuff, already has the website up and running and bringing in orders. Glory be, is that one smart boy. And he's going to be Mr. Barnett's assistant for six months, and then be promoted to manager when Barnett gets promoted to work in Washington D.C. And you heard what Hilda Mae said, her Frances is comin' in on the bus tonight from

California. She's going to join us for your Christmas Eve church services tomorrow evening. You know, I been thinkin' about somethin'. Young Frankie and my Henry are about the same age and…hmmm."

"Don't you go playing matchmaker again, Henny. But I must tell you, that's all great news. This will be a wonderful Christmas."

"Yes, if only we could have a white Christmas or if…"

"Keep wishing and hoping," said Grace, as she hugged Henrietta goodbye. As Grace walked through the town, it was a bustle of activity, as last-minute shoppers searched for that final perfect Christmas gift. This could be a wonderful Christmas, if only…

Bishop Kevin Donovan arrived that day, the day before Christmas Eve. He was a kindly man, and Grace found him to be very warm and very funny, something she did not expect from a man of the cloth of his stature. He loved to tell tales of growing up as a child in Belfast, Northern Ireland. His stories were so vivid in description, Grace felt she was there among the farmers, the shopkeepers, the neighbors, his brothers and sisters, and the everyday churchgoers. He told of the green fields of Ireland, the rough water of the seas that surrounded the emerald isle, and of their faith. Grace wanted to see it for herself. She wanted to see that and more. It had been almost a week, and not even shadows when she peeked. *It's not going to work. And it doesn't itch like Doctor Winston said it would. Patience, Grace.*

When she returned home that night, she thought of everything that had happened to her over the last few weeks, and she made a fateful decision. Reaching for her phone, she breathed deep and said, "Call Justin Reynolds."

The phone rang three times, and she heard a cheerful voice answer, "Hi Grace. How you doing?

"Fine, Mr. Reynolds. How are you?" She paused, not knowing exactly what to say.

Sensing her reluctance, he went right to the point. "You aren't going to join us in New York, are you?"

"No, sir. But how did you know that I had changed my mind?"

"Grace, I've been in this business for over thirty-five years, and I have a pretty good read on people. My feeling is that as much as you would like a professional singing career, you think you'd be giving up too many things to reach that goal. You have a spectacular voice, and your congregation should cherish the fact that they have you there singing for them."

She smiled, "Thank you. I've wanted to sing my whole life, but I enjoy teaching here. I enjoy my life here in Saint Michaels. I love the change of seasons here, I look forward to it. It brings peace and stability to my life. I love the people here, friends' neighbors, parishioners, and of course, my dad. He and I are very close. To leave all this for a singing career is something I gave a lot of thought to and decided...I want to stay here in Saint Michaels. I'm sorry. I hope you understand?"

"I understand completely, and should you ever change your mind, the offer is always open. Call me. Best of luck to you, and Merry Christmas, Grace."

"Merry Christmas, Justin, and thank you for being so understanding."

When she hung up the phone, she felt a tremendous weight had been lifted from her shoulders. Tomorrow was Christmas Eve, and now if only Sam...

# Chapter Twenty-Nine

The next day, on Christmas Eve, a light dusting of snow covered the streets and sidewalks of Saint Michaels, but it was gone with the dawn of the morning light. Grace lay in her bed, thinking, when she heard her father's knock on the door. "Grace? Gracie?"

"Yes, Dad?"

"You should eat something, we leave for Doctor Cassel's office a little later. And don't forget, we have our Christmas Eve services tonight with the bishop. We can't keep him waiting."

"I'll be ready in a little bit, Dad. Be right down."

"Don't be long, dear."

She felt rested and calm now that she had made her decision to stay. When she told her father, he sounded so pleased, but only said, "Whatever makes you happy, Gracie."

Sitting at her desk in her room, she heard the squawking sounds of seagulls pass by her open window, then suddenly heard the screech of blaring police sirens rush by on the street outside. Then another, and another. The sounds of loud voices and the banging of car doors made their way through her open window.

*What the heck is going on?* She quickly made her way downstairs. Near the living room were voices she didn't recognize. One of them said, "Here she is, here's the daughter."

Another gruff voice in the distance ordered him, "Bring her in here. Now."

She was afraid. Voices she didn't recognize filled the air. "Dad? Daddy? Are you okay? Where are you?" she shouted as she felt a hand take her by the arm, lead her into the kitchen, and place her in a chair. "Dad?" she repeated in terror. "Daddy?"

She jerked her arm away from the man's grip, shouting, "What have you done with my father? I want to talk to my father! And I want to talk to him now!"

"I'm here, pumpkin," called her father. "In the kitchen. Sit here, have some coffee." Her father sat next to her, guiding her hand to the coffee cup, whispering, "I'm right here. Everything is okay. These men are with the state police and are looking for Sam. Do you have any idea where he is?"

"Sam? My Sam? Sam Carpenter?"

"Yes, sweetheart. Do you know where he is?"

"In Philadelphia. I spoke with him late last night and...Dad, tell me what's going on?"

"Shh, quiet. From what I heard, they're expecting some VIPs to show up here soon. But they keep saying they need to talk to Sam. They're checking Philadelphia, looking for him. But they couldn't find him at his hotel room in Philly. That's all I know. The police are in the living room now, speaking with the bishop."

"Bishop Donovan? They're arresting the bishop?"

"No, sweetheart, I don't think so, they're merely speaking with him. But they need to talk to Sam for some reason. Don't ask me why, they just need to, that's all."

"Oh, Sam. What have you done?" she whispered to herself.

There was a commotion at the front door, followed by silence and mellowed reverential rumblings.

Her father touched her hand and whispered, "The Archbishop just came in, accompanied by a man in a long knee-length robe and a thick black beard. You sure Sam didn't say anything to you, anything at all?"

"No, nothing. Nothing at all. I tried his cell phone, but he didn't answer me. I don't understand, where's Sam?"


Sam Carpenter left Philadelphia after eating at his favorite place, Jack's Corned Beef. It was a small, back alley place, but they served the best corned beef sandwiches he'd ever had. He left an extra-large tip for his regular waitress. Why not, he figured. It was Christmastime, she could use the extra money, and it was his last meal in Philadelphia. He was going home, back to Saint Michaels.

The drive from Philadelphia to Saint Michaels took almost three hours, but he was happy. Spending time away had finally given him clarity in his life. He'd decided he was leaving Wanamaker's. He was going home, and he was going to marry Grace…if she would have him. He would tune organs wherever her career took her. There was always a need for organ tuners around the country. Impetuous, maybe, but he knew what he wanted.

He wanted to call Grace and tell her. Sam began to hum a Christmas tune as he crossed the Bay Bridge, glancing around for his cell phone. But his cell phone holder on the seat beside him was empty. In his rush, he had packed his cell phone in his luggage. He would get it when he stopped for gas.

Sam decided he wanted to go with her to the doctor, give her moral support, be there for her when Doctor Cassel removed the bandages, and she found out whether the operation was a success. She needed to know that he would be there and love her, no matter what happened after that. He smiled to himself as he joined in the singing of "Jingle Bells" along with the radio. As Sam made the turnoff from Route 301 to Route #50, on the final stretch home, he soon passed an all-too-familiar sign:

*Welcome to Saint Michaels*
*Population 1,038*
*Founded in 1677*

The traffic slowed as he made his way into town. Ahead, he saw flashing red, blue, and white police lights as he made his way down Talbot Street. *Must be an accident,* he thought to himself, as the cars crept along. Up ahead at the church, he saw at least fifteen state police cruisers, four local police sedans, a caravan of armored car vehicles, and four or five black Chevy Suburbans in the church parking lot. Secret Service? The local and regional television news stations had already set up camp surrounding the church. Officers roped off the church with yellow plastic police tape and held the onlookers at bay.

Mike Miller, a local Saint Michaels police officer, was directing traffic. Sam rolled down the window as he drove up. "Hey, Mike, what's going on?"

Mike took one look at Sam and shouted to a nearby plainclothes officer, "Hey, here he is, the one you been looking for, Sam Carpenter!"

A man dressed in a dark suit and tie, wearing an American flag pin on his lapel, approached his car. The tall man asked Sam, "Are you, Mr. Carpenter? Mr. Sam Carpenter?"

"Yes, yes, I am," he stuttered. "What's the problem, officer?"

"No problem, sir. Would you please park your car over there in the church parking lot and come with me?"

Sam heard the officer say into a microphone tucked inside his sleeve, "We have the goose. The goose has landed."

The crowd pointed at Sam as he followed the officer inside the rectory. Newscasters shouted questions he could not hear; he just turned, smiled, and waved. He was an innocent man. He had nothing to be afraid of…did he?

Grace's father was the first one to greet him, as he came inside with Grace standing behind him. "They've been looking for you, Sam. All day."

"I've been on the road for the last three hours. What's going on? What do they want with me? I've done nothing wrong."

Grace moved forward and asked him, "Why aren't you at work, Sam?"

"I'll tell you later," he said, kissing her cheek and squeezing her hand. "We have a lot to talk about."

"Yes, we do."

The bishop moved to greet Sam and introduce him to the man dressed in black. "Follow me, will you, please? There's someone I want you to meet." asked the bishop dressed in black pants and a clerics collar.

"Well, of course, Bishop Donovan."

They walked to greet Archbishop Stern and the man in black. Sam could not help but notice that the man had a familiar silver cross hanging from his neck. He offered his outstretched hand to Sam. "Good morning, my friend. You must be Mr. Carpenter. My name is Antonio Bennetti. I am a Knights Templar with the Royal Order of the Knights of Malta. I believe you have something which belongs to me…and to the order."

"I don't think so, sir. I've never seen you before in my life."

The mysterious Bennetti raised the cross in his hand. "But you have seen this, have you not, my friend?"

"Yes. Yes, I have."

He put his arm around Sam's shoulder and walked him to the front of the rectory, away from the prying ears of the others in the room. Four state troopers stood by the stairs and the doors. "You may not even know what precious cargo you have, my young friend."

"No disrespect, sir, but I'm totally baffled."

The tall man smiled and said, "We have a mutual acquaintance…in New York. A Hungarian. A Mr. Jasef Krasnik?"

"Oh yes, Jasef. Yes, I know Jasef."

"Well, he telephoned our offices in Malta a few days ago with some strange findings after he tested the metals in some of your bells. Where are those bells now, if I may ask?"

"They're in the storage room under the bell tower." Sam pointed in the direction of the storage room.

The dark-haired visitor motioned to one of his entourage and whispered something to him.

"Thank you, Mr. Carpenter," he said.

"What is this all about?"

"Please be patient. I'll explain everything to you and the rest of the group soon," he said, and then motioned for the archbishop. They huddled together for a few minutes until his entourage returned.

The archbishop smiled a broad smile as emotion flooded his face. "Ladies and gentlemen, could you all please have a seat? Father Bennetti has a few things he would like to say. Signor Bennetti, please. The floor is yours."

"Thank you, your Excellency," Bennetti replied. "My name is Antonio Bennetti. I am a Knights Templar with the Royal Order of the Knights of Malta. Many years ago— seventy years, to be precise—as the war was raging on in Europe, many churches sent their valuables, their gold, and silver to us on the island of Malta for safekeeping with the Order of Malta. As the Nazi scourge spread throughout Europe, it was determined that these valuables, the heritage and wealth of many European churches, were no longer safe on our island. It was decided that the best course of action was to melt down the gold, recast them as bells to disguise them, and ship them off to America for safekeeping. For security reasons, very few people knew the destination of the ships and future locations of the bells."

Grace felt her eyes begin to itch.

"The two ships set sail from Malta for America. One ship, called *Saint Paul*, went to the Gulf Coast and delivered its cargo to churches in and around New Orleans. The other ship, the *Holy Cross*, delivered its cargo up and down the east coast, but we lost track of it after it left Boston. It sank somewhere in the Atlantic. All the other bells have been accounted for, except for the ones we affectionately call 'the seven sisters.' For the last seventy years, they've been lost…until today. My security staff has just informed me that the missing sisters have been located right here in Saint Michaels."

He began to walk around the room. "So for the last seventy years, the church of Saint Michaels has had seven eighteen-karat gold bells hanging in its bell tower." Turning to Sam, he said, "They are not 'sour' bells, as you may call them, but instead golden bells, almost solid gold bells, Mr. Carpenter. Eighteen karat gold, my friend. Very valuable, worth millions and millions of dollars. Hence all the police and security, until we get them properly secured for safekeeping." He acknowledged Sam before continuing. Sam could hardly believe what he was hearing.

"We owe the highest debt of gratitude to Mr. Carpenter, to Bishop Donovan, to Archbishop Stern, and to the pastor of Saint Michaels Church, the Reverend William Albright, for keeping them safe from harm all these years. Thank you."

He clapped his hands and was joined in applause by the rest of those in the room. "To show our appreciation for your guardianship, we will be sending a sizable annual stipend to help maintain this church and keep it running for years to come. We will also be dedicating a plaque for the church outlining the history of the bells, and the role Saint Michaels Church played in their safekeeping and recovery."

Smiling before he continued, he said, "As an aside, I should say that church membership has been known to increase substantially, as well as tourism, any time one of our bells has been located. Everyone wants to come and see the place where the seven sisters lived for seventy years."

The pastor led the clapping when he heard this pronouncement.

"And finally," Signor Bennetti continued, "with the kind permission of the pastor, I would like to suggest a celebration of church services on Christmas Day to be officiated by the bishop, the archbishop, myself, and of course the pastor, Reverend Albright."

"With pleasure," said the reverend. *The school and the church are safe! They won't be closing! My prayers have been answered, at least some of my prayers,* he thought to himself.

"Now, if you'll excuse me," said Signor Bennetti, "I must arrange transportation home for our precious golden cargo and would like to thank you all once again for keeping them safe from harm. While they finish loading the bells into the armored trucks, I think now is probably a good time to speak to the press and share the news with the world. I would like to ask the bishop, the archbishop, and Reverend Albright to join me. Time to celebrate. And Mr. Carpenter," he said, as Sam stood, "You are now officially a celebrity. Congratulations."

"Thank you, sir."

Grace put her arms around his shoulders and said, "My hero." Her smile warmed his heart.

Her father approached both of them with a worried look. "I don't know what I'm going to do," he said. "Grace is going to be late for her doctor's appointment." He looked at Sam and said, "Sam, could you take Grace to Doctor Cassel's office in Cambridge? He has to change her bandages. Just routine, but I have services soon, and…"

"No problem, Reverend. Be happy to do it whenever Grace is ready."

"Ready," she said, grabbing her purse.

Once in the car, as they drove through the throng of reporters and gawkers, Grace reached out her hand to touch him. Then she asked quietly, "So why are you not at Wanamaker's today? Day off?"

"No," he began to say, then stopped. "I resigned today. Wanamaker's is a great place to work, but I realized that it wasn't for me. I thought it was, but I was wrong. I missed it here in Saint Michaels. I missed everything about it. This is home." He paused. "And I missed you. So wherever your new career takes you, I'll be there for you. Right by your side. Through thick and thin. Good times and bad."

"That sounds like a marriage proposal to me. Don't stop. Tell me more."

He pulled the car over to the side of the road and parked. "Grace, I may not be the best catch there is, but…I love you. I always have. I didn't want to say anything before to keep you from your career in New York, but…"

She placed her finger on his lips. "I called the talent agency last night and turned them down. I'm staying here in Saint Michaels. This is home for me too. I'm not going anywhere."

They both laughed. "So, we're both stayin' here, in sweet, beautiful Saint Michaels, Maryland. Land of pleasant living, as the slogan goes." He paused. "Grace Albright, will you..."

Her phone rang, but she ignored it. It rang again.

"Gracie, aren't you going to answer it?"

"Not while I have you in the middle of what sounds like a marriage proposal, I'm not." But the phone rang again.

"Go ahead, answer it."

"Hold that thought." She answered her phone as Sam listened intently. "Hello?" she said. "Yes, we're on our way. Yes, I know it's Christmas Eve. Yes, I know that the doctor does not normally work on days like this. We are about..."

"Five minutes away," whispered Sam, as he pulled the car back onto the road and sped up, the parking lot gravel spraying behind them.

"We're five minutes away. Please ask him to wait. We won't be long. Please? Thank you, thank you so much." She closed the phone. "Step on it, Sam! He didn't think we were coming, so he's leaving to go home."

Sam made record time as he headed to the hospital and parked. Soon they were led into the examining room together and told to wait for the doctor. They waited. And waited.

He could tell she was nervous. Her hands kept moving until she could wait no longer. "Turn off the lights, and close the blinds," she said. Then, slowly, she began to unwind the long bandage from around her head and face. The doctor had done the same exact thing on her two other visits. When the dressing was removed, the only protection that remained were the large cotton balls which covered her eyes. Silence.

Sam did not say a word.

Her voice was just barely louder than a whisper when she said, "Now open the blinds, slowly, and finish what you started in the car...the part about you not being a great catch and so on and so on."

He stood by the window and slowly opened the blind. "Oh yes, you would have to have me start there, wouldn't you?"

"Go on. You were saying," she said.

"As I was saying, I may not be the greatest catch in the world, but I love you, and I think that we should...I mean...will you marry me, Grace Albright? Will you be my wife?"

Grace was quiet for a long time, not saying anything.

"Gracie? Don't you have anything to say?"

She began to cry. "It's snowing outside. Sam, it's snowing!"

"Yes I know," he said not realizing what she really meant. Then in shock, he said, "Gracie? You can see! You can see. Oh, sweet…I love you, Grace Albright. I really do. I never ever wanted to be with anyone else." He hugged her and held her close as the tears rolled down both of their eyes. Even though her eyes were still blurry, Sam looked the same as she remembered, so handsome, so sweet, so…

"I knew you loved me, or at least I hoped you did…I hoped with all my heart." She stood, standing wobbly at first, as she regained her balance and her eyes adjusted to the light that had been denied to her for years. She could see. The door opened behind them, and the light switched on. The light was the brightest light she had ever seen, and she squinted to see who was there. It was Doctor Cassel.

"I guess maybe I'm a little too late," he told them.

"Doctor Cassel, I can see," she said, tears streaming down her cheeks. "It was blurry for a little while, but now I can see clearly. Oh, thank you, Doctor. Thank you." She started to leave the room, but the doctor stopped her. "Let me just do a quick examination first before you leave, just to be on the safe side. Okay? And you'll have to stay here for a little while, just to allow your eyes to adjust to the light. It's been three years, you can wait a little while longer while your eyes adjust. And don't worry, Sam will wait for you."

She looked at him and pleaded, "But Doctor Cassel, we have a church service starting soon that we must get back for…"

"I promise you won't be late. But I must insist. It's for your own good. We'll slowly introduce light to your eyes, a little bit at a time so you can get accustomed to it. Okay?" He turned out the lights in the room, casting them in darkness.

"But, but…"

"No buts about it. Sam, do you mind?" He pointed to the waiting room.

"I'll wait for you in the waiting room, Grace," Sam told her, reluctant to let go of her hand or be away from her.

"It won't take long. Please."

The exam took just under twenty minutes. Finally, Doctor Cassel gave her some eyedrops and wished her a Merry Christmas, still shaking his head in amazement. Then they went to the waiting room, Grace still